The Last Soulkeeper

G.P. Ching

Carpe Luna Publishing

Books by G.P. Ching

The Soulkeepers Series

The Soulkeepers, Book 1
Weaving Destiny, Book 2
Return to Eden, Book 3
Soul Catcher, Book 4
Lost Eden, Book 5
The Last Soulkeeper, Book 6

The Grounded Trilogy

Grounded, Book 1
Charged, Book 2 (Coming Soon)
Wired, Book 3 (Coming Soon)

"It is close at hand—a day of darkness and gloom, a day of clouds and blackness. Like dawn spreading across the mountains, a large and mighty army comes, such as never was in ancient times nor ever will be in ages to come."

-Joel 2:1-2

Contents

Chapter 1 *The Replacement* 1

Chapter 2 *Patrol* 16

Chapter 3 *Cord* 26

Chapter 4 *The Fourth Curse* 36

Chapter 5 *Empty* 45

Chapter 6 *Angel* 55

Chapter 7 *Hope* 67

Chapter 8 *Busted* 72

Chapter 9 *Visitation* 84

Chapter 10 *The Fourth Gift* 96

Chapter 11 *Sanctuary* 107

Chapter 12 *The Fifth Curse* 117

Chapter 13 *The Hedonic Party* 126

Chapter 14 *Connections* 133

Chapter 15 *The Fifth Gift* 144

Chapter 16 *Where Angels Fear to Tread* 150

Chapter 17 *For the Record* 160

Chapter 18 *A Demon's Plaything* 169

Chapter 19 *The Devil's Due* 178

Chapter 20 *A Light in the Darkness* 190

Chapter 21 *Preparing for War* 198

Chapter 22 *Labyrinth* 209

Chapter 23 *Plan B* 219

Chapter 24 *Consequences* 229

Chapter 25 *The Living Dead* 237

Chapter 26 *Healer* 249

Chapter 27 *Asher* 259

Chapter 28 *Hope's End* 268

Chapter 29 *The Still, Small Voice* 277

Chapter 30 *Winner* 288

Chapter 31 *The Last Soulkeeper* 295

Epilogue *The Service* 302

About the Author 311

Acknowledgements 313

Book Club Discussion Questions 315

Chapter 1
The Replacement

A uriel needed to feed. The torturous ache in her gut was only made worse by the scent of six humans, bloated with blood and sitting just a talon's strike away, hunkered over the conference room table at Harrington Enterprises. If it weren't for Lucifer's looming presence, she'd have stripped the flesh off any one of them before her victim had time to scream. But Lucifer, otherwise known as CEO Milton Blake, was running a tight ship these days, galvanized by Cord's continued absence. She'd witnessed his wrath enough times to know she would not willingly be on the receiving end of it, and at the moment, she could sense his fury brewing.

The dark one drummed his fingers at the head of the table, obviously annoyed. The heat of his soulless interior, the part of him connected to Hell, had passed the barrier of his skin and raised the temperature in the room several degrees. Even Auriel was uncomfortably hot. The human participants sported red faces and wet spots under the pits of their arms.

While Auriel hated the business world, she'd learned a few things about Harrington's operation. The purpose of this meeting was for the Harrington department heads to update Lucifer on the progress of their respective divisions. It was also their only chance to request more personnel or funding. Lucifer had come to rely on these meetings in Cord's absence. The human employees outnumbered the Watchers and were far more motivated to achieve success in their petty, limited lives. Unfortunately, the news today wasn't improving Lucifer's mood.

This was war. God had challenged Lucifer for human hearts. Six temptations versus six gifts, winner takes Earth for one thousand years. Lucifer had already cast three temptations: affliction, ignorance, and terror. In response, the Great Oppressive Deity had gifted wisdom, understanding, and a third gift she hadn't been able to interpret yet. Lucifer had been in the lead since the inception of the challenge ... that is, until that last, mysterious gift. Somehow, God had taken Cord—at least Lucifer thought He had—and with him Lucifer's control over his army of Watchers. The last gift was more than Cord's undoing though. She could feel it in the air. The humans changed in a way she couldn't put her finger on that day. Now, for the first time, the scorekeeper's scales tilted slightly in God's favor.

Auriel had worked hard to fill Cord's shoes. Too hard. But, just like Lucifer, she couldn't be in more than one place at a time, and the Watchers were growing too used to eating whomever they pleased whenever they pleased. If she and Lucifer couldn't get control of the Watchers, they would be at risk of losing this challenge. Auriel didn't want to think about what might become of her then.

"The problem isn't with demand, Mr. Blake," Mr. Adams said, loosening his tie against the heat. "We are moving more Elysium than ever. The problem is with the financials. We've given away too many pills. People are hoarding them and selling them on the black market. Meanwhile, my department is on the verge of bankruptcy."

A tooth-baring frown contorted Lucifer's mouth. "Why would people buy them on the black market and not from Harrington?"

Adams dabbed his temple with a tissue. "The distribution channels." He paused as if he thought the reasons were obvious. "Since the, er, anti-Elysium movement and the demon invasion, many of the doctors and hospitals we've worked with in the past won't sell the drug anymore for reasons of conscience."

Auriel inconspicuously wheeled her chair away from Lucifer under the guise of adjusting her boot. This wasn't going to be pretty.

"Reasons of conscience?" His voice, barely a whisper, held the promise of menace. "What business are you in, Adams?"

"The pharmaceutical business, sir," Adams said.

"Ah yes, we sell drugs for profit." Lucifer nodded. "I don't recall hanging out a shingle promoting our social consciousness. Who should take Elysium?"

"Elysium is prescribed for the treatment and management of the latest strain of bird flu," Adams recited.

"Blah, blah, blah." Lucifer made a duck face with his hand, opening and closing his fingers to mock Adams. "Everyone should take Elysium. Every man, woman, and child should be popping the stuff three times per day. I don't care if they need it. I don't care if it helps or hurts them. But I do care that they pay. They must all pay."

"But the doctors—"

Lucifer slammed a fist on the table and leaned forward until his nose was centimeters from Adams's. "Are you mentally impaired?"

"No—"

"Sell it on the street, you idiot. If the money is flowing on the black market, then *you* control the black market. And if doctors and hospitals won't sell Elysium, perhaps you could make things more difficult for them. Deny them Harrington Security. Let the demons eat them."

Auriel had to stop herself from cheering. This was the Lucifer she knew and loved, all-powerful and merciless.

"Yeah, about dat," Ted Kowalski interrupted in his thick Chicagoan accent. The man's corpulent body stressed the fabric of his white dress shirt, brown tie askew and bald head beading with sweat. "I'm not sure dat's the best strategy at this juncture. I think we oughta scrap the Demon Eradication System."

"What did you say?" Lucifer asked.

Sweat rolled from Kowalski's hairline to the round hump of his cheek. "I think it's time we phased out Harrington's Demon Eradication Systems. The things don't work. I been puttin' out fires for weeks. People are dying 'cause they trust in this product, and it's a lemon. Harrington's getting a black eye over this one. We'll be lucky to get out before the lawsuits hit."

Lucifer glared, lips peeling back from his teeth in an expression that couldn't be confused for a smile. "What department do you run, Kowalski?"

The man shifted in his chair, eyes darting around the room like a drowning man searching for a saving branch. None were offered. "Er, public relations."

"Public relations." Lucifer stood, leaning forward to plant his fingertips on the table. "I seem to recall the function of your department is to manipulate the public perception of our product."

Kowalski's jaw dropped. "We don't manipulate folks. We just manage the spread of information to the public."

"And why aren't you spreading the news that the eradication systems work?" Lucifer hissed. Auriel straightened in her chair at the foreboding sound.

The man rubbed his scruffy chin with his thumb and forefinger. "'Cause. They. Don't."

Silence. The other department heads froze in their seats. Lucifer strode around the table until he was standing next to Kowalski, the hip of his khaki trousers leaning against the table. "I am not paying you to be honest, Kowalski."

Kowalski's mouth bent into a frown, and his breath began to whistle in his throat. The nervous wheeze crept through his pseudo-confident exterior. He swallowed. "I ain't your patsy, Mr. Blake. I know what you're doing. I ain't gonna take the blame when the law comes down on us for this."

"You're not the man for the job, eh?" Lucifer said, eyes narrowing.

"I guess not."

Lucifer glared and leaned forward. Auriel knew what he was doing but suppressed her laugh. It wouldn't do to distract him. The dark one was allowing the man to glimpse who he really was, to see Hell through the window of his pupils. The wheezing grew louder. Kowalski coughed, his face turning the color of borscht before his hands began to flail at his sides.

"I think he's choking," Lucifer said calmly.

Kowalski slapped the table, airless, throaty grunts coming from his head.

Mrs. Anderson, vice president of human resources, looked up from her page of notes and slowly processed what was happening. "Maybe try the Heimlich?" she said slowly. She didn't move from her chair.

"I think he has asthma," Marketing chimed in. "Maybe we should call 911."

Lucifer didn't respond. No one reached for the phone.

Kowalski scratched at his ruby throat, eyes bugging and tongue extending from his mouth. A dying fish. He flopped to the floor, tipping over his chair in the process, and twitched on the low pile carpeting.

"Ms. Grimswald," Lucifer said to the mousy-haired secretary taking notes in the corner.

"Yes?"

"Please make a note that there is a position open in public relations, effective immediately."

"Yes, s…sir," the woman stuttered.

Lucifer spread his hands and addressed the room. "Meeting dismissed." He winked at Auriel. "Ms. Thomson, can you stay and help me deliver Mr. Kowalski to the nearest hospital?"

"Of course, Mr. Blake," Auriel said, grinning at the piece of meat now unconscious on the floor. The others rose from the table and filed from the room. No one even looked back to see what had become of Ted Kowalski.

As soon as the conference room door closed, Auriel begged Lucifer with her eyes.

"My gift to you." Lucifer motioned toward Kowalski.

"Thank you, my lord," she said, before pouncing on the body and using a talon to strip a bit of flesh from his neck. "His heart is still beating."

"You deserve the best, my pet. You've served me well these weeks."

She nodded, slurping in the next strip.

"I fear we may never recover Cord," Lucifer said, "and we can no longer afford to wait for him to return."

Auriel nodded. Finally. She thought he would never admit they'd lost him for good. "Then he *is* dead."

"It appears so."

She wiped the back of her hand across her bloody lips. "The Soulkeepers are behind this. Call Malini's soul to you and rip the truth from her filthy mouth." Auriel bared her fangs.

Lucifer scowled, turning his back to her as if he had a secret to keep. But then, Lucifer always had secrets. It was not her place to know or ask about his reasons, and she was smart enough not to press the issue.

"It is done, Auriel. He is dead. We must name another."

"Who shall we call? If only Mordechai or Turrel were still with us, what an awesome power we would make." She licked her lips.

Lucifer growled. "But they are not. No, the one we call forth must be supreme in his depravity. Intelligent and ruthless."

Auriel stopped eating and pointed a bloody talon in his direction. "You have someone in mind."

"More than one someone."

"Who?"

"The Wicked Brethren."

"I have not seen or heard of the Wicked Brethren in decades. They've gone their own way. Haven't lived in Nod in millennia. Never followed the quotas. What makes you think you can rein them in?"

"Because I hold their dark hearts in my fist," Lucifer snapped, balling his hand in front of her face.

Touchy, touchy. Auriel backed off immediately. The Wicked Brethren were a family group of six brothers, angels that fell with Lucifer and killed brutally in the early days. Made Watchers like the others, the brethren claimed one critical difference; they paid allegiance to each other and no one else, not even Lucifer. Each had come to serve a particular vice in the human world. Over the centuries, three had met their end, victims of the urges that drove them. The other three had stayed rogue, the last she'd heard, living and feeding on villagers in rural Romania. Lucifer had allowed it to this point, Auriel supposed, because the brethren had a nasty habit of impulsivity that made them poor candidates for close living.

Perhaps desperate times called for desperate measures. Lucifer needed a monster. Cord's replacement must both wreak destruction on the humans and control the legions of Watchers on Earth. If he could enlist the brethren for those duties, he'd be more powerful than ever.

Auriel held up a disembodied finger between her own. "I miss Cord," she murmured, then popped the digit between her teeth.

"There is only one way to gain the allegiance of the brethren," Lucifer continued. "We must get Damien to agree to help us. He has always been their leader."

"Yes, my lord, although I found Asher quite entertaining for a number of years." Asher was the pretty one. Always had a thing for the ladies, even the human ones. She supposed with the elimination of the compact between God and the Devil, he was exercising that particular vice again. Since Noah, human sexuality had been off-limits. Not anymore.

"Asher is too easily distracted. I will call Damien to me, and we shall enlist him in our cause. He will bring the others."

Auriel nodded. She finished her meal and wiped what remained of Mr. Kowalski off her face with a tissue from her pocket. "I am ready, my lord."

Eagerly, Lucifer closed his eyes, and Auriel understood he was sending his call through shadow, a talent he alone possessed. The Devil owned the stuff Watchers were made of. Once he connected with the thumbprint of Damien's black heart, he would pull his essence into his presence. The call could not be refused.

Auriel wasn't at all surprised when three funnels of darkness channeled into the conference room. The brothers always stuck together. She surveyed the brood as one by one they fully formed. Their massive shoulders seemed to fill the open space around the table, despite this being the largest conference room in the building. She'd forgotten how formidable the Wicked Brethren could be.

Damien's gray-green eyes narrowed with suspicion. Dressed in a business suit the color of money and Italian loafers, he looked like the typical executive. Auriel's eyebrow arched when she noticed his dark hair was peppered with gray. His appearance, like all of the Watchers, was an illusion. He didn't *have* to have gray hair or slight wrinkles around his eyes if he didn't want them. But why would he want them? Upon further thought, she remembered Damien's particular vice was greed. Perhaps his appearance facilitated his priorities, this illusion serving him well in the business world. Rumor had it he was exceedingly rich and even owned a castle in Romania.

Next to him, the lustful Asher turned his bright smile her way, his movie-star good looks giving Auriel a warm, melty feeling. His sandy blond coif, wild on top and short on the sides, made his aqua eyes dazzle. She knew it was an illusion, but somehow Asher wore it better than the rest.

Near the back of the room, the silk-shirt-wearing Levi checked his jeweled rings to ensure he hadn't lost any in his travels. He was wearing a decidedly Greek illusion these days, with longer dark waves and olive skin. Levi's vice was envy and thus he was the least predictable. The only certainty was his desire to obtain whatever anyone else had, whatever that might be.

"You called," Damien said, straightening his suit and adjusting the shiny watch on his wrist.

"Yes, I did. I am in need of your services."

"The brethren are very busy, my lord. We cannot offer you our assistance at this time."

"I'm not asking, Damien. I'm enlisting you," Lucifer said in a deadly quiet voice.

Damien stepped back. "Now is not a good time. I respectfully decline."

"I respectfully do not accept your decision," Lucifer growled.

"Why us? Why now?"

"The apocalypse needs you. If I am to win this challenge—and if I win, you win, Damien—I require your assistance."

Levi groaned, throwing his head back and spinning in the swivel chair where he'd taken up residence. He'd hooked one tall boot over the arm of his seat and looked decidedly pirate-like. "Sounds like a lot of work. Why should you get to call the shots after all these years, Lucifer? The Wicked Brethren have done splendidly on our own for centuries. Find someone else to help you." He waved a hand in the air.

With a growl, Lucifer extended one hand and clenched it into a fist. Levi stopped spinning. The demon writhed in pain, face reddening as his hands gripped his neck.

"You have done fine on your own, Levi, because I have allowed it," Lucifer said. "Do not forget that I own the very stuff you are made of, down to your black heart." He flicked his hand open and the demon flew out of the chair and smashed against the back wall, his overdeveloped muscles leaving a dent before he slumped to the floor.

Damien's eyes shifted from his brothers to Lucifer. "What is in it for us?"

It always came down to greed with Damien. The sin was both his greatest strength and weakness. This was good. Lucifer had taught Auriel that a servant with no desires couldn't be properly motivated. One thing about the Wicked Brethren, their desires were as strong as their physiques.

"If you help me, and I win the challenge, you will become Earth's princes. Each of you will be given your own domain to rule as you will, and all of the riches of that domain will be yours."

Sprawled on the floor where he'd fallen, Levi started to snore. Asher, who had strutted across the room to Auriel's side, turned toward the brother and laughed. "Seems Levi could do without ruling anything."

"Levi," Damien said. The brother stopped snoring and got to his feet, brushing himself off.

"This conversation bores me," Levi said.

Auriel could sense Damien fighting with himself as his eyes darted between Levi and Asher. Was freedom such a strong motivator?

"Nothing compares to serving Lucifer, Damien. It is its own reward," she said.

Lucifer grinned at her comment. "Come, my pet," he said to her. He wrapped one arm around Damien's shoulders, and then took Auriel's hand. At the moment her fingers touched his, smoke swallowed the three of them, wicking them from

Harrington to a rooftop in the sky. Auriel gasped at the grandeur of the panoramic view.

"Where are we?" Damien asked.

"The roof of the Empire State Building."

"Why?" Damien stared across New York City, pursing his lips as if this side trip was highly inconvenient.

"Only to show you all that could be yours." Lucifer motioned toward the city with his open hand.

Auriel stiffened. She'd been promised the world. Was not New York part of the world?

"The city of New York?" Damien clarified.

"And every other major city. You will be my second. The world and all the riches in it will be yours. When I win, you can bathe in the jewels of the humans you eat for lunch."

His second? Auriel was his second. She clenched her fists at her sides.

Damien's battleship-green eyes reflected the city. He licked his lips. "The world economy, all the money in all the world, will be mine to rule autonomously," Damien said, not a question but a demand.

"Of course. But all or nothing. You must convince your brothers to join me as well or no deal."

Damien clasped his hands behind his back, his face growing stony with thought. Auriel found herself wishing he'd say no, suddenly threatened by the Wicked Brethren's presence. Her wishing was futile.

"Consider it done," Damien said.

Lucifer's self-satisfied grin said it all. He reached out a hand and sealed the deal with a firm handshake.

A strange foreboding made Auriel's insides itch as she watched the arrangement, but there was no going back. Cord had been replaced.

Chapter 2
Patrol

Midnight. The witching hour. Jacob wove through a cluster of trees by the full moon's light, then raced across an open stretch of frozen grass. He leapt over the occasional human remnant, a foot, a thumb, a chunk of unidentified organ, in pursuit of a Watcher on a killing spree. His patrol team had tracked the beast for twelve blocks, but this was the first they'd made visual contact, and Jacob was not about to waste it.

His mother, Lillian, ran beside him, about one hundred yards to his right, dagger glinting in her hand. She was almost fifty years old, but her Soulkeeper powers made her lithe and spry, and able to wield any weapon upon first contact. She had no problem keeping up with his inhuman pace.

The third member of their patrol team, Cheveyo, circled west, hoping to head the creature off. The Hopi Soulkeeper was as fast as he was deadly, and he knew exactly what he was doing. There was a risk of getting too close. If the beast sensed Jacob, it could pass into shadow and escape, an end that would mean more work for the three of them to meet their nightly quota. So far, though, that hadn't happened. This Watcher staggered at a half-hearted run, seemingly drunk from his overindulgence on human flesh.

Still, an experienced Soulkeeper never underestimated a Watcher. A flash of leathery wing dodged behind a tree ahead. Jacob sped up until his quad muscles burned, breath coming in huffs, the water in his flask humming to be used.

A bloody arm flew at his head.

"Eww." Jacob ducked the disembodied limb. White flesh slapped the grass behind him. He didn't miss a step. Focused, he called the water, an arc driving from his flask into his palm, the spray forming a broadsword of ice perfectly balanced in his hand. He bounded off a park bench and ricocheted into the air, over the Watcher's head. The Watcher attempted to dodge left. Jacob's sword came around. The Watcher ducked, and the icy blade nicked its wing.

Poof. The Watcher twisted into shadow and disappeared.

"Damn," Jacob cursed. A blob of oily blood plopped to the grass near his toes.

"It hasn't gone far," his mom said. She'd closed in for the fight. "I can feel it."

"Me too," Jacob agreed, turning in a circle. "Did you see how sluggish it was? It could barely move."

"No self-control," Lillian murmured. "Gorged with blood."

Back to back, mother and son circled, blades at the ready. *Snap.* Jacob cranked his eyes north in time to see talons falling from the tree branches. He dove out of the way, swiping at the Watcher as he rolled. *Contact.* Only the wound wasn't enough to kill. The Watcher landed on Lillian, knocking her to the grass. His mother dropped to the snow at an awkward angle, her dagger trapped beneath her body.

"Mom!" Jacob reacted, swinging his sword at the creature's neck.

Boom. Another Watcher barreled into him. *Where did it come from?* Jacob took an elbow to the eye before he could land a sidekick in the center of the thing's chest. The Watcher transformed into a black mist on contact.

"No way," Jacob growled. Slicing the foggy air where the scaly flesh had been moments before, his enchanted weapon snagged. He yanked. *Ha.* The Watcher formed on the ground, leg spewing black blood. "Not fast enough with the quick change," Jacob said. Boot planted on the beast's neck, Jacob plowed his blade into the empty heart of the demon. The Watcher exploded, chunks of scaly flesh flying across the park on impact.

"You just never know how these things will die," he said, grinning. He wiped the oil slick from his eyes with the sleeve of his coat and turned back to help his mom. He didn't have to follow through. The Watcher had already released her and was backing away, skin bubbling and eyes bulging.

"About time, Cheveyo," his mother said, accepting Jacob's hand and trying to stand in the slippery muck of black blood and snow. She'd barely found her footing when Cheveyo's Watcher exploded, ensuring every exposed surface in a ten foot radius was completely coated in black excrement.

Cheveyo shook his shoulders like a dog, sending black droplets in every direction. "I will never get used to that," he said.

"Ugh. Do you mind?" Lillian spat. She tried to use the scarf around her neck to wipe her face, but the Watcher blood was everywhere.

"You'll get used to it," Jacob said. "Give it five hundred or so more times." Cheveyo's gift was kick-ass. The guy could possess Watchers, but since the stuff Soulkeepers were made of could not coexist with the stuff Watchers were made of, his presence destroyed them from the inside out. His soul automatically returned to his body when he was finished.

"Are you hit?" Cheveyo asked Lillian, pointing to a slice across her chest. White fluff poked out of the rip in her jacket.

"No," Lillian said. "Just my coat. It didn't break the skin."

"Cool. So that's quota, right?" Cheveyo asked.

Jacob nodded. "Yep. Counting the one in the zoo, we killed our three for the night." Weeks ago, Malini had set a quota for Watcher deaths, a strategy to shift the Soulkeepers' role in the war from defense to offense. Sometimes they killed more but rarely less. Jacob felt like they'd made a real dent in Lucifer's arsenal, and Malini said the scales now tilted slightly in God's favor.

"Sweet, because it ain't getting any warmer out here, and I'm starving." Cheveyo took off in the direction of Sanctuary. The place they called Sanctuary was the basement of what used to be a Catholic church and their new mission control since the portal to Eden was destroyed six weeks ago.

"Hold up, Jacob. I need to talk to you," Lillian said, slowing her steps to put room between herself and Cheveyo.

"About what?" Jacob asked, matching her steps. He would have loved it if the three of them could have poofed back via the enchanted staffs, but they rarely used them to travel anymore, especially not for quota. For one, they were unwieldy once the team got where they were going. And, more importantly, Malini was afraid the sorcery that powered them might draw Lucifer's attention.

"About the extra mouth we have to feed." Lillian looked at Jacob pointedly.

"You can't blame Hope—"

"I'm not talking about Hope, Jacob. Of course, I don't blame the baby." Lillian quieted. The only sound was her feet crunching on the frozen ground.

"You're talking about Cord."

"Yes."

Jacob took a deep breath and blew it out. "Malini thinks he could be useful to us. She's been talking about making him part of the team."

"That's what I'm worried about. Grace and I agree we can't trust him. Sure he looks like an angel, but he used to be a Watcher."

"He says that life is behind him. He bleeds silver. He's an angel now."

"But we can't trust him. She needs to keep him locked up until we know for sure what we are dealing with." Lillian pulled the sections of her coat together and crossed her arms against the chill air. Spring might be on the horizon during the day, but at night, Chicago was in full winter.

"Malini told me…" Jacob hesitated. He wasn't supposed to share what his girlfriend learned in the In Between. Seeing the future was an untrustworthy discipline, and the Immortals practically spoke in code.

"What, Jacob?" Lillian pressured.

"She said Cord might be important to our cause in the future. Mara said so."

His mom wiped a bit of black blood off her cheek and scratched her nose. The blood caused irritation if left on the skin too long. They needed to get back to Sanctuary and clean up before they were all itching from head to toe. "It's not that I'm unhappy with Cord's change. I think his transformation made a difference in morale," she said.

Jacob nodded. "No doubt. The team didn't think we had a chance until his conversion. Now everyone is wondering if it's real, and if it could happen again."

With a deep sigh, Lillian nodded her agreement. "I still don't trust him. Having him in the pantry is better than having him on the streets, but I question whether he's somehow getting information back to Lucifer."

"Mom, Cord was Lucifer's right-hand man. If he *were* still working for the Devil, something would have happened by now. It's been weeks. Lucifer has had more than enough time to counter an attack or call our souls to him. He would have sent a legion of Watchers to kill us in our sleep. Or worse, he'd come himself and pick us off one by one. Angel or not, Cord is out of the mix. No way is he feeding information back to Lucifer."

"We hope."

"Oh come on, you have to admit that things changed once we had Cord. The Watchers seem disorganized. I saw a survey on the news today, less than fifty percent of Harrington Security users are satisfied with the product. I've got to think Cord's absence has something to do with that. Malini says his conversion was part of the third gift."

"Maybe."

Jacob stroked the stubble on his chin. "Why do you think Lucifer hasn't called Malini's soul to him? We know he can. He did it when he held Dane in Hell. What's stopping him?"

"I wish I knew." Lillian shook her head. "It has to have something to do with the third gift, but none of us really know for sure, do we?"

"Malini said she can't fully explain the third gift or Cord's conversion, but she knows it is helping us. The immortals say it has something to do with baby Hope. She has the Soulkeeper gene."

Lillian frowned. "I believe Hope is important. How could the daughter of Abigail and Gideon not be? But this lull in Watcher activity isn't going to last forever. We are in the eye of the hurricane. The fourth curse has to be coming soon. We can't take any chances."

"Yeah." Jacob crossed the street, squinting at Cheveyo far ahead in the darkness. He silently prayed the newest Soulkeeper wouldn't encounter more Watchers on his own. He'd handle a loner like a rock star, but if there were others, the pack might snack on his body while he possessed the first one. Jacob picked up his pace to close the space between them.

"About Cord," Lillian pressed again.

Jacob groaned and tipped his head back.

"I'm serious. People are starting to talk behind her back. Malini won't listen to me. You have to convince her to keep him right where he is. Letting him out could be a disaster."

"Okay, okay, I'll talk to her."

"Good."

"But I believe in her, Mom. Malini is rarely wrong. If she says Cord is going to play a role in this thing, and that we might need him, I'm going to back her up."

Lillian sighed. They'd reached the alley behind the row of abandoned buildings near Sanctuary. She placed a finger over her lips, reminding Jacob they were in the quiet zone. Surveying the area, she skirted down the alley toward Sanctuary. The entrance to their basement camp was through a rectory with an underground passageway to the church basement. Jacob jogged to keep up with her. Once safely inside where Cheveyo waited for them, Lillian stopped and listened. It was procedure. All three team members must leave and return to Sanctuary together and ensure they were not followed.

In silence, the three listened and waited, senses tuned in for anything with black skin that might have trailed them home. Jacob couldn't trust his ability to smell a Watcher since he was covered in black blood, but he listened. The only sound was the wind blowing past the creaky rectory entrance. He remembered how he'd had to fix that door after he tore it off its hinges trying to get to Malini. Maybe he needed to tighten a few screws. At least the lock still worked, even though it would be useless against a Watcher who wanted in. It was the holy water they'd soaked the door in that might keep the real baddies out.

"Clear," Cheveyo said first.

"Clear," Jacob repeated.

Lillian listened with her eyes closed for one second more before confirming. "Clear."

Cheveyo ran for the stairs to Sanctuary.

"I expect you to believe in her," Lillian continued. "I believe in her too. I just don't believe in Cord, and I don't think we should ever make the mistake of trusting a former minion of Lucifer."

Jacob jogged down the stairs, stripping off his blood-covered clothing and dumping it in the basket they kept for quarantine at the bottom. "I'll see what I can do. But I'm telling you, Malini has her own mind. She's not going to change her opinion because of me or anyone else."

Chapter 3
Cord

Bonnie rested Hope in the crease of her lap and engulfed her tiny hands inside her fists. The baby's alabaster fingers squeezed her thumbs with a healthy grip. "Hope-ho-ho-ho-Hope," Bonnie cooed. Hope squealed, legs kicking and mouth bending into a toothless smile. Bonnie loved the moments when Hope made her forget that she lived in a basement of a church during the apocalypse.

Hope coughed, and then coughed again. Bonnie sat her up and patted her back. She spit up into the rag in Bonnie's hand.

"We need to talk." Malini's shadow crept over her, causing Bonnie to look up. The Healer was pissed—arms akimbo, jaw set.

"Yeah. I think you need to heal Hope. She keeps coughing up her formula."

"Grace says babies do that sometimes. That's not what I need to talk to you about."

"Then what?"

"You, torturing Cord." The accusation snapped like a whip between them.

Bonnie tossed the rag on the floor and lifted Hope to her shoulder. She stood so that she was eye to eye with Malini. "I don't know what you're talking about."

"Come with me." Malini took her by the elbow and forced her into the kitchen. Past the stainless-steel countertops and industrial appliances was a deep, walk-in pantry with a steel-grate door housing a massive padlock. Behind the door, a black-haired, blue-eyed angel glowed faintly, fluffy white wings drooping from his back. Cord.

Malini pointed at the tray of food placed a few feet from the door. Vegetarian. That's what angels could eat. Meat made him gag or vomit. She'd figured it out the hard way.

"You said I was responsible for feeding the angel. I fed the angel," Bonnie said.

"Cord, please attempt to eat the food Bonnie has prepared for you," Malini said, sweeping her bangs behind her ear.

Cord approached the door with a sigh, reaching through the grate for the tray. His fingers fell short of their goal. He tried a different hole, lower to the floor. Even lying on the cold tile and pressing his arm through to the point of his shoulder, his fingertips barely brushed the edge of the offered tray.

"What do you have to say for yourself?" Malini stared at Bonnie accusingly.

Bonnie didn't flinch. She stroked the back of Hope's now sleeping head on her shoulder, searching her brain for an excuse. "I didn't want to get too close. I don't trust him—as I've told you time and time again. He tried to kill me. He shredded my face." Bonnie pointed to her fully healed cheek.

"It's cruel, Bonnie. Don't think I haven't noticed that he's lost weight. You barely give him enough to eat as it is, and now you leave it out of his reach? If I hadn't stopped in here, he wouldn't get anything at all."

"So what? What good is he sitting in this pantry? He may look like an angel, but he's a Watcher, Malini. Lucifer's second. We should have killed him the moment he showed his face here."

"And you are going to enforce that opinion by starving him?"

Bonnie shrugged. "He's the enemy. No one except you thinks we will ever be able to use him. How is letting him rot in this pantry better than executing him?"

Cord retracted his arm and retreated to the wastelands of the empty pantry as if Bonnie's words had injured him. He wrapped his wings around himself, burrowing into an inner world of feathers.

Malini took a step toward Bonnie until their noses almost touched. Her silky, black A-line bob framed her face, bordering a stare that turned from brown to black with her anger. "Listen to me, Bonnie. I don't know what your problem is with Cord. You know as well as I do that, if he were working for Lucifer, we would have suffered the consequences by now. I've made the decision to keep him here for a reason."

"Fine. Get someone else to feed him."

"No." Malini's jaw clenched. "You need to do it."

"Why?" Bonnie's icy voice was edged with anger. Hope wriggled on her shoulder at the sound.

"Because my Healer wisdom tells me it's the way it has to be."

Bonnie snorted derisively, removing the red stone from her neck and tossing it at Malini, who caught it before it could strike her face. "I'll pass on your Healer wisdom. Thanks."

Malini wrapped her fingers around the stone, forming a fist. "Back down, Bonnie."

Using Hope as a shield against the fury rolling off Malini, Bonnie tried to cross the kitchen for the door. Malini planted one hand on her chest and stopped her short.

"Push the tray where he can reach it," she said through clenched teeth.

Bonnie jerked away and stepped to the tray. With Hope still nestled on her shoulder, she kicked. The meal skidded into the grate, toppling the bowls. Cereal and fruit sprayed across the floor of the pantry.

Obviously starving, Cord snatched a slice of banana from the tile and began to eat.

Malini shot Bonnie a deadly look and grabbed a rag from the counter. "Cord, wait. I'll get you some clean food. Don't eat off the floor." She moved for the locked door.

Bonnie wasn't about to stick around to watch her clean up the mess. She shot out of the kitchen and into the living area, planning to take Hope to the church foyer, where she could be alone.

A commotion from the stairwell cut off her progress.

"Quota in the bag," Cheveyo said, wiping black goo off his face with a towel. Jacob and Lillian came in behind him. All three paraded in front of her on their way to the bathrooms to get cleaned up.

Once they were out of earshot, a sharp tug on her elbow spun her around. Surprisingly, it wasn't Malini but Bonnie's twin sister, Samantha, and she didn't look happy. "Why are you giving Malini such a hard time about feeding Cord? I heard you yelling all the way out here. Doesn't she have enough to worry about without babysitting you and our stupid angel prisoner?"

"Just the point, Sam. Why are we keeping an angel prisoner when we can barely care for ourselves? Why me? Why do I have to feed him?"

"Why not you? Malini says it's important. She's the Healer. Her role as a Soulkeeper is to choose for the greater good. Why can't you just trust in that?"

"Because." Bonnie sighed. "I do trust Malini okay, completely. It's not about her."

"Then why?" Sam jerked her elbow again, demanding the truth. Hope began to fuss on her shoulder and turned her head to look at Samantha.

"You're upsetting Hope," Bonnie said.

Samantha arched one red eyebrow. It was useless to resist. Her twin could practically read her mind thanks to their metaphysical connection. Their Soulkeeper powers didn't just give them the ability to share mass and copy others' appearances; they shared thoughts and feelings in a way only they could understand. By the look she wore, she'd caught the scent of insincerity and would hound Bonnie until she broke.

With a deep sigh, Bonnie resigned herself to share her innermost secret. "He makes me really uncomfortable," she whispered.

"I think, if he were dangerous, something would have happened by now."

"No, not because he was a Watcher."

"Then why?"

Bonnie glanced over her shoulder to make sure no one else was listening. "Because he keeps saying he thinks *I* changed him. He says he looked at me and, *abracadabra*, he was an angel."

Eyebrows descending, Samantha processed that for a moment. "We don't actually know what changed him. It seems like a sort of sweet thing to say."

Bonnie shook her head. "No, it isn't. It's manipulative. He almost killed me on that stairwell in the Harrington building. Do you remember how he shredded my face? I'm lucky to be alive."

"I remember."

"Well, he looked straight at me then, and he didn't change. I've reminded him of this repeatedly."

"And?"

"He still looks at me like … like I saved him." Bonnie spat out the last words and pressed her lips into a straight line.

Slowly, Samantha nodded. "I think I understand."

Bonnie breathed a sigh of relief.

"I understand that you are not afraid of Cord. You don't *really* believe that he is still a Watcher or somehow working for Lucifer." Samantha pointed one tapered finger toward her chest. "You're afraid that he is saved. You are afraid he's been redeemed."

"What?" Bonnie shook her head.

"You don't want him to be an angel because that would mean he has been forgiven by God even after all of the bad stuff he did, especially to you."

Bonnie turned her back on her sister, but Samantha didn't stop.

"You want Cord to pay for what he did to you, but if he's a changed man, you can't exact your revenge. Worse, it means that God has forgiven him for all the evil he brought down upon all of us, and that's not okay with you. The idea that you might have been the vessel for his redemption is the worst possible slap in your face, because you *want* to see him pay."

Bonnie's eyes darted around the room. She shifted from foot to foot, her sister's words sinking in. "So what?" Bonnie said, voice rising. "So I hate him for almost killing me. No, I don't want him to be redeemed, and I don't want him to be forgiven. He remembers, you know. He remembers all the bad things he has done. He's the same person, no matter his current intentions. You're right, I *do* think he should pay, redeemed or not. What's wrong with that?"

"Because it's not God's plan for him or Malini's. How long should he pay, Bon-bell? How long should he be starved, ironically locked in an empty pantry of all places, before we give him a chance?"

"Oh, I'm all for letting him out," Bonnie murmured.

"You are?"

"Yeah. In order to kill him." Bonnie handed Samantha the baby and headed for the door. She needed some air.

* * * * *

"What are you doing in here?" Jacob asked Malini. After he'd showered, he was hoping to catch some Zs but was disappointed to find she wasn't in bed. They'd shared a bed since coming to Sanctuary. It wasn't sexual. All of the Soulkeepers slept in one room by necessity. There was no privacy. People slept wherever they found comfort, and for the two of them, it just worked out to be in the same place, even with all of their clothes on.

Malini not being in bed meant trouble. When the Healer couldn't sleep, it was a bad sign. He'd tracked her down to the kitchen, where she was watching Cord eat through the bars of the pantry.

"Bonnie hasn't been feeding Cord," she said. "She was starving him on purpose, Jacob. I just want to make sure he gets a decent meal. I'm afraid if I leave him alone, she'll find a way to take his food from him."

Jacob rubbed his eyes with his thumb and forefinger. "I think there's something you should know."

"What?"

"She's not the only one who would prefer Cord starve to death."

Malini turned a horrified visage in Jacob's direction.

"Okay, no one actually said they wanted him dead." Jacob held up his hands in mock surrender. "I was exaggerating. But public opinion is he should stay locked up—that we can never trust him."

"Who said this?"

"My mom, but she says everyone is talking about it."

Her hands balled into fists. "Behind my back."

"Malini—"

"What, Jacob? What reasoning does 'everyone' give for leaving part of the third gift locked in a pantry?"

Jacob frowned. "Listen, people are just confused about what he is. Angel or not, he has a Watcher's history. He's a liability. He's an unknown risk."

She rubbed her forehead as if she had a headache. "My instincts tell me we need him. I think we are supposed to let him out. I think he's supposed to be part of the team."

"He could mean the death of us all." Jacob pointed at the steel grate. "What if the only thing keeping us safe is the door to that pantry? What if you're wrong?"

A red-hot blush crept over Malini's face. "I. Don't. Know." She turned on her heel and burst from the kitchen.

Jacob crossed his arms over his chest. "That went well," he said under his breath.

Chapter 4
The Fourth Curse

High above the city of Chicago, Damien answered Lucifer's call, arriving at the door to the largest penthouse in the world as if he was coming home to a long-lost friend. From the moment he was ushered into the place, he reveled in the reek of money and greed, his vice of choice. He could smell it here in the leather grain of the furniture, the rich woods, the high-end appliances. Even the carpet oozed luxury and affluence.

"Welcome, Damien," Lucifer said toward the floor-to-ceiling windows overlooking the city.

Why wouldn't Lucifer turn to face him? Damien didn't ask, and he certainly wasn't going to confront the Devil on his manners. Next to Lucifer, the blond Watcher, Auriel, stood with her back to the view. She exposed her teeth in what Damien presumed was a smile, but the envy wafting from the female could rival Levi's.

"Yes, welcome," Auriel said.

"I am here alone as requested," Damien said. "My brothers are waiting for me in the place you've given us to stay."

"Comfortable, I presume," Lucifer said without removing his eyes from the twinkling city lights.

"Much smaller than this place."

"As it should be," Auriel snapped. "Who are you to have a grander home than Lucifer?"

With a wave of his hand, Lucifer dismissed her comment. "We have work to do."

The pout that crossed her face before she was able to disguise it made Damien grin.

"Where should we start?" he asked.

"Your brothers. I have positions for each of them."

Damien sighed. "Each of them? You must know that Asher finds it difficult to focus with all of the new … human delights, and Levi will not be easy to keep happy." In fact, Levi spent hours or days brooding over his place in the universe, and Asher often disappeared for days at a time.

"Believe me, they can't be any worse than what we have today."

Auriel visibly cringed.

"You can tell your brothers, I have carefully considered their skills for select and privileged roles in our ranks. You, of course, will be responsible for keeping them in line. I have full faith in your abilities."

Auriel's mouth dropped open, but Lucifer did not acknowledge her reaction. Her jealousy pleased Damien, his innate voracity for wealth transferring to the Devil's attention.

"What do you have in mind?" Damien asked.

"For Levi, a job worthy of envy. He will command my legion. He will have ultimate power and responsibility for the other Watchers. This was Cord's position before he disappeared, and it has been woefully neglected as of late. My army is in need of a heavy hand." Lucifer turned his head to throw a pointed look at Auriel.

Damien straightened. "Perfect." The highest position was the only position for Levi, although he supposed his brother would find something to be envious of in time.

"Asher is a different matter entirely." Lucifer pivoted, finally, from the windows, pointing a finger in his direction. "How does he feel about politics?"

Damien rubbed a hand over his chest and sighed. Who knew what Asher was feeling? His lustful motivations were fleeting and varied. Still, pessimism would not do to close this deal. "They say politicians make strange bedfellows. Perhaps Asher would enjoy politics."

"Good. I will name him to the Council for the Eradication of the Unholy. I may have additional use for him in the future."

Damien nodded. "It's a good fit. And what of me?"

"That depends on you, Damien."

Damien eyed Lucifer suspiciously, waiting for an explanation. None was immediately offered.

"Auriel, I believe we've waited long enough to release the fourth curse, don't you?"

The blond Watcher batted her lashes as if she were just waking up from a long nap. "Yes, my lord."

"What do you think my fourth curse should be?" Lucifer asked.

"I think—" Auriel started.

"Not you, Auriel. I'm asking Damien."

Auriel slunk back, turning her crossed arms toward the wall of windows, her scowl reflecting in the dark skyline of the city.

Damien hesitated for a moment. Was this a trick? Did Lucifer actually expect him to choose the fourth curse? The brethren had heard of the challenge. All of the Watchers had. Why would the dark one trust such an important task to him? Unless he'd already chosen, and Damien was simply the vessel. And if that were the case, there was only one temptation apropos.

"Greed," Damien rumbled.

"Absolutely," Lucifer said. "So far, the good people of this city and country have survived by sharing what they have, but what will happen when we release you, my dear friend?"

"Me?"

"I've recently learned that Harrington could expand its reach if we entered the black market. We need to profit from the humans' efforts to survive our apocalypse."

A tingle rose from his core and settled in the hollow of his chest. "You want to control the competition?"

"Yes. Nothing shall be bought or sold anywhere without allegiance to me."

Damien rubbed his chin. "And you want me to make that happen?"

"I want you to use human greed to my advantage. You will become the greatest gangster the world has ever known."

"How?"

"Every business in this town with a Harrington Enterprises Security System has sworn allegiance to me. You will deliver the message that, from now on, a medallion isn't enough. Protection will require a mark, my mark, burned on the back of their hand. You shall be the source of such a mark. Nothing shall be bought or sold without the Harrington seal, both buyer and seller. You will tell them it is for their protection, by order of the Council for the Eradication of the Unholy. Without a seal, how can we tell for sure the person is not a demon? Make certain the police are the first to incorporate this change in policy. Anyone they catch buying or selling goods without my mark gets arrested."

"What if they don't comply? The humans have their own laws, their own consciences."

"My fourth temptation is greed. Our first step is to make the humans desire financial wealth above all things. Once their greed has taken hold, they will do anything to obtain more money, money they can only get by swearing allegiance to me by taking the mark."

"And how do we ensure their greed?" Damien asked.

Lucifer reached into his pocket and retrieved a hundred-dollar bill. Damien rubbed his hands together; this was getting good. Pinching the edges, Lucifer stretched the C-note above his head and gazed at it reverently. A barrage of guttural syllables poured forth from the dark one's throat, echoing unnaturally in the room. With a flash of fire, the bill dissolved into a thick green smoke that wafted toward the ventilation system.

"In a few hours, the population of oxygen breathers will be extremely receptive to any opportunity you put before them," Lucifer said.

"And then?"

Lucifer offered his hand. Tentatively, Damien accepted. At first, the handshake seemed as any other, Lucifer's beaming smile accompanying the rhythmic pumping. But then, Damien's palm began to burn. He tried to yank his hand away, but Lucifer wouldn't let go.

"Stop. STOP," Damien cried. Blood oozed from their clasped palms, the internal workings of his hand liquefying within the devil's grip. The sorcery wormed through the back of his hand and turned his fingernails black, even through his illusion. Damien dropped to his knees, jaw clenched from the pain. "Lucifer!"

The dark one retracted his hand. "I've given you my mark."

Damien lifted his trembling hand and looked at his palm. His skin throbbed red but was otherwise normal. On the back, however, a circular image was branded—a pentagram with ancient runes in each sector of the star. Damien had lived among men for ten thousand years and could speak a hundred languages, but he'd never seen symbols like these.

"This is my seal, Damien. It gives you alone the ability to hold your illusion in the sunlight. If you brand another with this seal, it will bind them to me. When you go to the police, tell them that if they do your bidding, they will be rewarded with a percentage of the money we earn in the street. Mark them with this seal, and there will be no turning back without the price of death."

"Yes, my lord." Damien flexed his burning hand and smiled at the mark. What power this would give him.

"Then go to each of the shop owners. Anyone doing business must serve me. If they agree, shake on it. This brand will burn itself into their skin, and they are mine."

Damien nodded. "And what of the workers?"

"All who work must take the mark. If the humans want to work to earn money to feed themselves, they must commit to me. And something else." A slow smile spread across Lucifer's face.

"Genius, I'm sure."

"Everyone who obtains the mark gets a job. Hire them at Harrington if you have to."

Damien grinned. "You are truly diabolical, Lucifer. No one buys, sells, or earns without aligning with you?"

"Exactly."

"And we corrupt the police to enforce your new law?"

"You are correct, my greedy friend."

"I can't wait to get started."

"One more thing, before you do."

"Yes?"

"We've lost a number of Watchers recently. Auriel tells me the bodies showed signs of holy intervention. The Soulkeepers are here. They're hunting us."

Damien emitted a low growl.

"They've blocked my power. I can't determine where they are hiding."

Auriel turned away from the window, eyes widening with surprise. "You never told me."

"I'll tell you when you need to know, Auriel," Lucifer snapped. He waved a hand in the air, and, in a flash of fire, a parchment formed in his hand. "This document contains the names and photographs of all the known Soulkeepers." He handed it to Damien, who unrolled it and inspected each of the ten faces.

"What shall I do with it, Lucifer?" he asked. "Do you want me to find them?"

"Give this list to all who wear my seal. Any who see these ten must report them to you immediately. If they bring me a body, I will reward them beyond their greatest imagining."

"And if I see one?"

"Kill on sight," Lucifer said. "Beware of this one." His finger landed on Malini's russet skin. "This is the Healer. Beware. She is stronger than she looks. If you find her, you must bring her to me."

"So be it." Sirens and shattering glass attracted Damien to the window. With his demonic vision, he could see the streets below swarming with people, pushing and shoving each other, arms laden with goods. "Looting." The word sent a pulse of pleasure through his body.

Auriel placed her hands on the glass next to Damien, watching the chaos below. He could tell she longed to be part of it, to be in his place. He relished the sense of power the brand on the back of his hand gave him. Whatever Lucifer's history with this one, she seemed to have fallen out of favor. In truth, Damien was only excited about taking her place because of how he might benefit from the experience. A short-term grovel at Lucifer's feet could gain him and his brothers an independent and permanent empire of wealth. But, the gravy on top was her pain. To have gained what she lost made his skin buzz.

"It appears the fourth temptation has taken hold," Lucifer said. "Go, Damien. Show no mercy. Teach the humans about our new order."

Damien nodded and slipped from the room, disappointed to leave the opulence of the penthouse, but excited about the possibilities of running this city and beyond.

Chapter 5
Empty

Bonnie stood across the street from the convenience store with the Harrington Demon Eradication System octagon in the window, hoping today would be easy. The Soulkeepers had been lucky the last several weeks. They'd kept up on their Watcher kill quotas and gathered supplies without much in the way of trouble or injuries. However, luck could be fleeting. Supplies were hard to come by these days, and more shops than not had the Harrington logo. Those that didn't often had nothing on their shelves.

She'd done this dozens of times since moving into Sanctuary, but somehow today seemed different. Her gut ached with the sense of holding a position too long, innards stretched and twisted to their breaking point. Maybe it was her argument with Malini about Cord. Maybe it was the anger she nursed toward Lucifer over what he'd done to Abigail and Gideon. All she knew was she was twitchy and uncomfortable, even before walking into the place.

It wasn't easy to stay safe without showing any of the weapons that could keep her that way. She'd dressed in layers: jeans and a T-shirt, followed by two sheathed daggers, one on each wrist, and a longer blade that fit along her calf under her pant leg. A sweater went on next, followed by a jacket, a hat to cover her pinned-up red hair, and sunglasses. A switchblade fit in her jacket pocket. Chances were, if attacked, she'd reach for her sister not the blades, but it was always a good idea to have a backup plan. Plus, even meshed together into the giant ogre body they preferred to fight with, she and Samantha would need a weapon.

"You ready to do this?" Samantha said, looking decidedly like the Stay Puft Marshmallow Man in her down-filled coat. Bonnie knew she was loaded to the gills with weapons too.

"Yeah. Where's our third?"

Ghost materialized at Samantha's side, a hatchet from Eden in his hand. "Ready as I'm going to be." He slipped the weapon into a secret compartment inside his coat.

Bonnie looked around her, but there was no one watching. "Jeez, Ghost, could you be a little more careful flaunting the hatchet? We're in public. It's not going to help if we get arrested."

"No one notices me, Bonnie. That's part of my power. Trust in it."

"Like they didn't notice when you were trying to kill Cord?" During their Harrington mission, Ghost had captured the Watcher Cord and had a knife to his neck when a crowd of do-gooders saved the fallen angel.

"That was different. They noticed Cord screaming and came to *his* rescue. They didn't actually notice me until the very end."

Samantha placed her hands on her hips and cocked her head, frowning. "Jesse…"

"I'll be more careful," Ghost grumbled. "Who has the money?"

Sam raised her mittened hand. "Malini gave me five hundred and the list. We're out of almost everything. We might need to make multiple trips. Jacob said not to avoid the Harrington Security places. He thought the others might be too unpredictable, especially with the weird looting last night. Hope needs formula."

Bonnie and Ghost nodded.

"Let's do this. I want to be done before dusk," Bonnie said.

The three crossed the street and Ghost opened the door for the twins. A bell chimed over Bonnie's head.

"Welcome to Harold's," a man called from the front of the store.

Bonnie couldn't see him because of the placement of the shelves, but she returned a polite greeting. She pulled a cart from the corral at the front of the store. "Let's divide and conquer," she whispered to the others. Sam and Ghost each grabbed a cart and headed down separate aisles.

Squee, squee, squeeeee. It would figure she'd get the cart with the squeaky wheel. Bonnie groaned. The front left barely reached the floor and spun noisily every time she advanced, but she was feeling too anxious to waste time going back for another. She attempted to ignore the annoyance and mentally ticked off the items she retrieved from the shelves: formula, diapers, antibiotic ointment, paper towels. Her cart was full in no time. She met Ghost at the end of the aisle.

"I think we should check out and take a load back to Sanctuary," she whispered. "This is as much as we can carry."

He nodded. "Wait. There's a customer."

Sam joined them at the head of the aisle, eyeing a shelf of shampoo to keep herself busy and avoid suspicion. Soulkeeper protocol was to avoid contact with the public as much as possible. High noon, Bonnie wasn't concerned the woman buying a gallon of milk and a loaf of bread was a Watcher, but humans tended to want to talk and talking wasn't good for keeping a low profile, especially when both shopper and clerk were wearing medallions with Lucifer's face on the back.

"She's gone. Come on." Ghost led the way to the counter. Bonnie followed. Since Sam had the money, it made sense for her to go last.

"Good afternoon," the cashier said. Bonnie noticed his name tag read Mr. Harold. Did he own Harold's or was the name a coincidence? She didn't risk the small talk to ask. A small patch of bright red blood soaked through a bandage on the back of his right hand. Bonnie frowned at the injury. Her stomach churned with nervous energy.

"Afternoon," Ghost said, reaching to unload his basket onto the counter.

"Wait a moment, son. I need to see proper identification before I can ring you up for that."

"Identification?" Ghost asked.

"Your Harrington medallion. We don't serve demons here. No medallion, no service, unless of course you have one of these." He peeled back the bandage to expose a scabby red burn in the shape of a pentagram with symbols in each of the star's sections. He'd been branded. Bonnie forced herself not to jerk away from the bloody mess and rancid smell. She held her breath.

"Oh, is this something new?" Bonnie said, digging in her collar as if trying to find the chain to her medallion.

The man narrowed his eyes. "Haven't you read your email? This is the Harrington upgrade, Demon Eradication 2.0. A medallion used to be enough to protect you. Now the demons are posing as humans. If we are going to beat these monsters, we've got to make sure they are not among us. From now on, you'll have to have one of these to buy or sell anything, even to work, by dictate of the Council for the Eradication of the Unholy."

"So, the brand is to make sure demons don't buy anything?" Samantha asked. The last word petered out as if she'd run out of breath. Before this, medallions were used for protection, not identification, and their money was always good enough. Bonnie's heart sank as she met her sister's gaze. This meant trouble.

"You have a day to get yours from city hall. Tomorrow, even a medallion won't be enough." Mr. Harold's lips pulled into a straight line. "Now let's see those medallions."

Ghost backed away from the counter. "On second thought, I don't think I'll be needing anything today." He abandoned the cart and moved for the door.

Bonnie found Sam's hand and pulled her past the end of the counter. "Thanks anyway."

Mr. Harold eyed the three carts. His face reddened. "Hold it right there, kids. You can't leave this stuff here." His hand reached out for Bonnie's shoulder but snagged her crocheted hat instead. As he pulled back, her red locks fell around her shoulders.

"Sorry," he said, handing her the hat. "If you don't want this stuff, you need to return it to the shelves."

Bonnie tucked a strand of hair behind her ear and grabbed the corner of her cart, pulling it toward her body. "Okay." Mr. Harold glared at her with a look that could cut glass. "We're going to put it all back," she said.

"Please remove your glasses," Mr. Harold said.

"Why?" Bonnie asked.

Mr. Harold bent down to retrieve something from under the counter, revealing a poster on the wall behind the register. Bonnie glanced at the notice and froze. Her picture, all of their pictures, stared back at her from under large red letters that read *Wanted Dead or Alive*. She hadn't noticed it before because Mr. Harold's body had been blocking her view of it from the counter.

"What the hell?" she murmured.

Mr. Harold straightened, pointing the long barrel of a gun in her direction. Bonnie dodged left, and the shelf behind her head exploded. *Damn*. Bonnie thanked the Lord he wasn't a good shot.

"Soulkeepers," Mr. Harold growled.

A random woman in one of the aisles screamed at the sound of gunfire and kept screaming as Bonnie raced for the exit. Ghost had already grabbed Sam and was dragging her through the double glass doors.

Bonnie's hand connected with the door pull, but she didn't have a chance to open it. A man tackled her from the side, knocking her into a display of postcards. She toppled with the rack, glasses flying from her face and skimming across the floor. Using her superhuman speed, she ousted herself from under the man and flipped to her feet, pulling the switchblade from her pocket. The door was blocked by another store patron. In fact, every human in the place was closing in, and Mr. Harold still had the gun. A large, scary-looking gun.

"Wait, you don't understand," Bonnie said, holding her hands up. Mr. Harold's finger twitched. She grabbed the man beside her, pulling him into a chokehold and pressed her blade into his jugular. "Don't shoot. You'll hit him." These were humans, not Watchers. *Don't panic*, she told herself. *You are stronger and faster.*

She glanced out the window, looking for Ghost and Samantha. Unfortunately, she found both of them running for their lives from a crowd of humans, some with baseball bats. Help was not coming. Rattled, she looked back at Mr. Harold.

From behind the barrel of the gun, the man bared his teeth. "Unfortunately, I can't let you go, Soulkeeper. There's a price on your head. You're dangerous."

Bonnie's pulse pounded in her ears as she sidestepped along the window toward the exit. She didn't make it. The gun fired. Instinctively, she blocked the bullet with the man's body. There was no time for guilt. She tossed him aside, then dove through the window, somersaulting over the patch of grass out front. As she bolted toward the alley across the street, gunshots bombarded the ground around her. More shattering glass.

Digging deep, she scrambled between buildings. Dead end. The alley was segmented by a stretch of chain link. The stomp of feet behind her motivated a vertical jump worthy of an NBA star. Not good enough. She slammed into the top of the fence and tumbled over, limbs flailing. Her landing was hard, enough to buckle her knees. The crowd behind her screamed obscenities, their bodies slamming into the chain link, but she didn't look back. Panting, she darted from the alley and wove through a parking lot at super-speed, racing for safety until her legs burned so badly from the effort she couldn't take another step.

She took cover behind the base of a massive concrete statue. As she tucked her hair back into her hat, she got her bearings. The park near Sanctuary. Almost home.

Pain shot through her torso. Or maybe the pain had been there all along, but she hadn't noticed with the adrenaline pumping through her veins. The front of her coat was covered in blood. She unzipped the puffy, purple jacket and tried to pull it away from her chest. It snagged, and a sharp pain shot through her. A large piece of glass had passed through the down, next to the zipper, embedding itself in the space above and to the left of her belly button. With a shaking hand, she grabbed the edge and pulled.

It wasn't the smartest thing she'd ever done. A gurgle of blood followed the glass out of her body. Pressing her hand over the hole, she stumbled forward. Sanctuary. She had to get home, or she was dead for sure.

Her head swam. Black dots danced in her vision. Bonnie moved as fast as possible toward checkpoint one. She paused. Safe. With her last bout of energy, she sprinted for the rectory, slipping inside the door and closing it behind her. Checkpoint two. Her chest felt heavy when Ghost and Sam weren't there, or maybe it was the wound that bled through her coat. She couldn't hear anything outside, but even if she had, she couldn't wait a moment longer. She needed help.

Light-headed, she staggered down the steps and spilled into Sanctuary, barely able to stay upright. "Help," she rasped. Her voice wasn't working properly, and there was no one in the large open room. "Help," she rasped again. Where was everyone? She stumbled toward the kitchen, thinking Grace might be inside.

The door pushed open. The kitchen was empty aside from Cord, who locked eyes with her through the bars of the pantry door. "Help," she mouthed. She flopped to the floor in the doorway, unable to go a step farther. If she were going to die, she would do it here. Vision darkening, her only regret was Sam. She wouldn't get a chance to say goodbye. But there was no choice. Welcome unconsciousness overcame her.

Chapter 6
Angel

Blissful warmth washed through Bonnie's body, soothing the ache that had taken over everything moments before. Light turned the inside of her eyelids red. At first, she kept them closed, afraid of the pain of staring into the sun, but eventually her logical mind roused and remembered she wasn't outside. She cracked one eye, then the other. The glow above her surrounded two beautiful blue eyes and a straight white smile.

"Cord?" she asked.

He retracted his light, folding the white aura inside his skin. His hand lifted from her chest, and Bonnie thought she might cry from the loss of the warmth that went with it.

"I am sorry I broke the rules and left the pantry, but you needed my help," Cord said.

Bonnie sat up and glanced to where she'd pulled the glass from her chest. The skin under the hole in her shirt was a fresh pink color, completely healed.

"You fixed me," she said.

"I aimed for pressure to stop the bleeding. Surprisingly, I was able to do more." He flexed and stretched his fingers, full lips slightly parted.

Bonnie could relate. She was feeling rather amazed at the moment as well. Speechless, she blinked at his hands and then glanced over her shoulder at the pantry. It was still locked.

"H-how did you get out?" she squeaked.

"I blended with the light and passed through the bars."

"Could you do that the whole time?" Bonnie's gaze connected with his.

Cord spread his hands and shrugged. "I never tried until now."

"All those times I left your food too far away for you to reach ... weren't you hungry? Why didn't you try then?"

His face fell. "I didn't know I could. I didn't want to risk angering you and the other Soulkeepers. You've been good to me, keeping me alive after what I've done. It wasn't important enough."

"And I was?"

Cord's blue eyes met hers, but he didn't respond.

The sound of pounding feet announced the arrival of Dane, Ethan, and Grace, who was holding Hope on her shoulder. They appeared in the doorway to the kitchen next to Bonnie's feet. The three Soulkeepers gaped at the scene on the kitchen floor.

Cord leaned over Bonnie protectively, one wing spread behind her back and the other shielding her lower legs.

Grace's eyebrows shot toward the ceiling. "Bonnie, you're bleeding. Do you need Malini?" Her mother's eyes darted between Cord and the bloody stain on Bonnie's shirt and coat. Dane and Ethan did the same.

Bonnie folded her legs underneath her and stood. "Cord healed me." She parted her coat to show her healthy, pink skin.

Three sets of eyes widened in her direction.

"Where have you guys been, anyway?" Bonnie asked. "I yelled for help."

Grace found her voice. "We were soaking weapons in the holy water upstairs. We thought we heard something and came down to see. We would have come sooner, but we thought the others were here. Where is everyone?"

Cord answered. "The one called Ghost came and got them. He said he needed help. I heard from the pantry."

"Oh dear Lord," Bonnie said, "my sister! The humans were chasing them too."

"Too?" Grace gasped. "Why were humans chasing you?"

"Our faces are everywhere, Mom. We are America's most wanted. And get this—all of the posters say we are demons in disguise."

Grace shook her head.

"Why would they think that?" Dane sputtered.

"How did they get our pictures?" Ethan asked.

"There's more—" Bonnie began, but at that moment Malini, Jacob, and Lillian stormed into Sanctuary, pausing deer-in-headlights style behind the group in the doorway.

"Thank goodness you made it back," Malini said. She cringed at the blood on Bonnie's jacket and reached for the wound.

Bonnie held up her hand and shook her head.

Lillian frowned at the scene, looking first at the blood on Bonnie's chest and then reproachfully at Cord. "How did you get out? What did you do to her?"

"He didn't do anything but heal me," Bonnie said softly.

"The light." Cord pointed at the large fluorescent above his head. "I traveled through the light to help her."

At that moment, Cheveyo, Samantha, and Ghost rushed in. Sam paled when she saw Bonnie covered in blood.

"I'm fine," Bonnie said.

Sam shouldered her way into the kitchen and tossed her arms around her sister's neck. "Oh, thank God. We thought…"

Ghost drew in a relieved breath. "We thought you were dead."

"I'm fine," Bonnie repeated. She couldn't think of anything else to say, and currently, her neurons were swarming with questions, about Cord and about herself. She'd almost starved the angel who had saved her. A black hole of guilt opened behind her breastbone and pulled her heart into the pit of her stomach. She pushed Sam away.

"We need to talk about what happened today at the grocery," Bonnie said.

Samantha quickly agreed. "It's bad. I think Lucifer has handed out his fourth curse."

Ghost nodded, focusing on Malini. "Worse than anything we expected."

"You heard them," Malini said to the group. "Emergency meeting. Cheveyo, go get Father Raymond." Cheveyo gave a two-fingered salute before jogging up the stairs.

Cord turned back toward the pantry, but Bonnie stopped him by gripping his wrist. He met her eyes in silent exchange. She couldn't say all was forgiven. She still remembered the way it felt to have his talons shred her face, but he was different now. She finally accepted the obvious.

"Where do you think you're going, Cord?" Malini asked, breaking their connection.

The angel glanced at her hopefully, wings tucking down the length of his back as he straightened his posture.

Bonnie's lips parted as she searched Malini's face.

"We are not going to keep a bona fide angel locked up in the pantry, especially not one who can heal. Get out there and grab a chair. You're officially part of the team."

Bonnie couldn't miss the way Cord's face glowed as he left the kitchen, but she did catch the disappointed look Malini shot her.

"You were right, okay?" Bonnie said. "I'm sorry I fought you on this. It won't happen again."

Malini smiled and held the door open for her. "Good. Come on. Sounds like you had a hell of a mission this morning."

Bonnie nodded. "Unfortunately, that expression is more literally true than any of us imagined."

* * * * *

The Soulkeepers gathered around the conference table they'd acquired a few weeks ago, fidgeting in the padded chairs. Bonnie grabbed a dry erase marker and headed for the board. "The shop owner had a symbol on his arm, like this." She tried her best to draw the pentagram with the symbols accurately. "He said no one could buy or sell anything without it."

"And what's worse," Ghost interrupted, "when we tried to leave, people hunted us in the street like animals. Our faces are on wanted posters all over the city. Ordinary humans were climbing all over each other to take us down."

Samantha hugged her abdomen. "Yeah, I heard them say there was a reward for us, dead or alive."

Malini cursed. "Are you sure it wasn't isolated? Maybe they were influenced?"

"No." Sam shook her head. "When Jesse dematerialized to get help, I saw a police officer in the street. I ran for him, thinking he would help me, until I saw the mark on his hand. Even the cops are in on it."

"Mr. Harold told us that the brand is part of Harrington's new security requirements, Demon Eradication 2.0. People have twenty-four hours to get the brand from city hall. After today, no one can buy or sell anything, or work for money without the brand," Bonnie said. She capped the marker and returned it to the tray at the bottom of the board, then sat down at the table next to Samantha.

"This one, even I should have predicted," Father Raymond said, holding up a Bible. "Revelation 13:16-17 *And he causes all, the small and the great, and the rich and the poor, and the free men and the slaves, to be given a mark on their right hand or forehead, and he provides that no one will be able to buy or sell, except those who have the mark.*"

Hope began to fuss in Grace's arms. The older woman stood from her chair and paced to comfort her.

"It's the fourth curse," Malini said. "It's not enough to buy the Harrington Eradication system or sign the contract anymore. Now, if you want to eat, you have to have his seal burned into your skin."

Jacob cleared his throat. "So, uh, we knew this was coming, right?"

Eleven pairs of eyes came to rest on him. Tugging the string on his hoodie, Jacob shrugged. "We knew there would be six temptations and six gifts. It's been three weeks since

Lucifer unleashed terror on the human race in the form of the apocalypse. It was only a matter of time before the other shoe dropped."

"Jacob's right," Malini said. "I think we all knew something like this was coming. I just didn't expect him to use the humans like this. We've always counted on the sun for protection. Now we'll have to be as careful during the day as we are in the darkness, not just from the Watchers but from the humans."

"Malini," Lillian said. "I hate to be the bearer of bad news, but we are gravely in need of supplies. We might have enough to feed everyone tonight, but Hope is running out of formula and if we don't replenish our stores, no one eats tomorrow."

Malini stalked to the whiteboard. "Ideas, let's have them people."

"I could go alone," Ghost said. "I could blink inside, grab what we needed, and blink out."

The black marker squeaked across the board.

Cheveyo piped up. "You still gotta get to the store, man. If what Sam says is true, walking down the street could be deadly for you."

"Plus, you can only carry what you can fit in your arms," Sam said. "No offense, Jesse, but it won't be enough to feed us all."

Father Raymond raised a hand. "My face isn't on the list."

"You can't get the mark, Father. It's your soul," Grace said.

"No. But I still have the rectory's car. It's small, and it's buried in the rubble, but if you can get it out and working, I can provide transport for Ghost. I can drive to the front of a store, and he can use his gifts to take what we need, right?"

The group nodded hopefully.

"We'll have to be careful," Malini said. "Ghost's power is limited. We use him too much and he'll be sick. Plus, we'll have to remove him from rotation."

Lillian nodded. "We'll need to ration our supplies."

Malini agreed. "Priority one is Hope. If nothing else, Ghost and Father Raymond can get diapers and formula. Now, what else? How do we get food?"

"We could use the enchanted staffs," Dane suggested.

"Too dangerous," Malini said. "We still don't know why Lucifer hasn't called our souls, but the staffs work due to a spell Abigail and Gideon performed before they became human. It's possible the sorcery could leave a trail Lucifer could follow to us."

Dane leaned back in his chair and crossed his arms.

Bonnie placed her hands on her hips and stared at the board as if she were looking through it. "Sam and I could try to replicate the cashier we saw at the store—Mr. Harold. We should be able to recreate the symbol on his hand by illusion."

Malini wrote a number two and jotted *Bonnie, Sam, symbol* under Ghost's suggestion. She paused, presumably waiting for someone to rip the idea apart. No one said anything. The room grew quiet. She turned back toward the group. "Any other suggestions?"

Dane and Ethan became obsessed with the carpeting, and the others refused to look Bonnie in the eye. The team was relying too much on her and Sam, and honestly, just the thought felt like a one-ton boulder on her shoulders, but what other choice did she have? She saw pity on each of their faces, but no one spoke up on her or her twin's behalf, not even Jesse.

"Bonnie shouldn't have to go again so soon after getting hurt," Cord said hesitantly, as if he wasn't sure he was allowed to speak. "I could travel by light. If you give me a list, I can pass in and out of the store unseen."

Bonnie blinked at the angel, torn between wanting to hug him for offering and the terror that came with trusting the unknown.

Lillian shook her head. "None of us has any idea what he can and cannot do. Not for sure. He could go back to Lucifer." The table erupted in grumbles of agreement.

Malini tipped her head and pointed a hand in his direction. "He can travel by light. He proved that with Bonnie. He can leave anytime he wants to."

"But he won't," Bonnie said, compelled to stick up for him. "I believe him when he says he won't."

Malini stared at the angel with her lips pressed together. "I believe him, too."

"Believe him or not, he can still only carry an armful at a time," Ghost said. "Unless we are going to send Father Raymond out twice."

"We can do that," Father Raymond said. "It will simply take longer."

"Maybe we could go together." Bonnie blurted before she could think about what she was saying. Silence pressed against her. Her mother's mouth dropped open. "It makes sense that only one of us would take on the image of the shop owner. He was a big man, and even if we chose another human, it will be suspicious if we go together. If I transform into Mr. Harold, Cord can blend into the light and stay with me to protect me and to help carry. Plus, I can keep an eye on him."

Samantha opened her mouth to protest, but Bonnie saw Ghost's hand clamp down on her sister's fingers. She closed her mouth again. *That's right. Can't risk losing your girl.* As for Bonnie, she had nothing to lose. She was like Cord in that.

Somewhere deep inside, she knew that this was Cord's one chance to redeem himself to the group. Maybe the tar trap of guilt that had formed in the center of her chest caused her to care more than usual for the angel. Maybe thankfulness for him saving her life drove her suggestion. Then again, maybe it was something more. She didn't want to admit the last. The idea that she might actually care for the reformed Watcher who'd almost killed her made her shiver. She decided not to analyze it.

"It's settled," Malini said. "Dane and Ethan, help dig out the car. Ghost and Father Raymond will go tonight for the essentials. Bonnie and Cord will go tomorrow. Let's hope this works."

Chapter 7
Hope

Malini bounced Hope in her arms, wishing Father Raymond and Ghost would get back soon with her formula. The sun was down. Dane, Ethan, and Jacob had already left on Watcher patrol. Malini was beginning to worry that something had gone wrong, and now was not the time. Hope's last bottle was empty, only half the ounces the babe usually drank, and she'd thrown up most of it.

The baby's piercing blue eyes misted over, and she scrubbed her face with her tiny, uncoordinated hand. Hope's eyes would forever remind Malini of Abigail's, and the shape of her face was all Gideon. What would her parents think of her letting their daughter go hungry?

"Don't take this the wrong way, but do you know what's wrong with her?" Cheveyo asked. Off rotation for the night, he was on his way to laundry duty with a basket of black-blood-stained clothes under one arm.

"I think she's hungry," Malini said.

"Hmmm." Cheveyo continued to stare at Hope, eyebrows low and close together. "No. I don't think so. She's coughing all the time and not keeping her food down."

Malini frowned. "I've noticed. I've been giving her healing energy. Maybe she has a touch of the flu or something."

"Yeah," Cheveyo said. He didn't move.

"Are you going to do laundry?" she asked.

He nodded, staring at Hope with that worried expression on his face.

"Is something wrong, Cheveyo?"

The Hopi boy dropped the basket and plopped down on the end of the bed. "I haven't been around many babies since I became a Soulkeeper. Well, actually I've never been around babies. If I'd grown up on the reservation, I would have. Everyone there takes care of everyone else's baby. It's a Hopi thing. I was raised by my Caucasian mom."

"I remember."

"Anyway, I don't know much about babies." He bobbed his head.

Malini met his dark brown eyes. He was staring at her with an intensity she'd rarely seen in his usually laid-back personality. Something was up. Either he had a confession to make or he was going to admit his undying love for her. She hoped it was the first.

"Cheveyo, are you procrastinating on the laundry or is there something you want to say to me?"

He sighed heavily and wiped his palms on his thighs. "It's just, I don't know if this is important or not. Maybe it's nothing. Maybe it's completely normal. I haven't been a Soulkeeper that long, and I don't want to freak anyone out over nothing." He stopped short, toying with a loose thread on her bed covering.

Frustrated, Malini reached out and shook his arm. "Out with it."

He leaned in, looking right, then left across the empty room. "Hope's soul is *different*."

Malini turtled her head back on her neck. "What do you mean?"

"I can sense souls. That's my gig, you know. For example, yours is like this nice green haze around your body. I can't actually see the color. It just feels green. Abigail was like a cool breeze. That's how I found her in the kitchen in Lucifer's penthouse. Every person's soul is unique, but so far they've all had one thing in common."

"What?"

"They are all slightly bigger than the person's body." He nodded and stared at her expectantly.

A strange foreboding frosted the tips of Malini's fingers and toes. She moved Hope to her shoulder facing away from Cheveyo as if her tiny ears wouldn't hear if her eyes couldn't see. "Are you suggesting that there is something wrong with Hope's *soul*?"

Cheveyo cringed. "Well, uh…" He reached for the laundry basket. "Like I said, I'm new. I could be wrong."

"Wait. I'm sorry. I didn't mean to snap at you. Tell me what you were going to say." Malini forced her expression to stay neutral.

Tucking his long hair behind his ears, Cheveyo stared at the carpet. "Her soul is small for her body." He pointed at a spot between her shoulder blades. "It just sort of hovers around her heart. I wasn't going to say anything because I thought it was from being a baby, but then I noticed a change."

"Change?"

"Yeah, like when she was first born it took up most of her torso, and now, it's smaller. Or maybe her body has grown. I don't know. I just thought it might have something to do with her being sick."

Malini tipped Hope back into her lap, searching the baby girl's face. She'd fallen asleep on her shoulder, and the precious bundle breathed peacefully in her arms. "Thank you for telling me, Cheveyo. I know that wasn't easy for you. Like you say, it might be nothing. Maybe that's how babies are. We'll watch her and see."

Cheveyo breathed a sigh of relief. "Cool. I knew you'd know what to do." He popped off the bed and lifted the basket into his arms. With a short "see ya later," he disappeared in the direction of the laundry room.

A tiny cough brought Malini's gaze back to the rhythm of Hope's breathing. The foreboding tingle hadn't left her. In fact, it had spread, chilling her entire body. She prayed Cheveyo's observation was a mistake, a harmless reality of her babyhood. If it wasn't, he was wrong about one thing: Malini had no idea what to do about a problem with Hope's soul.

Chapter 8
Busted

"Are you there?" Bonnie asked, scratching the back of her right hand. The brand itched terribly. It was an illusion, the same as Mr. Harold's graying brown hair and wide shoulders. She hoped it was dry skin and not an omen of things to come.

A twinkle caught the corner of her eye in the early morning light. Cord whispered, "I am here."

"I'm nervous. What if I didn't get the symbol exactly right? I only saw it one time."

"I'll protect you."

The caring in his voice made her turn away, fearful the hot creep up her neck might reveal how much the words meant to her. With a deep breath, she approached the store on the corner. They'd chosen this one, on the outskirts of the city, precisely because it was as far away as possible from the shop whose owner's image she was wearing. The place was called Quik N Smart. She hoped she could be both today.

Hyperaware of Cord's presence, she opened the door, trying not to jump at the *bee-boop* of the chime as she crossed the threshold. The place was empty. Good. She retrieved a cart. Milk, meat, cereal, canned goods. Quickly, she navigated the aisles. When the cart was overflowing from the haul, she took a deep breath.

"Here goes nothing," she whispered and headed for the counter.

The woman behind the register gave her a tight smile as she approached. She was young and beautiful, dark like she might be Middle Eastern or southern European. Maybe both. She scratched her neck beneath her mass of dark waves. A nervous tic?

"Good morning," Bonnie said in Harold's deep baritone, praying the girl didn't know the shop owner.

"I need to see your hand," the woman said. Again with the scratching. She was nervous. Question was, about what? The plastic name tag on her shirt read Candace.

"Sure, Candace," Bonnie said with a smile meant to put her at ease. Inside, her stomach twisted as she offered up the symbol.

"Yours looks new. Still red around the edges," Candace said.

Working hard to remain calm, Bonnie nodded and began to unload the cart. Candace typed something into the computerized cash register, and then began to scan the items one by one. At first, Bonnie thought the woman must be new. She flipped each item multiple times before finding the code to scan, then bagged it carefully. Minutes ticked by. Bonnie glanced at her watch. Could anyone really be this slow?

A bead of sweat dripped from her hairline. Something was wrong. Her intuition was banging pots and pans together in her mental kitchen, yet the woman seemed perfectly calm behind the counter. Maybe Bonnie was just paranoid.

"That will be two hundred twenty-five dollars."

Bonnie dug in her pocket for the cash Malini had given her, counted it quickly, and handed the wad to Candace. The woman slowly sorted the bills, turning and flattening them.

"You know, since Harrington added these tattoos to their protocol, you wouldn't believe the number of people who come in here without one. It's amazing what people will try to get away with. I mean, can you imagine the nerve?" She laughed nervously.

"I can imagine," she murmured. A cold ripple traveled the length of Bonnie's spine, clenching the muscles in her jaw as it flowed through her nervous system. The clamor of her intuition made her fingers twitch.

"Do you think it's fair? I sold my soul for this brand, and the protection it gives me. That's what it says in the small print. Lots of people don't read the small print, but I did.

When you get your brand, you swear to align yourself body, mind, and soul to Milton Blake and Harrington Enterprises. Seems odd for a corporation to ask for your soul, but this *is* the apocalypse."

Bonnie reached for one of the grocery bags, but Candace knocked her hand away. "Why should someone else get to keep their soul and still eat?" She folded the money and slid it into her pocket.

"What are you doing?" Bonnie asked.

Candace snorted derisively. "Do you know how you can tell a brand isn't real?"

Bonnie took a step backward, shaking her head.

The woman offered her right hand. A twisting length of blackness squirmed beneath the skin of her mark, causing the symbol to warp and bubble under the light. "It started this morning. See the worm? These things are alive, now. It's a fail-safe. Makes it easy to see who's not playing for our team."

Bonnie bolted for the door, but it was too late. Three huge men in police uniforms stood in the doorway.

Candace called out, "I was beginning to worry this one would leave before you got here."

One of the men adjusted his cap. "Nice work, Candace."

The second man pulled a nightstick from his belt and slapped his hand with it. "Sir, you need to come with us. Everyone is required to get the Harrington seal."

"It only hurts for a moment," the third one said. "You'll hardly notice the pinch."

The three men blocked the doorway, shoulder to shoulder. There was no way Bonnie could move around them. Her eyes flashed to the windows. *Security bars. Damn.* Frozen with fear, she shivered in Mr. Harold's skin.

"Move. MOVE," Cord shouted. A force yanked back her elbow and then an entire shelf of beauty products crashed to the floor between her and the men. Her muscles engaged, and she stumbled toward the back of the store. Cord formed at her side and pushed her toward a door. She opened it.

"Storeroom. No windows," she said. The rattle and crash of the men climbing over the fallen shelves caused her heart to hammer behind her breastbone.

"This way." Cord corralled her into the filthy confines of the men's room, locking the door behind him and pointing at a small window near the ceiling. "Out."

The policemen banged on the door, shouting warnings and threats through the barrier, and then the metal on metal of someone inserting a key in the lock caused a new kind of fear to bloom in her chest.

"Now, Bonnie." Cord punched through the window and propelled her through the jagged hole. She belly-crawled into the alley behind the store, glass scraping the front of her body.

"Where do you think you're going?" said a voice from the shadows. Holy hell, a Watcher. The demon was huge, twice the size of an ordinary Watcher and with an attitude that was almost palpable. He stood in the shadows, large and dark, with a silk shirt and gaudy rings on his fingers. "I can smell you a mile away, Soulkeeper."

Cord materialized beside her. The Watcher's eyes widened at the sight of the angel, and he hissed like an animal. With both hands, Cord pushed Bonnie toward the street.

The Watcher attacked. *Smack.* Angel and demon collided in a shower of sparks. Smoke billowed from the places of contact: hands, chest, and the side of one leg. Cord groaned, and the smell of burning flesh filled the small space.

"What are you waiting for? Run," Cord commanded.

The Watcher's illusion broke as the struggle moved into daylight, but even in shadow there was no way anyone would mistake the two in the alley as human. The fight was too fast. Too brutal.

Bonnie backed toward the street slowly, wondering if she should help Cord. His eyes met hers. Cord lowered his shoulder and barreled into the Watcher again. "Run!"

This time, she obeyed.

The journey home was a blur, but Bonnie finally tumbled into Sanctuary, huffing from the run. "Help. You've got to help," she insisted. A cold breeze blew through the room from behind her.

"Is the door open?" Malini asked, staring up the stairwell. "What happened?"

"Yes. I'm sorry. It's Cord." Bonnie braced herself on her knees.

"Dane, go lock up," Malini ordered. He nodded and bounded up the stairs.

"Please," Bonnie rasped. "There's no time. He'll kill him."

Malini placed an arm around Bonnie's shoulders, infusing her with healing warmth as the other Soulkeepers circled them. Samantha leaned worriedly over her sister. "What happened?"

"The brand won't work. The real brand ... is alive. It moves. When we tried to use this"—Bonnie rubbed the back of her hand—"we were caught. The police came and then a Watcher attacked us. Not just a Watcher ... he was huge—some kind of mega-Watcher or something. I only got away because of Cord."

"Where is Cord now?"

"Fighting the Watcher in the alley behind Quik N Smart. We have to help him."

Malini hugged Bonnie's shoulders. "Sam, come help your sister shift back into herself. Bonnie, don't worry; we'll help Cord."

Samantha reached for Bonnie's fingers. The change came quickly, but it did nothing to improve Bonnie's distraught state.

"Please, help him," Bonnie said again.

"No need." Cord formed in the middle of the room, under the brightest lightbulb in Sanctuary. Silver-white blood dripped from a swollen wound on his face, and one wing hung limply from his back. He collapsed on the nearest bed, which buckled under his weight.

"Easy," Jacob said, obviously recognizing it was his bunk. Malini quieted him with a glare.

Bonnie rushed to Cord's side, and Malini followed.

"I don't think I can heal you," Malini said. "It doesn't work on angels."

"Don't concern yourself. I'll heal myself in time."

"But how did you get away?" Bonnie asked. "When I left, the Watcher had the upper hand."

Cord's head rolled to the side so he could see her better. "Once I knew you were safe, I broke away and dissolved into the light. He couldn't follow. Watchers travel through shadow."

Bonnie sighed, dropping onto the floor next to the bed.

"We're glad you made it out alive," Malini said.

Cord pushed himself into a seated position and wiped some silver blood out from under his eye. "I am worried for you," he said, eyes falling on each of them and then lingering on Bonnie. "I know the Watcher who attacked Bonnie and me. He's not a typical Watcher, and he never works alone. He's one of the Wicked Brethren."

"The Wicked Brethren?" Malini asked. "Who are the Wicked Brethren?"

Propping himself up on his elbows, he searched Malini's face and then Bonnie's. "You've never heard of the Wicked Brethren?"

Malini shook her head.

"Very well, gather around and I will tell you the story."

As it was the middle of the day and Father Raymond and Ghost were back from their latest supply run, the Soulkeepers and Hope, on Grace's shoulder, circled Cord. When the sounds of shuffling died down, the Watcher turned angel began to speak.

"In the beginning, before the garden, before Adam and Eve, all angels lived to serve God. Time is irrelevant in Heaven, but there is space and all of God's creation has order and duty. Lucifer was one of seven powerful and stunning brothers, the light of Heaven in many ways. They were as close to God as any of us.

"When God decided to make man in his own image, it became clear to us he meant for humans to hold a special place in Heaven. Angels would become the servants of this new creation. Some angels accepted God's will without a second thought, but Lucifer and his six brothers began to talk about the unfairness of it. Angels, as the more powerful beings, should be above men, and, in fact, Lucifer often wondered why he couldn't be above God. He and his brothers began to plan a coup against God.

"All knowing, God intercepted Lucifer's attempt and gave the archangel Michael authority to cast him and his brethren out. Michael tossed the seven Wicked Brethren from the edge of Heaven, Lucifer and his brothers."

"The Devil had brothers?" Ethan asked.

"Not brothers in the sense of human brothers. Angels don't have sex and don't have babies, but they do have family groups. I digress. The seven Wicked Brethren were cursed to be the vessels of the seven deadly sins. Pride, lust, wrath, gluttony, sloth, envy, and greed. All of their selfish wickedness multiplied exponentially upon their fall and populated their seven bodies with these vices."

"Wait, what about the other Watchers?" Jacob asked.

"About a third of the angels followed Lucifer over the edge. These became his Watchers, less powerful copycats of the brethren. He lured them into his kingdom with the promise of power, but instead, he made them slaves."

Malini cleared her throat. "So there were seven Devils? How did Lucifer become *the Devil*?"

"As I was saying, each of the seven Wicked Brethren took on one of the seven deadly sins. Lucifer's vice was pride. He truly believed he was as good as God and that sin, that vanity, defined him. His brother, Satan, took on the vice of wrath."

Ethan flinched. "Wait, Lucifer and Satan aren't the same person?"

Cord lowered his chin. "They are now. Within moments of reaching Earth, Satan, consumed with anger, challenged Lucifer's supremacy. Lucifer won the battle and ingested Satan, taking on his vice."

A collective *ewww* rose up from the group.

"Pride and wrath, an exceptionally evil combination," Lillian said.

"Yes, and a deadly one," Cord agreed. "Another brother, Belphegor, was embodied by sloth. He fell asleep watching the battle between Lucifer and Satan, and rumor has it, has never awakened. His sleeping form was long ago swallowed by the Earth."

Grace adjusted herself in her chair and huffed skeptically. "Pure poppycock. There is plenty of laziness to go around today."

"Oh, the seven Devils are not the source of sin, Grace, simply slaves to it. The sin is a curse they carry, and while it is true they tempt humans with their sin of choice, if you kill the demon, the sin remains."

Bonnie leaned her face into her hand. "What about the rest of them?"

"Beelzebub embodied gluttony. He was killed in the Middle Ages by a band of Huns who didn't appreciate his rabid consumption of their sheep. They were able to behead him in battle. One of the only successful demon killings by humans."

"So is Lucifer the only brother left alive?" Ghost asked.

"Unfortunately, no. Mammon, the embodiment of greed, has done well for himself over the years. Last I heard, he was living in a castle in Romania and was worth close to one billion dollars."

"You mean he has been here the entire time? I thought all Watchers lived in Nod?" Malini asked.

"Most Watchers moved to Nod after the flood. God made it difficult for them to stay above ground. The sun caused them pain and drained their powers. However, Mammon was quite cunning and took up residence in the dark forests of Europe, where he was able to survive with the remaining brothers, rarely seeing the sun. His brother Asmodeus, vice of choice lust, was active among humans until the time of Noah when his, um, lustful wings were clipped. He moved in with Mammon after that incident, as did Leviathan, the demon of envy. The three remaining Wicked Brethren never fully accepted Lucifer's leadership. They went rogue, living among men and becoming more powerful over the centuries. They've changed their names over time to blend in. Mammon is now Damien Bordeaux—"

Lillian gasped. "I've heard of him. He's an oil tycoon."

Cord nodded. "Asmodeus is now Asher James."

"The rock star?" Ghost asked. Every face turned toward him in surprise. "He was a popular name in Europe during the seventies. I came across some albums during a Sex Pistols phase I was going through."

"Yes. And Leviathan is now Levi Kostopoulus. You won't have heard of him. He is a European crime boss."

Jacob shook his head. "This is a fascinating story, but why are we talking about the Wicked Brethren now?"

With a deep sigh, Cord flopped backward on the bed and stared at the ceiling. "Because, the Watcher I fought today outside Quik N Smart was Leviathan, otherwise known as Levi Kostopoulus. I cannot stress enough that Levi would not be here if Damien and Asher were not also here. My guess is that Lucifer has chosen my replacement. The Wicked Brethren have joined the war.

"If I'm right, things are going to get worse for you fast. A lot worse."

Chapter 9
Visitation

Malini tossed and turned under the covers, sleep seeming as elusive as the mythical unicorn illustrated in the scrolling Celtic pattern on the ceiling. It wasn't just her growling stomach that kept her awake or worry for the team of Soulkeepers out killing their quota of Watchers. What Cord had told her of the three Wicked Brethren truly disturbed her. Three ruthless demons, each with their own favorite vice, and barely contained by Lucifer himself.

How could the Soulkeepers help God win the challenge when they couldn't even feed themselves? There was nothing left in the kitchen. Ghost and Father Raymond had come through with diapers and a can of powdered formula for

Hope, but they'd never survive on what Ghost and even Cord, when he was healed, could carry.

The problem was the humans. Those who had sold their souls were guarding the infrastructure for everything from food to medicine. Malini was sure there were still good people in the world, but like her and the rest of the Soulkeepers, those good people were in hiding, struggling not to give in to Harrington's tactics.

It was time for her to go to the In Between, to read Lucifer's tapestry, and make a plan to combat this latest curse, but she hesitated. Her vision had limitations. The future was only predictable in terms of the past and constantly changing. Worse, Lucifer and the Watchers didn't have their own life threads. In their case, her immeasurable powers were reduced to following the space they left behind in the human world, a decidedly fuzzier discipline.

Resolved to try her best, she repositioned her head on the pillow and emptied her mind. Before she could cross over, the bed bounced, jerking her back into the present. An arm flopped across her stomach.

"Everything'll be okay," Jacob mumbled without opening his eyes. A moment later, heavy snoring rose from under the curtain of his hair. Gently, she nudged him onto his side, and the noise quieted.

Malini smiled. "Thanks," she whispered. Her soul connected with the rhythm of his breath, grounding and sweet, a forever reminder of why she did this every day. Love.

Life was nothing without love, and love didn't exist in Lucifer's world.

Clearing her mind again, she passed into the In Between on an exhale, her breath carrying her over, her body a fallen leaf on a gentle breeze. But when she landed, she paused. She was not in her usual place of arrival, Fatima's villa, but in a forest, thick with massive pines and sycamores.

"What the hell?" She turned a circle. Where was her fabric? Where was Fate?

Her eyes locked on a young girl, willowy and wide-eyed, standing among the branches. Poised in a simple navy dress, her long, golden-brown waves glinted auburn in the ambient light. She looked familiar, but Malini couldn't place her.

"Who are you?" Malini asked. "Why am I here?"

"Hope," the girl said. Her piercing blue eyes blinked innocently.

"Hope?" Malini asked.

The girl stared at her expectantly but said nothing.

"Can you speak?"

More staring. "Hope," the girl said again.

Malini narrowed her eyes, taking the wisp of a girl in from head to toe. The In Between was constructed of consciousness, every pine needle or blade of grass created by someone's thoughts and feelings. Only three people lived here permanently: Fate, Time, and Death. So who was responsible for Hope?

Hope. Only one other Hope existed in the Soulkeepers' world, and she was sleeping in a makeshift cradle in

Sanctuary. Hands on her hips, Malini met the girl's gaze and tried to riddle her out. Her eyes were an exceptional color, like thin ice over ocean. They reminded her very much of Abigail's. The shape of her face, the line of her nose, the undertone of her hair, undeniably Gideon's.

The Healer gaped at the girl. How was this possible? Hope was a baby; this girl was at least fifteen, but there was no denying the resemblance. Her eyes were Abigail's. "You can't be…," she whispered.

The girl wrung her hands, looking as if she might cry.

Malini approached cautiously and reached out to touch the girl's shoulder. She was solid, real, and a complete mystery. "Hope's mother, Abigail, visited the In Between when she was rescued from Lucifer's prison. She was pregnant," Malini said.

Hope looked away and brushed her fingers through the needles of a pine tree. A wave of innocent loneliness passed behind her eyes. Her lips parted on a sigh.

"Are you saying you are her?" Malini watched the girl pick a pinecone from the tree. Her mannerisms were so like Abigail's. "I don't understand this. On Earth, Hope is a baby. She's only a few weeks old. Who are you?"

The girl crossed her arms over her chest and frowned. Malini had never seen someone look so … lost. Her gaze floated toward her feet, eyebrows knit, shoulders hunched over her crossed arms. Then, as if someone had flipped a switch, she confidently squared her shoulders and looked directly into Malini's eyes. "I. Am. Hope."

A laugh erupted from Malini's throat but dissipated when it hit the air between them. She stepped back, scanning Hope from her ballet flats to her long loose waves. The cut and stitching of the navy dress she wore looked handmade and ancient.

"Impossible."

Folding her hands, Hope's face twisted into a grimace as if Malini had insulted her existence.

"I'm sorry, Hope. I don't mean you are impossible. I mean..." Malini hesitated, afraid to say it out loud. "Would you mind coming with me to visit a friend?"

Hope shrugged. Malini took the girl's hand gently and led her through the forest. She didn't know the way. She trusted her Healer instincts, setting one foot in front of the other by faith.

Soon, the trees grew farther apart, and a great marble statue of an angel marked the rolling hillside. Even from a distance Malini could clearly see the scales now tilted in Lucifer's favor. *Great.* The Wicked Brethren and Lucifer's mark had shifted the course of the challenge faster than Malini expected. All of these weeks of Watcher quotas and she had barely made a dent.

She forced herself not to dwell on the scales, and instead completed her journey to Fatima's villa. As expected, Fate waited for her at the table on the veranda, sipping tea with Henry and Mara. All three stood as she approached, and stared apprehensively at the girl by her side.

"Welcome, Malini. Who have you brought with you today?" Fatima asked.

"I've brought no one." She widened her eyes and dropped her chin. "This is Hope. I found her in the woods behind your house."

With a laugh, Fatima shook her head. "No. She is not my construct. Where did she come from? Mara? Henry? Is she yours?" Fatima glanced inquisitively across the table.

Mara shook her head and turned toward Henry in silent questioning.

He stood, folding one arm across his waist and the other behind his back. His unnaturally straight posture made it impossible to forget he was the immortal Death. "She is not ours. Where did she say she was from?" Henry asked.

"She didn't," Malini said. "She is simply here. Don't you think she resembles two people we knew well?"

Fate snorted in rejection of the thought that Hope could be "simply here," but when she squinted in the girl's direction, her skepticism faded. "Impossible. Henry?"

When it came to souls, no one was more expert than Death. Henry stepped around the table, removing his gray riding gloves along the way. Toe to toe, he placed one palm against the skin of Hope's neck, just above the V-neck of her dress.

"You're scaring her," Malini said, noticing Hope shiver.

"Only a moment longer," he said.

Squeezing the girl's hand, Malini attempted to send her comfort through the connection, but her Healing powers didn't work the same way here as on Earth. Still, it seemed to help. Hope's breathing slowed and her shoulders relaxed.

"It is her," Henry said slowly. "She is Hope."

"What?" Fatima said. "Don't be ridiculous."

"The fingerprint of her soul is unmistakable. She is here, and she is also there. I can see her in Sanctuary. Her soul is split." Henry shoved his hands inside his gloves and took a step back to get a better view of her. "I have never seen anything like this before."

"She is a Soulkeeper," Mara said. "Perhaps this is related to her power."

"But she's a baby," Fatima whispered.

"Only, this part of her isn't," Malini stated firmly.

Henry's mouth dropped open. "I am mistaken. I *have* seen something like this before."

With a sharp exhale, Fatima gestured with one of her eight hands, continuing to weave with her other seven. "Please, enlighten us."

"Malini." His black eyes fell heavy on her face. "When she is on Earth, a portion of her soul remains here, acting as a guide to those who use the stone to seek her counsel."

Mouth gaping, Malini looked at Hope with new eyes. It was true; a portion of her soul, the ancient part associated with her power, was available here to anyone who sought her wisdom using the enchanted stone. She'd been told that part of her had appeared as both man and woman, young or old, depending on the needs of the visitor, and she had no knowledge or memory of what her guide said or did.

"Hope is a Healer," Mara said.

Fatima cleared her throat. "Highly unusual if true. All Healers I have ever known have had to pass my trial, just as you did, Malini. She has not been through the trial."

Pondering the possibilities, Malini's gaze fell on the teapot between them. It was bone china with a floral pattern Malini thought must be from the Victorian era. Things in the In Between were all mixed up; time and space, past and present, all blended together. Maybe this Hope was not the same Hope as the baby on Earth, but a future version, a timeless echo of who she would become.

"Perhaps she's a Soulkeeper with the potential to be a Healer," Malini said. "But why is she here? Did I have a guide here before I passed the trials?"

"Not that I know of," Fatima said. "The Healer's power is eternal, but your power connected to you after you agreed to the test and accepted your role. Before that, it belonged to the existing Healer, Panctu. Every Healer's experience is different."

"But there is always an immortal who issues the challenge," Henry said, spreading a hand toward Fate. "And always one who gives the new Healer a gift." He looked pointedly at Malini's right hand, the skeletal hand he'd given her during her test.

"What does it mean?" Malini asked, staring at the girl. Hope frowned under her inspection, bowing her head.

"She is a *gift*," Mara said. "The only Soulkeeper not on the list Lucifer obtained from Abigail. God has sent us a secret weapon."

"One who can't speak or explain who she is," Malini stated. "A complete mystery."

At the last words, Hope began to shake and cry. Confused, Malini pulled her into a tight hug. "We will figure this out, Hope." She glanced at Fatima, who did not look convinced. "We all will."

* * * * *

There were no answers in the In Between that night, and Malini fell back into her body even more frustrated than when she left. Jacob rolled over next to her and resumed his rhythmic breathing. Silently, she crawled out of bed and tiptoed to the kitchen for a glass of water. She was surprised to find someone else on the other side of the door.

"Dane? What are you doing up?" Malini whispered.

"I could ask you the same." Dane leaned against the stainless steel counter, holding up his glass.

Out of habit, Malini glanced at the pantry, but Cord had taken to sleeping upstairs next to the holy water font. She couldn't blame him for not wanting to spend another minute behind those steel bars. She shuffled to the sink and selected a glass from the cupboard.

"I couldn't sleep," Malini said.

"Me neither. I'm starving. I was hoping the water would trick my stomach into feeling full."

"I'm hungry too." Malini lifted the glass to her lips and pivoted to face him.

"But that's not why you are up, is it?" A wrinkle formed between Dane's eyebrows.

"You know me too well."

"We've been to Hell and back." The corner of his mouth tugged upward. "Come on, Mal. Tell brother Dane what's going on."

Malini swallowed another gulp while she considered the ramifications of sharing what was troubling her. As the Healer, she knew better than anyone how misleading the In Between could be, but maybe, just maybe, Dane could help.

"I met Hope in the In Between tonight."

Dane blinked at her. "I don't understand. Do you mean you took her with you to the In Between?"

"No. I met a piece of her soul in the In Between. The immortals and I believe Hope is a Healer, and as such, an ancient part of her soul resides in the In Between."

The wrinkle was back on Dane's forehead. He shifted from foot to foot. His full lips parted slightly. "Abigail's baby, Hope, is a Healer."

"Yes."

"But I thought there had to be a test? Didn't you have to wrestle a snake and battle a cemetery of Watchers?"

Malini nodded. "Every Healer's experience is different, but yes, that was mine. Usually one of the immortals gives the Healer a gift, too." She flexed the fingers of her right hand, the hand of Death. "Hope's situation is highly unusual.

Even Fate can't remember a time a Healer's guide formed before the person became a Healer."

Dane scratched the scruff on his cheek, the result of living without a razor for several days. "I borrow powers. I could see if I could borrow Hope's. Maybe she is a Healer, but we just don't know it yet. It's not as if she can tell us."

"You've never borrowed my power, Dane. We've always assumed it would be too dangerous. Everyone on the council agreed. We don't know what it will do to you."

"I won't take it. I'll just try to sense if it's there."

Malini nodded. "Deal. Thank you."

"Hey, Mal."

"Yeah?"

"I thought a second Healer only came when the first had reached the end of her life. You told me Panctu was ready to die when you were put to the test."

"True. Two Healers are rarely on Earth at the same time. One allows the other one to die."

"So the fact that she exists could mean…"

"That my expiration date is up? Yeah. That's occurred to me."

"Oh my God, Mal—"

"Don't be overly dramatic. We don't know anything yet. In fact, can we keep this between us? I don't want the other Soulkeepers to worry, especially Jacob."

At first Dane shook his head, but the longer Malini pleaded with him, her eyes misting in desperation, the more he seemed resolved to keep her secret. The last thing a starving group of Soulkeepers needed was to think their Healer was dying.

Dane reached over and pulled her into a quick hug. "Don't worry. It's in the vault. Plus, it's probably not true. We don't know anything for sure yet. As soon as I'm alone with Hope, I'll check her out. Until then, no need to worry."

Malini shuddered in relief, exhausted tears welling in her eyes. "Thanks." She nodded and pushed him away, wiping her cheeks. "Now, try to get some sleep. Healer's orders."

He released her and returned to bed.

She crawled in next to Jacob, but sleep did not come easily, and when it did, her dreams were filled with navy blue puzzle pieces that refused to fit together.

Chapter 10
The Fourth Gift

On the corner of Michigan and Wacker, two men huddled in the cold behind a cardboard sign that read *Please Help.* An empty pie tin, pinned to the sidewalk with a chunk of concrete, rattled and scraped in the blustery weather. Both men wore dark glasses and heavy coats that offered little protection against the intense late winter chill. They'd waited a long time for help, but the sun had started to set on another day, and there was nothing in the tin.

"Lord, what if there is not a generous heart left in this city?" Gabriel asked.

God adjusted his dark glasses. "There is always one."

"Couldn't we simply give the gift?"

"Not this time."

A man in a camel-hair coat kicked the tin as he passed. He did not apologize, or turn his head to acknowledge the misstep to the two men. The behavior was unexceptional; most people passing didn't make eye contact. Gabriel scowled at their shuffling shoes. It was one thing not to help, but another to dehumanize.

"What if there isn't anyone left *here*?" he pressed. "I can hardly remember what a decent human looks like."

God sighed. "This gift must multiply a characteristic that is already in the heart. If I force generosity, I am no better than a Watcher influencing a human. Free will works both ways."

With a disenchanted grumble, Gabriel repositioned the pie tin and leaned back against the building. Thousands of people had passed them since they began this campaign to find a generous heart. They'd been kicked, spat on, pummeled with garbage, but no one, not one person had offered them anything but this advice: *Get off your asses and allow a Harrington mark on your hand. They're hiring down the street.*

Frustrated with the lack of compassion, Gabriel tugged his coat tighter around him. He was less convinced than God that there was anyone left in the city worth saving. In fact, he'd lost a good dose of faith in humanity over the last two days. The Soulkeepers were all but starving in their under-church safe house. The Wicked Brethren now worked for Lucifer, and Damien had wasted no time taking control of most of the businesses in town, if not directly then indirectly by pressuring the owners. Finding anyone to stand up for what was right wasn't going to be easy, especially considering that doing so meant they might never eat again.

Slush sprayed across the sidewalk as the car parked in front of them pulled into traffic. As Gabriel glared through the window at the departing driver, a young man on a bike took the open parking spot. Dressed in jeans and a shiny blue down coat, the young rider looked directly at Gabriel as he adjusted his bike helmet, an expression of unadulterated empathy warming his chilled expression.

Blink, blink. A surprised Gabriel lowered his sunglasses. The young man's dark eyes darted to God and then back to Gabriel. Shaking his head, he pulled a key from his pocket and unlocked the delivery cart attached to the back of his bike. With both gloved hands, he retrieved a large package wrapped in brown paper, then locked the cart again. He waited.

Gabriel wasn't sure if he should do something, maybe say hello or smile, but since God hadn't reacted to the young man's presence, neither did Gabriel. A moment later, another man arrived with a hot dog cart. The cart owner parked and opened his umbrella.

The bicycle man walked to the vendor and handed the package to the other man, who quickly but smoothly transferred it inside the cart. In exchange, the vendor provided the first man with an identical package that gave off a subtle fog like hot breath against cold air. The men exchanged words.

A queue had formed behind the bicyclist, men and women who pulled off their gloves in preparation to show their marks. But Gabriel noticed the vendor did not remove his gloves. Nor did the bicycle deliveryman. No one in line seemed to question this because of the extreme cold and the vendor's more permanent station on the sidewalk, but Gabriel did. Especially when the vendor wrapped three steaming hotdogs in brown paper and rested them on top of the deliveryman's box. No money exchanged hands. No gloves were removed.

While the vendor began doling out hot dogs to the waiting customers, the young man returned to his bike and rested the large package and the three hot dogs on the curb. He unlocked his cart and put the large package inside. Then he approached Gabriel.

Gabriel stiffened as the man neared. Could this be it? Could this be the one they were waiting for? Two of the hot dogs landed in the tin. Gabriel almost cheered.

"You gotta keep movin', you two. You stay in one place too long, and they find you."

"You have a kind and generous heart," God said, tilting his face up. He removed his glove and offered his right hand.

Entranced, the young man accepted, whispering, "You better keep those gloves on. There are only a few of us left. We've got to be careful."

"Generosity is more contagious than you might think," God said. "Perhaps all you need to expand your operation is a leader."

Gabriel watched the coupled hands glow slightly, and the man's dark eyes light up from within. With his free hand, God reached into his coat and presented the young man with a copy of *Tom Sawyer*, an original by the looks of it. The illumination of their touch passed to the book. The man blinked rapidly and released God's hand to accept the gift.

"Listen, uh, we will be at Randolph and Franklin tomorrow, same time. The carts always move. Never the same place twice. I'm sorry, but I can't guarantee anything beyond that. My brother and I need to stay ahead of the law."

"From now on, you will display a sign—the book I've given you and others like it. The book will be the symbol of your secret society."

The man laughed, running his palm over the cover of the book. "We don't have a secret society. It's just us. Two brothers who don't want to be owned."

"Not anymore," God said. A warm breeze originated from God and spiraled around the man, who inhaled deeply, staring at the book as if he were seeing it for the first time.

It was done. The fourth gift had been given.

In a fog, the young man returned to his bike, blending into the edge of traffic.

"The gift is given, Gabriel. See that the Soulkeepers get the message."

* * * * *

Jacob's stomach growled, loud enough to garner Malini's attention. She veered closer on the busy sidewalk, rubbing her mittens together.

"The cereal wasn't enough for you?" she asked.

"Uh, no. A bowl of Fruity Pebbles is not dinner. I'm starving," Jacob whispered.

"I know," she said sadly.

The box of cereal and some milk was all Ghost could carry, and every time Father Raymond drove him around, he took a chance of getting caught. He was thankful for what little they had, he really was, but it was taking its toll. Everything was harder. He'd lost weight and felt tired all the time.

"It's almost over. Help is coming," Malini said from behind her scarf and dark glasses. She'd been visiting the In Between for any sign of impending relief.

"But you don't know how or when."

"No." She shrugged. "Please refrain from quaking in the presence of my awesome power."

Jacob laughed as they turned the corner toward Grant Park. Lillian was their third tonight. She'd circled a few blocks over in an effort to lure Watchers into the open.

"That's strange," Malini said.

Jacob followed her line of sight. A sophisticated woman in a white peacoat and heeled black boots sat on a park bench reading *Tom Sawyer*. "What's so strange about that?"

"It's four degrees out, Jacob. Kind of cold for reading outdoors."

"I guess."

"And why *Tom Sawyer*? It's not exactly a popular book these days. I haven't even found a bookstore open since the Watcher invasion."

"Huh." Jacob looked right then left. "Uh, Malini?"

She was still staring at the book. He grabbed her chin and turned her face toward a vendor's cart at the end of the block.

"That guy is glowing," she said.

"Yeah. Like an angel." Jacob walked toward the cart, his gloved hand automatically finding hers.

"Pizza," Malini said wistfully.

He pulled her into line behind a man who already had his right glove off. His branded symbol shimmered in the moonlight, the black worm she'd heard about causing his skin to ripple.

"What are we doing?" Malini asked under her breath. While the angelic glow from the vendor did seem like a sign from God, this was dangerous. People who had sworn allegiance to the Devil surrounded them. Watchers around every corner might smell them and attack. Killing Watchers was their goal tonight, but since the fourth curse, they had to be careful not to draw human attention, too.

Jacob nodded toward the angelic glow behind the cart and shrugged. Hunger kept him in line, and Malini seemed resolved, as well.

"Should we try to bring some back?" he whispered.

"Too dangerous."

By the time they reached the cart, Jacob's mouth was watering so much he couldn't speak. Luckily, Malini could. "Two slices of supreme please." She held out a twenty.

The man glanced down at the money in her gloved hand and paused. Jacob prepared himself to run. Had he imagined the glow? A trick of the moonlight by a hopeful and starving mind?

The vendor nodded and reached into his cart. "Good to see you two again." He grasped the money from her hand and handed each of them a gigantic slice. "Don't forget to visit us in the future at the locations listed on the napkins." He handed them each a generic paper square as blank as it was brown.

Greedily, Jacob snatched the plate, while Malini nodded and accepted her change. Wrapping his gloved hand around the greasy slice, he raised the pizza to his lips. The cheese burned the roof of his mouth as he scarfed down a bite, but he couldn't stop. Hunger drove him to swallow chunks without even chewing, the spicy sauce staining the skin around his mouth. When he'd eaten enough to remember she was there, he glanced at Malini and noticed she was doing the same.

"I feel so guilty," she said around a mouthful. "The others must be starving. But I can't stop. I'm so hungry."

"Maybe they can get their own." Jacob glanced back to see the vendor's glow leach from his body and disappear into the streetlight above him. "I think the vendor was possessed."

"By an angel," Malini said. "You couldn't smell him?"

"I smelled Heaven, but I thought it was the pizza."

She nodded, chewing. "We have to find a way to bring more to Sanctuary."

"What was that about the list of locations on the napkin? Mine is blank."

"I have a theory about that. Come. There are too many people here." She led him deep into the park, off the path, and inside a cluster of evergreen trees. "I used this once with Abigail. Blessed ink. Only appears with help from one of us." She handed him the empty plate and removed the mitten from her left hand, her healing hand. Gripping the napkin, her power flowed into the paper in veins of pale yellow that bled out through the fibers, wet paint sinking into canvas. When the spreading blotch reached the corners, words appeared on the napkin, addresses. The title of the list read, *The Tom Sawyer Society*.

"Are all of these people working together?"

Malini's grin shone in the moonlight. "I think so. Jacob, this is the fourth gift. This is what we've been waiting for. The people who have refused Lucifer's mark are organizing. They are subverting Lucifer's power."

"You know that from a list of names and addresses on a napkin?"

"*Tom Sawyer*, Jacob."

He stared at her blankly.

"You never read it?" she whispered.

He shook his head.

"*Tom Sawyer* is all about rebellion. It's about understanding that society and the people in power can be wrong. Over the course of the book, Tom goes from a spoiled boy to one who stands up for his friends at his own personal expense. The Tom Sawyer Society is doing the same thing. They are standing up for their right to their soul and refusing popular opinion that Harrington's way is the only way."

"That's good news."

"Do you know what this means?" She grabbed his face and kissed him, lips coming away saucy. She wiped her face on her sleeve and laughed. "Everyone is going to eat tonight."

The corners of his lips lifted but never successfully accomplished a full smile. A wretched moan from the other side of the tree grabbed his attention. Jacob covered Malini with his body and moved her deeper into the branches. Through the gaps between limbs, he saw a Watcher pulling its victim into the park. The human was still alive, her head bouncing against the frozen grass.

"Time to get started on that quota," Jacob whispered. He reached for the flask on his ankle while Malini tucked the mitten she was holding and the napkin in her pocket. Side by side, they silently jogged along the tree line, the snow barely dusting in their wake. The Watcher paused, leaning down to cup the weeping woman's neck and pull her limp, wasted body toward his teeth. Her hair was already matted with blood, and she was so thin, Jacob was sure she couldn't survive if she lost much more. Maybe the thing had tortured her before tonight. She already looked like a corpse.

"Now," Malini said.

With practiced execution, Jacob bolted directly at the Watcher, raising his sword. As expected, the thing dissolved into a ripple of darkness. Also, as expected, Malini was there, circling to the back of the beast while it was distracted with Jacob's attack. Her hand caught the middle of the ripple, wrenching it from shadow and slamming the smoking black flesh to the snow. Jacob leapt to avoid the victim as his sword swept downward. The snakelike face had a moment to register terror before its head was detached from its body. Malini released her grip on its chest and buried her burnt hand in the snow next to the bubbling black remains.

"Good job." Jacob wiped his boots on clean snow and channeled the sword back into his flask.

"Jacob?" a weak voice cracked. "Malini?"

He turned toward the victim, whose raspy voice came from a heap of skin and bones curled on its side in the snow. When he approached her, he tried to help her up, but she was too weak. He ended up kneeling in the snow with her cradled in his arms.

"Do I know you?"

Dull green eyes met his.

"You don't recognize me anymore?"

His heart turned to lead and sunk into his stomach. "Katrina?"

She nodded. "I'm sorry, Jacob," she rasped. "About everything." She closed her eyes and went limp in his arms.

"Malini, I need your help."

Chapter 11
Sanctuary

Jacob had his doubts Katrina would live. He'd only seen one other person look as far gone as she did, and that was Dane, the day he floated into Eden after his time in Hell. She was a skeleton, hunched and gray, hair thin and dirty.

"Cord, hold her up and give her healing energy," Malini ordered. "Jacob, you feed her this." Malini handed him some soup they'd obtained from the Tom Sawyer Society after calling off the night's patrol.

"It only works if I can touch her skin," Cord said.

Malini unzipped Katrina's jacket, covering her nose at the smell of body odor that escaped as she removed it. The sleeves got caught on her gloves, and Malini reached down to remove them. She paused, holding Katrina's right hand.

"What if—?" Jacob started.

Malini shook her head. She yanked off the glove. An audible sigh of relief filled the room as everyone saw Katrina's skin was unmarked.

Cord adjusted Katrina in his arms, causing her head to loll to one side. A soft glow radiated from the angel, through the exposed skin of Katrina's back, lighting her torso from within. Her eyes fluttered. Jacob raised the spoon to her lips.

"Keep it up. We need her conscious."

"Malini, perhaps we should gather a team to go obtain more supplies from the Tom Sawyer Society," Lillian said.

Grace, who was bouncing Hope on her hip, nodded. "Everyone is starving. We must go sooner or later."

"Perfect," Malini said. "I'll go too. It's almost dawn, and there will be too much for one team to carry. You can't call attention to yourselves. Wake Father Raymond. He can take one team and the others can go on foot. Leave Hope here with Dane."

Malini glanced over to the bed, where Dane snored peacefully.

Grace nodded.

A few moments later, Sanctuary was bustling with Soulkeepers readying themselves for the mission, and then the room emptied. The quiet left behind was almost deafening.

Jacob spooned another helping into Katrina's mouth.

She woke with a start, took one look at Cord, and screamed.

The angel broke apart, leaving Jacob to catch her falling head. "Relax. Katrina, chill. It's okay. It's okay."

"I thought I saw ... Cord. Oh my God, am I hallucinating?"

"Uh..." Jacob sat her up, propping pillows behind her back on the bed they'd made for her. He spooned another bite of soup and brought it to her lips. She opened her mouth like a baby bird. "Where have you been, Katrina?"

A deep breath rattled in her chest, fighting against whatever muck had taken root in her lungs and sending her into a fit of coughing. Jacob backed off a little, hoping to avoid the germs.

"When I left home at Christmas, I went back to school. My roommate didn't want to let me back in my dorm, but it was paid up for the year. I lived on Elysium until they stopped giving it away a few weeks ago."

She paused, suddenly intent on her soup. She lifted it from Jacob's hands and spooned in another bite.

"Then what?" he asked.

"I had a friend who also relied on Elysium. He suggested we go to where Elysium was made to try to find a clinic or something to get our medicine. So we came to the city." She paused again, her face going stony as if she were blocking out some unwanted memory.

"And then what?" Jacob prompted.

"I'd rather not talk about how I survived until now." She finished the soup and set the empty bowl on the table. "Earlier this week they changed the rules, and you had to get that brand thing on your hand to buy any Elysium. I swear to God, Jacob, that was my wake-up call. I didn't mean for it to get this bad. I didn't." A tear navigated the corner of her eye and worked its way down her cheek.

Jacob ran a hand through his too-long hair. "I'm glad you didn't get Lucifer's mark."

"They tell you before you get it," she said, voice breaking.

"Tell you what?"

"At city hall. I went all the way to the chair. You sit down in this plastic chair with the built-in desk, the type they have at the DMV, and this man comes in and says, 'Katrina Laudner, do you commit your soul to Milton Blake and all of his aliases for eternity?' What type of corporation asks you to commit your soul for eternity?"

"One managed by the Devil," Jacob said.

"I never believed you before. I wanted it to be innocent."

"I know."

"I left without getting the brand. I haven't taken Elysium in three days."

"I thought you were dead when we found you."

"Me too. I let him find me. I knew how to avoid them, I did. I wanted to get caught."

"We can help you." Jacob placed a hand on her shin.

Katrina nodded, eyes pleading. "I'm ready to get better. I want my life back. I want my soul back."

He reached for her hand and carefully hugged her brittle body. "I'm so glad, Katrina. I've really been worried about you, but there are two things you've got to know."

"What?"

"First, once you are well enough, you need to go back home to Paris. Uncle John and Aunt Carolyn have been tortured since you left. Think about it. It's the apocalypse. They probably assume you're dead. I know I did."

"Fair."

"Second, you didn't hallucinate Cord."

"Huh?"

"Cord," Jacob called. The angel appeared behind his right shoulder. "He's an angel now, and he's helping us."

Katrina took one look at Cord's glowing body, his white wings outstretched, and promptly passed out again.

Jacob sighed. "I think that went well."

* * * * *

In the far corner of the room, Dane bounced baby Hope on his lap, holding her up under her shoulders. She loved to play this game. He'd sing to her, a song his mother used to sing to him, something about riding on a horse and falling off. When he got to the falling off part, he'd straighten his legs and gently roll her backward so she could see the world upside down. He always made sure to hold her firmly, to keep her safe. He didn't want anything to happen to Hope.

It was more than a familial sense of protection that made him passionate about her well-being. Malini had confided in him that Hope was not only a Soulkeeper, but also a Healer. Healers were rare. The rarest of all Soulkeepers. There was usually only one on the entire Earth at a given time.

Dane was the only one besides Malini who knew Hope's real secret: her existence could mean Malini's impending death. Which was why he'd waited until now to do what Malini had asked him to do, to use his power to try to learn more about Hope's. No one could know. Knowledge of Hope's power might mean either a false hope or a source of anxiety for the Soulkeepers. After all they'd been through, they didn't need either of those things.

He glanced over to make sure Jacob and Cord were still distracted with Katrina and then brought his knees up so that he was eye to eye with baby Hope. "I'm going to try to do this as gently as possible, sweetheart, but to be honest, I've never had it done to me, and I have no idea if it hurts."

Hand on the bare skin of her arms, Dane cast his power into her. On his end, it always reminded him of fishing, that moment when the pole passes over your head, and the line goes out until the lure plunks into the water. There was a toss at the beginning on his part, and then the other person's power would hook onto his own, and he would reel it in. Only, this cast didn't catch on anything. Hope's ice-blue eyes stared up at him innocently, seeming oblivious to what he was trying to do.

"You don't have a Soulkeeper power inside of you," he whispered, eyebrows sinking over his narrowed eyes.

Hope focused on his face and kicked her feet.

Dane glanced up again toward Katrina. It looked as if she was asleep, and Cord and Jacob were headed toward him.

"We're on laundry detail. Let us know if Katrina wakes up?" Jacob said.

"Sure." Dane nodded, shifting Hope into the crook of his arm.

The two disappeared through the staircase to the rectory, lifting the overstuffed bin of Watcher-blood-soaked clothes. As soon as they were out of sight, Dane shuffled to Malini's bed. An overturned milk crate served as a nightstand and was covered in odds and ends, but on top, as if it were left for him, was the red stone. He hooked a finger into the leather strap and returned with Hope to his own bed.

Nestling into his pillow, he tucked Hope into the crook of his arm. Her eyes drooped like she might fall asleep.

"Hey, baby girl. Not quite yet, okay. I want you to look at something." He dangled the red stone from his fingers in front of her face. When her blue eyes locked onto the red, he relaxed and gave himself over to the pull of crimson.

Red washed through the room, solidifying around him in shingles of reflective glass. He gripped Hope more tightly as he washed away in the red tide, but somehow, when he landed on the other side, his arms were empty. A stone veranda came into focus, followed by the face of a beautiful young woman seated at a table, a cup of tea in her hands.

"Are you?" he asked.

"Hope."

Dane stared at her blankly, the unsettling blue eyes, the golden-brown hair, the face that reminded him of Gideon's.

He pulled out a chair across from her and allowed his knees to give out. It was her, really her, all grown up.

"Are you inside of Hope on the other side? Are you her soul?"

Hope tilted her head to the side, frowning. She entangled her fingers on the table in front of her, face twisted as if truly disturbed.

"You can't speak? I mean, beyond your name." Dane rubbed his forehead, trying to puzzle her out.

She shrugged.

Dane leaned back in his chair and rubbed his chin. "Wait a minute, Malini said you are the part of Hope that is eternal, the equivalent of her guide." He glanced toward the sky, racking his brain. "But I've met Malini's guide. He only answered my questions about the future. Is that how you are?"

A smile spread across Hope's face, and she straightened in her chair, hands trembling excitedly.

"Let's test the theory," Dane said. "First, the obvious. Will baby Hope, the one on Earth, become a Healer?"

Hope glanced toward the sky, and Dane wondered if she would read the clouds like Malini's guide had, but instead flower petals fell from the light above and landed on the table. Hope scanned the pattern.

"Y...yes," she said carefully, as if she were just learning to manipulate her lips into words. "If ... the Soulkeepers can connect us. If you fail, she will die, and I will cease to exist."

"Why?"

Hope looked at him mournfully.

"Oh, that isn't about the future, is it? How about this? Why will baby Hope die in the future if I don't connect you to her?"

She smiled sadly as more blossoms rained down. "My soul is fractured. Part of me stayed here when my mother came that should have moved on. Eventually, the baby will outgrow the portion left inside of her, and this will result in her death unless you can reconnect me with her."

"How will I do that?"

"You won't. Another will release me."

"How will you be released?"

She opened her mouth to speak, but nothing came out. "I can't see it clearly."

Dane rubbed his forehead. "Healers can't see their own futures. Malini has the same problem. It must be a difficult fate to know everyone's future except your own."

Hope ran her hands through the scattered flower petals on the table.

Cautiously, he reached for her, his hand landing on hers. He attempted to cast his power into her, but nothing happened.

"Damn," he said. "I guess my physical body isn't here, only my consciousness. I can't use my power to get you out of here and back in your body because my power is still in my body." Dane retracted his hand. "Which means, Cheveyo won't be able to get you out either."

Large blue eyes blinked at him.

"And I can't bring your body here. I tried."

She nodded, tears welling over her lower lids.

"I'm not going to give up, Hope. Malini and I will find a way," Dane said. He squeezed her hand. As Dane said his goodbyes and allowed himself to fall back into his body, he wanted desperately to be telling the truth.

Chapter 12
The Fifth Curse

Lucifer poured a glass of scotch at the wall-bar in his high-rise penthouse, swirling the thick amber liquid in the bottom of the glass. The alcohol itself did nothing for him, but a man had killed another man for this particular bottle, and the residue of sin pleased his palate. Murder begot an acrid aftertaste you didn't find with other indiscretions.

"The brethren are late," Auriel said from the living room.

Buzzkill. Lucifer rolled his eyes. Her demands for attention were increasingly bothersome. "Relax, Auriel. The brethren are stepping off the elevator now and will be here momentarily."

As if on cue, the door opened and three massive bodies filed into the room. Damien, in his suit and tie, crossed to

Lucifer to shake his hand in a sickeningly human gesture. What self-respecting demon shook hands? If Damien weren't uniquely qualified for his position, he'd snub the fallen angel. How he hated aligning himself with the brethren. He would ingest them all and be done with it if he could be in more than one place at a time. Damn his limitations. For now, he'd have to use these three for his purposes.

Unsurprisingly, Asher walked directly to Auriel without saying hello, and Levi sneered from the doorway, no doubt coveting the grandeur of his penthouse. "Come in, Levi," Lucifer said. "I'd like to start with you."

"As you should, my lord. I have important news to share with you."

Of course he did. Levi was only happy when the entire conversation revolved around him. Lucifer expected as much from the embodiment of envy.

"Please, Levi, share your latest wisdom with us."

Tossing the waves of his dark hair from his eyes, Levi stepped to the center of the living room and spread his hands. "I thwarted an attempt of a Soulkeeper to obtain supplies this week."

"Excellent," Damien said.

"But they have a secret weapon," Levi said. "An angel."

Lucifer raised his eyebrows, suddenly more interested in the conversation. "An angel? Are you sure?"

"I fought him, hand to hand. He slipped into the light and evaded me."

"Who was it? Do you remember the name?" Lucifer asked. A messenger angel was a bad enough foe, but if God dispatched an archangel to aid the Soulkeepers, the situation was exceedingly more complex. Archangels wielded unparalleled power. An archangel had tossed him and the other brethren from Heaven.

"The angel looked familiar, but I can't be sure."

"Who did you think it looked like?"

"He looked like ... The resemblance was..." Levi paused, and then removed a disc of stone from his pocket. "See for yourself," he said. He passed a hand over the disc and an image of the angel appeared life-sized before them.

Auriel gasped so loudly it was almost a scream. "Cord."

Lucifer could feel Hell rising within him. Heat sizzled through his skin, reddening it, and echoes of the souls of the damned pounded behind his ears. "How is this possible?" he hissed.

"The third gift," Auriel said. "We never knew exactly what it was, only that it pitched the scales. God flipped him."

"SHUT UP!" Lucifer snapped, pointing a finger in Auriel's direction. "Do not say that name in front of me." In fact, his anger was not at the name itself but at the ignorance of her words. The Great Oppressor hadn't just given the Soulkeepers Cord, He'd given them *hope*. He'd given them protection. This was the reason Lucifer hadn't been able to call Malini's soul to him. The presence of an angel was the ultimate metaphysical protection and would block any attempts of him or his Watchers to divine their location. No doubt, Cord's talents were being employed to obtain the supplies he'd worked so hard to keep from the Soulkeepers.

Lucifer scowled at the four faces that stared at him. He pointed at the one he considered his second. "Damien, tell me some good news."

"Your mark is a huge success. Earnings on Elysium are up as are earnings on Harrington Security systems. Over forty percent of the registered population has obtained the brand, and it is simply a matter of time until the rest fall to us. One hundred percent of business owners and all law enforcement still working in the field have adopted the mark. Even better, as Levi said, we've successfully thwarted the Soulkeepers' attempt to obtain supplies. I suspect our policies will be the demise of the Soulkeepers before long, and we will eventually win this challenge."

Lucifer groaned. "You are a fool. The scales barely tip in my favor."

"How is that possible?" Levi asked.

"Because they have Cord, you imbecile. And another gift has been given, the fourth."

Asher took his hands off Auriel long enough to ask, "What gift?"

"I don't know exactly. The Great Oppressor's gifts are often insidious, but I would guess that the Soulkeepers are eating well tonight."

Levi sneered.

"We are still in the lead, but I am running out of cards and this next play has to count."

"What will the next curse be?" Auriel asked.

Pacing to the windows, Lucifer coupled his hands behind his back. "You say over forty percent and counting have my seal?"

Damien nodded. "Yes. We are overrepresented among the poor, but some of the most influential in the country have sworn allegiance to you, as well."

"We need to secure popular opinion. Asher, what is the status of your work on the Council for the Eradication of the Unholy?"

"Pleasurable," he purred. "Senator Bakewell is a faithful ally. The president is so afraid of the Watcher invasion he has given us carte blanche."

"But still there is more to do."

"Of course. Per your request, we haven't influenced all of Congress. The president and many of the American leaders have refused your mark. There are several congressmen who even now are working to undo what we've done. They speak of civil liberties and freedom of enterprise."

"I despise order," Lucifer said. "Government is for the powerless."

"We've allowed the humans to go on as they have before because a certain level of comfort is conducive to our ends." Damien paced to the bar and poured himself a jigger of scotch without asking. Rankled, Lucifer balled his hands into fists to keep from ripping the brother's head off. The demon sipped, closing his eyes and smiling at the flavor. "To win human hearts, you must have ultimate control. People who feel safe and free tend to grow consciences."

Noting the shift in Lucifer's attention, Levi piped up, "But the brands mean the humans *have* dedicated themselves to you. What more control is needed?" He twisted one of his many rings on his finger.

"The humans are mine today but brands can be removed." Lucifer swirled his scotch at the bottom of his glass. "Free will is an ugly reality. We must create a world where the humans are dependent on me and me alone for their safety and security. They must credit me, not their country or their democracy, for their freedom or else we risk losing them to their own ideals. What I want is to create a government I control. The humans must turn to me for leadership. I will be their hero. I will be their king."

"How will we win such loyalty?" Levi asked.

Lucifer grinned. "How do you feel about a run for office, Asher?"

The Watcher raised his eyebrows. "Which office?"

"President, of course. I promise you, your campaign will be fully funded."

Asher gave a deep bow. "It would be my sincere desire to be served in this capacity."

To be served. Lucifer chuckled at Asher's play on words. The brother was perfect, a self-centered figurehead that would lead the country into ruin while upholding his every political whim.

Out of the corner of his eye, he noticed Auriel place her hands on her hips, obviously jealous of Asher's assignment. Her envy almost rivaled Levi's. He snorted. There was always one whiny cog in the wheel. He'd eliminate her now if he didn't think she'd serve a purpose in the future. Like it or not, she was powerful, and he needed every Watcher he had to win this challenge. Afterward, he could eliminate any he chose.

"But what is the curse, my lord?" Damien demanded, bringing him back into the now. "Or is Asher's politics punishment enough?"

Lucifer glanced around the room, fully satisfied with himself for his ingenious idea.

"The fifth temptation is anarchy. People, after all, desire nothing more than to do what they want when they want. Asher and I are going to set them free. Free to be controlled by us."

With a flourish of his hand, talons grew from the fingertips of his right hand. He sliced into his wrist and dribbled black blood into his empty scotch glass. The wound healed, but the blood in the glass throbbed with an incorporeal heartbeat.

"You are my vessel, Asher." He handed him the glass. "Drink this and all who hear your voice will be extremely interested in your political platform. Drink this, and you will be able to walk in the sun without losing your illusion."

Asher nodded. "And what is my political platform, my lord?"

"Why, you represent the Hedonic Party, and your mantra is '*Take back what's yours. Total freedom. No consequences.*' We will create a government of the people and for the people who have Harrington's best interests at heart."

"I love politics." With a charming half smile, Asher lifted the glass as if to toast Lucifer and tossed the black blood to the back of his throat. A moment later, his smile turned to agony. He bent at the waist, a sound like a bark squeezing out of his constricting throat.

Lucifer poured another scotch at the bar, sipping the drink as he watched the macabre spectacle. In obvious pain, Asher writhed on the carpet, eyes bulging, stomach rippling from the evil at work within. The whole business was nothing short of poetic.

With one final heave, Asher's body accepted the curse, limbs falling limply to his sides. He rolled onto his face and knees, arms useless weights. Precariously, he struggled to his feet, his illusion lapsing with the pain and effort. Black snakeskin peeked through tears of flesh at his hands and face.

"Asher?" Lucifer said firmly.

The brother shivered at the Devil's voice. His movie-star good looks snapped into place on a sharp inhale. "Yes, my lord."

"Stop wasting my time. You have work to do." Lucifer motioned toward the three brothers. "You all do." With an obedient bow, Asher turned on his heel and left, Damien and Levi following close behind.

When Auriel moved to join them, Lucifer called her name. "Auriel."

She stopped short. "How may I serve you, my lord?" she asked enthusiastically.

Lucifer fixed her with a cutting stare. "Stay here, and most importantly, stay out of the way."

The words knocked Auriel off balance, sending her staggering toward the windows.

Lucifer ignored her, passing her stricken form to join the rest of the brethren.

Chapter 13
The Hedonic Party

"Watch it." Dane jerked Ethan out of the way. The bullet skimmed past the Soulkeeper's head as the car holding the shooter jumped the curb and skidded toward them sideways.

"What the hell?" Ethan's power slammed into the vehicle, tipping it on two wheels.

At first, Dane thought their winter gear had failed them and that the bullet was meant for him. All of the Soulkeepers were on America's most-wanted list, after all. But the man in the car was looking behind him. A boy in a red hoodie paced toward the car, gun sideways in his hand and pointed at the man behind the wheel, who still had his own gun drawn.

"You're dead," Red Hoodie yelled, pulling the trigger.

It was Ethan's turn to pull Dane out of the way of the bullet.

The back window shattered as the other man floored the accelerator and pulled into the street.

Boom. The driver's gun went off and Red Hoodie collapsed, twitching, to the sidewalk. The driver sped away, going the wrong way down a one-way street.

Dane watched the shot boy's blood drip off the curb and run into the sewer. "Should we help him?" he muttered.

"Too late," Ethan said. "And by the looks of things, we better move."

Dane glanced up to see a group of three red hoodies heading toward them, and they looked pissed. The three Soulkeepers dodged around the corner at super speed, searching the shop windows for help.

"Here," Cheveyo said, pointing to a copy of *Tom Sawyer* propped in the window of a place without a sign. It might have been an antique store or a secondhand clothier from the looks of it. The building was painted chalky white, and besides *Tom Sawyer*, the window was filled with junk.

"Let's hope they have what we need," Ethan said, yanking open the door. Dane led the way inside, Cheveyo closing the door quickly behind them.

"It's like the Wild West out there," Cheveyo whispered. "It's the middle of the day. Those were humans. What's going on?"

Dane shrugged and shook his head.

The dark room was crammed with furniture and miscellaneous décor. Haphazard stacks of junk seemed held up by will alone. Ethan and Cheveyo dropped into a single-file line behind Dane in order to navigate the piles.

"Belongs on an episode of Hoarders," Cheveyo whispered.

"Turn your pockets out," a gruff voice said from the back of the store. Dane had to lean to the right in order to see the man with the gray beard and a shotgun pointed in their direction. The wrinkles on his face made him look at home among the ancient artifacts, but his trigger finger seemed spry enough.

Dane turned out his pockets and held up his hands.

"You buyin' or sellin'?" the man asked.

"Buying," Dane answered. A dark foreboding in the pit of his stomach warned that the copy of *Tom Sawyer* in the window might have been just an old book and not a symbol of an underground revolution. "We were interested in the copy of *Tom Sawyer* you had in the window."

"Yeah?"

"Yes, sir, and we need more *Tom Sawyers*. A few bags full."

"That's a lot of reading. Can you pay?"

Dane nodded.

The man stood. "Warm in here. Why don't you take off your gloves?"

"I'd rather keep 'em on if you don't mind."

"I do mind." The man grabbed Dane's right hand and peeled his glove back before he could protest. At the sight of his smooth, bare skin, the man nodded and smiled a mouthful of yellow teeth. "You must be brave or stupid coming by here today. It's war outside that door."

"We noticed."

"Stay here. Don't touch anything unless you want to lose a finger." The man hobbled past them, scanning the store right to left. When he reached the front door, he twisted the deadbolt and pulled *Tom Sawyer* from the window. "Our policy is one customer at a time, for safety's sake. Our safety mostly."

Shotgun still gripped in his hands, he walked to the far corner of the store, where a giant trunk leaned against the wall. "Well, come on. I haven't got all day."

Ethan glanced back at Dane and carefully navigated the rows of junk toward the man with the shotgun. Cheveyo wasn't quite as careful. He tripped over a plate of armor on the floor, the clang of metal ringing out awkwardly around them, and tried to steady himself on a small side table. The wood leaves of the table snapped on his hand like a bear trap. At super speed, Cheveyo retracted his touch, barely saving his fingers. He widened his eyes at Dane.

"I warned you not to touch the antiques," the man said sternly. Cheveyo crossed his arms protectively and gathered in the space in front of the chest. The man unlocked the padlock and flipped open the lid. Three knocks on the bottom and the wood swung open to reveal a passageway. "Tom will be waiting for you on the other side."

Dane nodded and ducked inside.

"This is cozy," Cheveyo said as the lid closed behind him and the sound of the lock sliding into place echoed in the tunnel. "I wonder if we are at risk of losing a limb or being shot back here too."

"Definitely the most elaborate so far. The Tom Sawyer Society must have multiplied," Ethan said.

"Like the loaves and the fishes," came a voice from up ahead.

Dane emerged inside a warehouse with shelves and shelves of boxes. A black man with large brown eyes and an expression that seemed older than the rest of him waved them inside.

"I'm Tom. Come on in. Pick what you need. Everything's marked. Prices are high, and we don't have everything, but it is all available without a mark."

Cheveyo's mouth dropped open. "Wait, you're Tom? Like the Tom behind the entire Tom Sawyer Society?"

The man circled his neck and gazed pitifully at Cheveyo. "We are all Tom—everyone who runs a place like this. The guy up front? Tom. The guys in the back? All Tom. Get it?"

"Oh," Cheveyo said.

"If you're wondering, the first Tom was a bike messenger who decided he had to stop Milton Blake when he fed a bum on a street corner. Harrington is evil. A brand on your skin? It's a form of dominance over the branded, and it's only going to get worse now."

"Worse? I didn't think it could get any worse," Dane said.

"You haven't heard the news?" Tom asked.

Dane shook his head.

"Milton Blake's mentee, Asher James, was nominated for president at the Hedonic Party National Convention last night."

"Hedonic Party?" Ethan asked.

"You never heard of 'em?" Tom laughed. "That's because they didn't exist until earlier this week. Guess what their motto is."

"I have no idea," Ethan said.

"*Take back what's yours. Total freedom. No consequences.* They're selling anarchy, folks, and the sad part is you know that everyone with a mark on their hand will vote for him. They'll *have* to. Someone else is pulling their strings."

Dane glanced at Ethan and Cheveyo. "Are you saying that come November, if any of us are still alive, we could have a president who answers to Milton Blake?"

"Don't worry about November, my young friend. The Hedonic Party is now. People are signing up in droves, and they are living the lifestyle. The police are in Harrington's back pocket. There's no law anymore but Harrington law. Unfortunately, I think things are going to get much worse for the Toms."

Ethan tugged Dane's elbow. "Come on, Dane. This isn't getting the shopping done." Father Raymond was scheduled to drive by their starting point on the hour. If they wanted a ride back to Sanctuary, they'd have to hustle.

Dane nodded. Tom rolled him a cart from a corral, and Dane led the way to the rows.

"We're losing," Cheveyo said, lifting a box of cereal from the shelf and placing it in the cart.

"Don't be stupid. There's another gift coming," Ethan said. "We just need to be patient."

"You don't get it, Ethan." Cheveyo shook his head in frustration. "The people with that brand on their hand have sold their soul to Milton Blake. If there are more of them than us, they win. I'm pretty sure we're at the tipping point."

"Malini says people have free will. They can change, with or without the mark," Dane said.

"Yeah, but why would they?" Cheveyo asked.

"You're optimistic today," Ethan said sarcastically.

Halting abruptly, Cheveyo's usually cheerful disposition melted into something baleful. "You don't know, Ethan. You haven't had your people almost wiped out by a competing government. All of this? What's happening now? This happened to the Hopi." Cheveyo's finger pressed into Ethan's chest. "Starve them out. Poison their minds until they conform. And how many Hopi caved to the white man's game? Those were strong, proud, good people, Ethan."

"I'm sorry." Ethan looked Cheveyo straight in the eye. "You're right. I'm sorry. This is serious."

Cheveyo backed down, turning his attention to the list in his hand. With a deep breath, Dane met Ethan's gaze, trying to comfort him. He raised an eyebrow and shrugged before returning to their work.

Chapter 14
Connections

"Malini, we need to talk," Dane said, rushing into Sanctuary with his arms full of contraband.

"I know," she said. The look on her face was somber but composed. Dane had seen this before. In Nod, when she'd handed herself over to Lucifer, she'd had the same look. This was the Healer he was talking to, not his seventeen-year-old friend. "Come with me."

She donned her coat and led him outside, around the back of the rectory, to the cemetery where Abigail, Gideon, and Master Lee were buried. He sat down next to her on an iron bench facing the graves.

"Asher James has been nominated for president," he said.

"I heard. It's all over the television. I think it's the fifth curse."

"How do you know?"

"People are tripping over themselves, hanging on his every word. He was nominated only days ago by a party that didn't even exist days before that. Where is the opposition? I think Lucifer has given him a golden tongue."

"What do we do about it?"

"Try to survive until the next gift." With one toe, she rubbed a trail through the light dusting of snow on the packed earth. "And kill as many Watchers as possible while we are surviving."

Leaning forward, Dane rested his elbows on his knees, collecting his thoughts. "I did what you asked me to … with Hope."

"What did you learn?"

"That isn't just her guide in the In Between; it's a part of her soul. The part with her Soulkeeper powers. The part in her human body has no power. She said we must reconnect her to her body or she will die."

Malini turned her face to him sharply. "Said?"

"Her guide is the same as yours, Mal. She can only answer questions about the future."

"I should have known. Hope is sicker than yesterday. I can't heal her. I've tried."

"I tried too, I mean, to fix her. I can't borrow her power because I can't touch her in my physical form. Cheveyo can't possess her for the same reason. I can't bring her body over, and I can't bring her soul back. It's as though she's trapped in that stone. Her soul is being kept from her body."

"It is imperative that we solve this puzzle and reconnect her with her body."

"Of course. I don't want her to die," Dane said.

"We would be lucky if all we had to worry about was the death of a Healer."

"What are you saying?"

"Cord, show yourself, please."

Cord formed over Abigail's grave, a shimmer of light that solidified into a broad-shouldered angel with lapis eyes. "You called," he said.

"Can you tell us again about the day you were transformed?"

Folding his hands and bowing his head, Cord reverently began to speak. "I came here to kill you, all of you," he said. He pointed to a tall skeleton of a tree, still hibernating in the winter cold. "I waited in that tree and watched Gideon die at the hands of a Watcher who I didn't care to know. I followed Abigail's body inside, hoping to bring her back to Lucifer. What a prize she would have been. The only thing that stopped me was self-preservation. You, Healer, were too close, too dangerous." Cord licked his lips and turned his face toward the sinking sun.

"Go on," Malini said. "I know this is hard for you. It's painful to revisit who you were, but we need to go there. We need to know how you changed."

"I watched Hope's birth." Cord looked away, expression vacant and morose. "I planned to eat her, not simply because I was hungry, but for the purpose of torturing you. I waited for an opportunity to strike. You handed the baby to Bonnie, wrapped in a worn blanket. Then you ordered the rest of the Soulkeepers away."

Malini nodded. "To hide the RV and prepare a place for Abigail and Gideon's burial."

"I was alone with Bonnie and the baby." Cord rubbed under his eyes with his thumb and forefinger. "I crept up behind her, as quiet as a mist. Bonnie said, 'Let's see you.' I paused, directly behind her, because I thought she was talking to me, but she was talking to the baby. She lowered the blanket to expose Hope's face, but she must have heard me because she turned on her heel so that we were eye to eye. I saw the baby nestled into Bonnie's neck beside the red stone necklace she used to wear, and a warm feeling, the love she felt for the baby, hit me straight in the heart. I was transformed."

"Back up," Malini said. "Were you looking at Bonnie or Hope when you changed?"

"Both."

Dane interrupted, "But you had seen Bonnie before, at Harrington, and hadn't changed."

"Correct. I almost killed her in the stairwell. We were face to face."

"So it must be Hope," Dane said, turning toward Malini. "That must be Hope's power. She can change Watchers into angels."

"I was thinking the same thing," Malini said. "The piece of Hope's soul in the stone must have worked with her body for Cord's transformation, but if we could unite her soul with her body—"

"There was another element," Cord said. "I felt Bonnie's love for Hope. I think it was the love that sparked the change, not the baby."

Malini rubbed her chin. "Perhaps Hope is like a lighthouse. Love lights the beacon and calls the fallen to change."

With his hands spread, Dane asked the obvious question. "How do we use this? Somehow, we need to get Hope in front of the Watchers. If we could start turning watchers, we'd win this war."

"I agree," Malini said, "but we can't be wrong about this. Taking Hope out of Sanctuary puts her at risk, not to mention Bonnie."

"Bonnie?" Cord asked. "Surely it wouldn't need to be Bonnie who delivered Hope's gift to the world. That honor belongs to the Healer."

Malini shook her head. "We need to reproduce what happened to you exactly. Soulkeeper powers are always changing and growing. Jacob started with the ability to move water, but he can also read and translate every other language on Earth as if it was his own. My speed and strength came long after I became a Healer. For all we know, something about Bonnie's power helped Hope's to work. If we use Hope in this war, it has to be Bonnie who pulls the trigger. You said yourself, it wasn't just Hope; it was the love you felt between the two."

"It pains me to think of her at risk," Cord said.

"I know," Malini said. "But it's necessary. She's on rotation tonight. Tomorrow, I'll talk to her about what we know. Maybe we can capture a Watcher and do a test run. Try to reproduce the phenomenon."

Cord frowned. "You know best, but I do not look forward to seeing Bonnie and Hope in the presence of such evil."

"I think the same thing every day," Dane said. "We don't have the luxury of safety."

The angel's glow faded a little as he nodded solemnly.

"Thanks, Cord, that will be all." With a gesture of Malini's chin, Cord dissolved into the light and disappeared.

Malini turned to Dane. "Remember, tell no one of this. I will talk to Bonnie tomorrow, but the less who know all the details the better."

"But—"

"I'm serious, Dane. I know you want to tell everyone why Hope is sick and how we think Cord changed. Don't forget what it means that she's a second Healer. The world only needs one."

"Maybe the others should know, to try to keep you safe."

"Every person who knows becomes a liability. Remember that Hope's greatest protection is the fact she is not on

Lucifer's list of Soulkeepers. The Devil doesn't know she exists. The less people who know, the greater chance of keeping it that way."

"I don't think anyone would tell, Mal."

"I'm not worried about them telling. I'm worried about the information being taken from them. Lucifer has ways. He can get inside your head."

"Right," Dane said. "Her secret is safe with me. The Devil will have to kill me before I share it."

"I appreciate that." She placed her mittened hand on his. "You're a good friend, Dane."

He lifted one corner of his mouth. "I try."

* * * * *

Cord formed next to the holy water font in the destroyed foyer of the church above Sanctuary. The hum of the blessed water soothed him, a sound he'd never heard before becoming an angel. He needed soothing. The idea that Bonnie might be put in danger because of his words weighed heavily on his heart, although he could not have lied about the incident. Lying was as foreign to him now as telling the truth had been as a Watcher.

As soon as he fully formed, he knew he was not alone.

Katrina dropped the dagger she'd been holding into the font and stumbled backward, bumping into a fallen statue of St. Joseph. She steadied herself, fear widening her eyes. He watched her gaze shift hopefully to the pile of blood soaked weapons on the floor.

"I'm not going to hurt you," Cord said, raising a hand between them. "I'm not the same person."

Her throat rippled with her swallow. "You look the same."

At first Cord was going to agree, but then he saw the faint glow of his raised fingers. He did not look the same. He did not bleed the same. "Do I?" he asked.

Katrina's shoulders relaxed slightly. "No, I guess not. I mean, your eyes are different, and your skin sort of glows."

He nodded. "I'm sorry to disturb you. I usually come here to be alone."

"I was thinking the same thing," Katrina said. "Plus, I wanted to make myself useful. Malini and Jacob have helped me so much."

"You look better."

"It's amazing what six meals a day and magical healing will do for a girl. I'm pretty sure I've broken some kind of weight gain record."

"Are you feeling *better*?" Cord asked as delicately as possible.

"Sort of. I'm better physically. Not passing out anymore. Am I still craving Elysium like oxygen? Yes. Sometimes the need for it cuts through me like a bolt of lightning, squeezing me in its grip until I think I can't stand it anymore. But I'm still here. The wanting hasn't killed me." She laughed a little. Her fingers found the dagger at the bottom of the font, and she lifted the now sparkling weapon from the water, placing it in the clean pile. "I wish it worked like this for me. The nasty Watcher blood just dissolves in the water. I'm healing, but the nastiness is still there under the surface."

"I'm sorry I possessed you," Cord said.

Katrina's gaze rose to meet his eyes. "You said yourself you are a different person now."

"It doesn't change the past. I'm sorry I possessed you and nearly killed you. I ate you alive from the inside out. Maybe I had something to do with your addiction to Elysium. Please forgive me. Please." Cord's voice caught on the last word, and a sure and certain truth ignited within him. He needed Katrina's forgiveness, needed it to his core.

"I've hated you for a long time, Cord. I blamed you for every hardship I've faced over the last year."

Something wet ran from his eye. Cord wiped the wet away and saw silver on his fingers. Angel tears. He stared at the strange substance on his fingertips.

"Does it make it better to hate me? If it helps you, then so be it," he said.

Katrina made a sound between a cough and a sob, causing Cord to lift his eyes to her. "Maybe it's time for me to let it go," she said. "The you I hated does not exist anymore. I'm in hate with a ghost."

"I exist. And I'm sorry for who I was. Sometimes my knees buckle under the weight of my past, but it is a burden I made for myself."

Katrina took a deep breath. "I think we have that in common. I can't even think about what I did to my parents."

"It's not too late," Cord said. "Your parents are still alive. You can make it up to them."

She nodded. "And I will. Father Raymond is going to drive me home to Paris tomorrow."

Cord smiled, but his heart still burned for the forgiveness he sought. It was hers to give or withhold, but he wished there was a way he could make it up to her.

"I forgive you, Cord," Katrina said suddenly. "I'm letting it go."

"Thank you." Cord blew out a relieved breath and bowed his head. "You do me a true service."

"It's not too late for you either," she said. "Lucifer is still out there, and you, more than anyone, have the power to help the Soulkeepers."

Cord raised his eyebrows. "I do?"

"Of course you do. Who knows Lucifer better than you? You need to help Malini intercept his next move. The Soulkeepers need you."

"Bonnie needs me?" Cord whispered. He thought about what Malini had said—at some point Bonnie and Hope would be put in danger to test the baby's abilities. Only he could make a difference. If he were able to use his angelic abilities to obtain information that would help the Soulkeepers win this challenge, maybe he could protect the two humans responsible for his redemption. He owed them that, didn't he?

"Sure. All of them do," Katrina said.

"You're right. I need to make it up to them by doing something that really matters. I need to help them thwart Lucifer."

Katrina nodded. "It couldn't hurt."

Cord walked toward the column of light where the sun shined through what remained of a stained glass window.

"Where are you going?" Katrina asked.

Cord glanced back at her. "To get started. Thank you, Katrina." Then he broke apart into the light, concentrating on his destination, Harrington Enterprises.

Chapter 15
The Fifth Gift

"Now this I could get used to," Gabriel said. He smoothed the lapels of the cashmere suit jacket he was wearing and took a seat in one of the early American chairs in the waiting area. God took a seat next to him, his tall stature and perfectly groomed hair an unusual look for the deity.

"Your name tag," God said, handing him a lanyard with the picture of his current image inside. The name read Mr. Gabriel Wingman. God placed his around his neck.

Gabriel laughed.

"What's so funny?"

"Mr. Iam Love? I am love? It's funny because it's true." Mr. Wingman smiled.

"I suppose. Stop laughing, Gabriel. We are going to meet with the president of the United States. We must present an air of solemnity."

"Why?"

"Because we want him to take us seriously and accept my gift."

"Can't he see you for what you are?" Gabriel asked. "He should be falling on his knees for the chance to be your vessel of change."

The Lord smiled. "Ah, Gabriel, you are a devoted and priceless friend. As before, we must allow this man to come to me of his own free will, and that requires we give him that freedom. My unshielded presence would most likely overwhelm him."

"Very well."

A thin and graceful woman with a short black bob appeared in front of them. "I am sorry about the confusion concerning your appointment. The president will see you now."

"Thank you." God nodded, and the woman opened the door to the Oval Office.

"Confusion?" Gabriel asked in a voice so quiet it was imperceptible by human ears.

"The president had a two o'clock appointment with the Israeli prime minister. Fortunately, I arranged for two o'clock to come twice today. Bending time wasn't quite as difficult as making everyone involved believe the duplicate calendar was perfectly normal. Tomorrow, they will remember it only as they might a daydream."

"Genius."

The president stood from his work and extended his hand. "Welcome, Mr. Love, Mr. Wingman. Please, have a seat. What can I do for you today?"

God pulled a sheet of paper from the portfolio he was carrying and placed it in front of the president before taking a seat in the hand-carved chair on the other side of the desk. The paper was blank.

"I am from a grassroots organization called the Cultural Conservation Society. Our goal is to survive the demon apocalypse while preserving the qualities most germane to our humanity."

"Right now I'm focused on the survival part, Mr. Love. We've lost too many citizens to this thing. Even the Council for the Eradication of the Unholy is struggling to keep the invasion at bay."

"Or perhaps the fox is guarding the henhouse," Gabriel said softly.

"What are you suggesting?"

The Lord quieted Gabriel with a raised eyebrow. "We at the CCS believe that Harrington Enterprises, Milton Blake, and his mentee, Asher James, have a conflict of interest serving on the council. Eradication of the demons would put Harrington out of business. Fifty percent of their profits come from their security packages, and now, with the mark required for everything bought, sold, and earned, they take a percentage of every purchase."

"Don't get me started on the branding." The president glanced at a picture of his wife and daughters on his desk. "It was all I could do to get an exemption for myself and my family. Bakewell called me an elitist."

"But you aren't, are you?"

"No." The president coupled his hands on his desk as though he were praying. "I am a man who believes in personal liberty. It's what this country was founded on. The idea of inserting something under my skin or anyone else's doesn't sit right with me. You know, they've never even explained how it works."

"Exactly." God held up his right hand, the clear pale skin indicating his aversion to Harrington's seal. "And now, Asher has been nominated to run against you in November. You know who is pulling his strings—Milton Blake. It would be a shame to lose your leadership, Mr. President."

"You don't understand. Everyone is afraid. It's anarchy out there. The council has unlimited power precisely because American citizens are terrified to leave their homes. Harrington promises safety. People won't like me taking that away from them."

"What if the Cultural Conservation Society could give you information so formidable that it could not be ignored and would give you the power to eliminate the council and take up the gauntlet against the demons yourself?"

The president rubbed his chin. "Go on."

"Turn the paper over," God said.

The commander-in-chief's eyebrows knit as he flipped over what he thought was an introductory letter on his desk. The photo on the other side elicited a gasp. Gabriel smiled.

"You will recognize that photo as the one taken at the Hedonic Party's National Convention a few days ago. This version was taken with an ultraviolet flash. You can clearly see—"

"Asher is a demon," the president said. "You two didn't tamper with this photo?"

"No, sir," Mr. Gabriel said. "He is what he is."

The president rubbed a manicured hand over his face. "We need to leak this to the press, but will anyone believe?"

"I have a better way, but first, I need your word, Mr. President, that you will align yourself with all that is good and human in the world and help Mr. Wingman and me stop Milton Blake. We can't do this without you." God extended his hand.

The president didn't hesitate. He clasped the Lord's hand. "You have my word. In the name of all that is holy, we need to work together to end this apocalypse once and for all."

A soft electricity burned along the Lord's arm and into the hand of the president. The man's skin lit up like a lightbulb, his chest swelled, and his eyes glowed with an internal light.

"I give you leadership," God said. "You, Mr. President, are the vessel. Speak the truth, and all who hear will come to follow you."

The president blinked rapidly. God retracted his hand. On the desk, a small vial appeared next to the picture.

"What's this?"

"The water in this vial is toxic to demons. If I recall correctly, the Council for the Eradication of the Unholy meets tomorrow morning. Place a few drops of this into Asher's drink and make sure the cameras are rolling."

"Yes. I know just what to do." He nodded slowly.

God stood. "I thank you for your time, Mr. President. You are a good, good man."

"Do you have to go so soon?" the president asked, sliding the vial into his pocket.

"Unfortunately, yes. You have work to do, and I fear I am a terrible distraction. But you will see me again someday."

"I look forward to it."

Gabriel opened the door for God, and then followed him out of the Oval Office. "Mission accomplished," God said. The graceful woman glanced up from her desk, but in the blink of an eye, the two men disappeared and so did the memory of why she'd looked up from her work. She shook her head and returned to what she was doing.

Chapter 16
Where Angels Fear to Tread

Cord arrived in the conference room at Harrington Enterprises, a silent cascade of molecules that blended seamlessly into the fluorescent light. He hovered there, listening. Katrina was right, the least he could do after all the pain he'd caused the Soulkeepers was to spy on Lucifer and help God win the challenge. This would be his true redemption.

When he saw what was on the table, he almost dropped from his hiding place out of shock. A woman was bound by the wrists and ankles to the conference table, surrounded by Auriel, Lucifer, and the Wicked Brethren. Fully conscious, she'd been gagged silent, but tears fell from the corners of her eyes. She knew her death was near. Cord sensed her despondency pressing in around him, as though the air was thick with her unanswered prayers. Her eyes snapped to his. No. She was simply staring into the light, and he was in the light. Still, it was unsettling.

With a heavy heart, Cord forced himself to look away to keep from helping her. It was for the greater good that he complete his mission and return to the Soulkeepers.

"Our market penetration is at forty-five percent," Damien said, words floating over the woman to the place where Lucifer sat at the head of the table, intermittently tapping a pen near the wretched woman's head. "Of course, that number is of registered voters. We know there are other humans avoiding the mark."

"Strong, but I want over fifty percent before elections in November. We must be prepared for the next gift. I don't like surprises," Lucifer said.

"We could force them, my lord." Damien steepled his fingers under his chin.

"No," Lucifer said firmly. "They must maintain their free will. The Great Oppressor will not tolerate a slip in this regard."

"The unaligned will bow eventually," Levi said. "We have not allowed so much as a block of cheese to pass to an unbranded soul."

"Hunger is a fine motivator, but I fear the Great Oppressor has a hand in their persistence. Last I checked, the human body could go no more than three weeks without food. I believe we are past that threshold, yet still the humans live. The fourth gift has come to pass."

"They are sharing," Auriel piped in. "Those with the brand are giving to those without."

"A silly, girlish theory," Damien said. "Those with the brand are not concerned for the welfare of others."

Asher waved one well-manicured hand. "It is beside the point. My campaign is skyrocketing. People will join me to reap the benefits of the Hedonic Party. No rules. No law. Do anything you want. Who could resist?"

"Yes," Lucifer said. "You are the key, Asher. If we can win the people's favor, we can win their hearts. Total freedom is in their best interest, after all. It's good for the economy."

Damien flashed a greedy smile.

Not to be outdone by his two brothers, Levi cleared his throat. "Don't forget, my lord, that forty-five percent of the population could be forty-eight tomorrow as my Watcher army continues to feed on those without a Harrington brand. I've succeeded in channeling the Watchers' appetites away from those with your mark."

A pleased smile turned Lucifer's lips. "Excellent. The number of Harrington Security complaints has bottomed out since the implementation of the seal."

"The coming spring will make it even easier for us to find the dissenters. No gloves to hide behind."

"Brilliant, Levi. They will join us, or they will die. And what of the Soulkeepers? Have you killed any?"

The three brothers became very interested in the table. Auriel smiled self-righteously.

"Have you found where they are staying?"

The brothers glanced toward the door.

"This is disappointing, brothers. I would have thought you could have flushed them out by now."

"It's the angel," Levi said. "He's blocking us. Maybe he's even spying on us."

Lucifer ran a hand through his well-groomed blond waves. "Cord," he whispered.

Auriel huffed. "Cord, an angel. It can't be true. Another Soulkeeper trick, my lord. One of them could change her appearance."

With an annoyed sigh, Lucifer narrowed his eyes at Auriel. "Copying an image is one thing. Blending into the light is quite another. Levi saw Cord blend into the light." He addressed Damien directly. "Increase police patrol. Offer an award of a day's pay for anyone who brings a friend in to be branded. Levi, keep the pressure on the Watchers to seek out our enemies for their next meal, and Asher…"

"Yes, my lord."

"Let's wow them tomorrow at the council meeting. We have to continue winning favor to our side."

Asher nodded.

"Very well," Lucifer said. "You may feed."

With a collective growl, Auriel and the three brothers dove in, tearing flesh and drinking blood. Cord wept silently at the senseless gore, the woman's pitiful, gurgling scream, and the awful slowing beat of her heart as it trudged toward its inevitable demise.

Lucifer stood from the table and walked toward the door. Where was he going? Cord prepared himself to follow, to obtain more information for the Soulkeepers. But instead of leaving, Lucifer reached for the light switch.

Cord realized what he was doing too late. He couldn't react fast enough to retreat into the light above him. The click of the switch plunged the room into darkness. Cord's body formed and fell, crashing into table and corpse before toppling past Levi to the industrial carpet.

"Break him," Lucifer hissed.

Levi obliged. Cord cried out as the Watcher's heel stomped on his wing, and the sound of his bones snapping resounded through the small room. The pain was infinite. He flapped his wings and tried to pull away, but the room was too dark for him to call any real power. For angels, sunlight was renewal and darkness a prison. Lucifer knew this.

"Cord. Good of you to join us. Where have you been?"

Cord pressed himself against the wall and remained silent.

"You've changed, my friend. Care to explain how this transformation occurred?"

Turning slightly, Cord refused to meet the Devil's eyes.

"The problem, Cord, is you are one sorry excuse for an angel. For as strong and ancient a Watcher as you were, you are a baby angel who doesn't even know that his tears stink of Heaven. How dare you come here?"

A whimper escaped Cord's lips as Lucifer closed in. The slither of evil flesh gripped his broken wing. The contact burned, but Lucifer did not let go.

"Where are the Soulkeepers? How did they change you?" Lucifer demanded, tugging sharply on the limp wing. Cord cried out, noticing the bone poke through his feathers. The entire appendage burned and throbbed. He bent over and hurled from the pain.

Lucifer lowered his lips to Cord's ear. "We can do this the hard way or the easy way. I hope you choose hard. I will enjoy watching you suffer."

Borrowing a move from his Watcher days, he forced himself to smile against the pain. He flashed Lucifer his middle finger. The Devil's fist pounded his cheek, sending him flying against the conference room wall. He crashed to the floor, his broken wing crumpling painfully under him. He was bleeding now where the bone poked through. Head swimming, he flailed helplessly in his own blood.

"Auriel, torture this *creature* until he gives us the information we want. Spare him no suffering."

"Of course, my lord," she said with a proud smile.

What little light there was in the room faded. Horrified, Cord recognized the cause. No source of natural light existed in this room, and the electric lights were off. The only reason he could see was by his own glow. The fading light then was an ominous forbearance, his body conserving its energy to nurse its afflictions. Without light to feed his healing, he was veritably doomed.

Auriel's face appeared in front of his slowly failing vision, her blond illusion coming and going with each blink.

"I've been waiting for a project worthy of me, Cord," she said through her teeth. "Welcome back."

Her fist connected with his temple.

* * * * *

"Have you seen Cord?" Bonnie asked Malini. "We're on deck for quota tonight. Sun's almost down."

"No." Malini tipped her face toward the ceiling. "Cord."

"See? He has super hearing. Why isn't he coming?" Bonnie asked.

"Cheveyo." Malini tapped the boy, who was stuffing his face with a ham sandwich, on his shoulder. "Have you seen Cord?"

He shook his head.

"What's going on?" Jacob asked.

"We can't find Cord," Bonnie said.

Dane turned in his seat. "Maybe he's in his room. He really likes to hang out by the holy water, especially when he's thinking things through." Dane raised an eyebrow at Malini.

Bonnie broke away from the group and jogged up the stairs, navigating the toppled pews and fallen statues. She passed through the door to what used to be the foyer of the church, where an enormous holy water font remained unscathed from the initial Watcher attacks. When she saw Katrina soaking weapons, she pulled up short.

"Have you seen Cord?"

With a haunting rattle, Katrina pulled the chain she'd been washing from the water and placed it on top of a pile of clean weapons. She nodded. "Sure, about an hour ago." Standing tall, she placed her hands on her hips and stretched her back.

"We can't find him. Did he say where he was going?"

Katrina narrowed her eyes. "Not exactly. He apologized to me, I forgave him, and then he said he was going to do something that really mattered to thwart Lucifer. He wanted to make it up to all of you."

Bonnie marched forward until she was almost on top of Katrina. "Why didn't you say anything? Where did he go?"

"I didn't think he meant now, like literally. I thought he meant over time … by working with all of you."

"But you saw him leave?"

"Of course, but he pops in and out of the room all the time. Where are you going?" Katrina called at her back.

Bonnie ignored her. With long strides, she returned to Sanctuary and stormed to Malini's side. "He's gone. Cord is gone."

"He's defected," Lillian said, standing from her place at the table. "I knew this would happen. We should have never trusted him."

"Shut up," Bonnie snapped.

Everyone stopped eating. Silence bombarded her in the form of pointed stares from all sides. A Horseman simply did not yell at a council member, but Bonnie needed to speak her mind.

"Katrina told me he said he was going to do something to try to make it up to us for his past. I have a terrible feeling he went to spy on Lucifer. The sun is going down; he travels through light. What if he gets trapped there? What if something went wrong?"

"Calm down, Bonnie. We don't know for sure where he went," Malini said.

"Or if he was telling the truth," Lillian said.

"He's an angel. He can't lie," Bonnie said. "I of all people didn't want to trust Cord, but he saved me *twice*. He's had ample opportunity to leave, Lillian, and he hasn't. He's on our side."

"Unless he was gathering enough to make a difference for Lucifer. He knows it all now, our quotas, our territories, the Tom Sawyer Society. Once he left, he couldn't come back. He had to earn our trust to learn the really important stuff, and now, what a surprise, he's gone." Lillian stood, coolly, and addressed Malini. "I think I should go on patrol tonight in his place. It could get ugly."

Malini gave a curt nod but placed her hand on Bonnie's shoulder. "We don't know why he left or what he's doing, Bon, but we have to close ranks. I trusted him completely. Personally, I don't think he left to betray us, but if he has been captured, he's a liability. He knows all of our secrets. Lillian is right. This could be very bad."

"So then we have to get him back," Bonnie said. "Let me take a team and see if we can't find him. Ghost could check the penthouse."

Malini shook her head. "We can't risk it. The fifth curse has been cast. We are down to the last blows of this challenge and God is losing. Cord knew the rule that no one was allowed to go out alone. No less than three, remember?" Malini held up three fingers.

A rattled sigh parted Bonnie's lips.

"He broke the rules and didn't tell anyone where he was going. I don't agree with Lillian that his intentions were evil, but his actions *were* deliberate. He has to live with the consequences. We can't save him this time."

Tears welled in Bonnie's eyes. She'd hated him. For months, she'd wished him dead, but over the last weeks, she was sure he'd changed. Just as she was sure that he had done something incredibly stupid ... for the greater good.

Samantha wrapped an arm around her shoulders and hugged. "Maybe Bonnie shouldn't patrol tonight, Malini," she whispered.

"No," Bonnie wiped under her eyes. "I'm fine. I understand, all right? I need to keep busy. Don't take that away from me."

Malini nodded her head. "Okay then, Bonnie, Sam, and Lillian, you're on tonight. Be careful out there."

Bonnie strapped on a set of daggers and donned her puffy purple coat, hat, and mittens. She hadn't eaten yet, but suddenly she wasn't hungry. She had a job to do, and it was going to take every ounce of courage and cunning she had left to do it.

Chapter 17
For the Record

Alfred Winston had been the president's friend for a good twenty years. He trusted the man, and the relationship had been prosperous, to say the least. Alfred didn't have an official title. His name did not appear on any record, anywhere, and he had never been photographed with the president. This meant he was perfect for a certain type of work, the type the president didn't want associated with himself or the White House.

Today, Alfred was dressed in a black suit and bowtie with an apron tied around his waist. In his hand was a pitcher of water, one into which he had emptied the contents of a small vial. He worked his way around the conference table, filling empty water glasses while men in tailored business suits filtered into the room chatting each other up. After some time, he relegated himself to the corner. The suits took their seats around the table, and Alfred angled himself so that the tiny camera in his boutonniere was pointed directly at Milton Blake and Asher James.

Senator Bakewell opened the meeting. "The Council for the Eradication of the Unholy will come to order. First order of business is Senator Worth's report on deaths by Watcher violence."

Alfred allowed his mind to wander to the problem at hand as the men took turns speaking. Earlier, he'd cranked the heat, and most of the men drank the water with gusto to cool off. Not Mr. James. His orders were to coax him specifically to ingest the liquid and get it on film. As he refilled glasses, he pondered ways to get Asher James to drink. He couldn't rightly hold the man down and force him to swallow.

Senator Bakewell blotted his vast forehead with his handkerchief, his face flushed red. "You, you there," he said. "Find a way to turn down the heat in here."

With a sigh, Alfred entered the hidden servant's door in the corner of the room and did as he was asked. The heat wasn't working anyway. He resumed his post as quickly as possible.

Mr. James still wasn't drinking, but Bakewell seemed distracted. He stared at Milton Blake as if seeing him for the first time. In fact, all of the men in the room had stopped talking and gaped in the direction of Blake and James.

"Is there a reason we've paused the meeting?" Blake barked, rapping his knuckles on the table.

Bakewell rubbed his eyes with the knuckles of his fists, blinked them closed and opened them again. "You look … That is, the lighting in here has given you a…"

"I see it too," Worth said. "Darkness."

And then the unthinkable. The brands on the back of their right hands began to smoke. The men screamed in pain. Bakewell plunged his hand into his glass of water. The others did the same. Blake and James looked at each other in obvious confusion, then pushed their chairs back from the table. It was now or never.

As if he were using the remainder of his pitcher to come to the aid of the burning men, Alfred lunged forward, splashing the contents over Asher James. Milton Blake cursed as rivulets stained his suit. Alfred did not regret the move. Mr. James began to smoke, and, with boutonniere camera rolling, Alfred recorded it all.

Asher's skin reddened and then split, peeling from his hands and face. To Alfred's horror, the scaly black skin of a demon peeked from underneath the human flesh. The man's eyes turned yellow, and the pupils changed to resemble a snake's. The other senators, including Bakewell, ran for the door. They didn't make it.

The demon dropped all pretenses of being human and, wings outstretched, attacked. Bakewell's neck spewed red blood, shredded by demon fangs. The man crumpled to the floor amid torrid screams. The demon who had once been

Asher James left Bakewell to bleed out on the carpet, and pounced on Worth. An ear slapped the wall next to Alfred's head.

"Don't you think we should find a way out of here?" Milton Blake spoke quickly to Alfred. How had he moved so quickly around the table?

Alfred nodded, forcing his paralyzed muscles to back toward the hidden service door. He pressed the corner of the wall, and the section popped open. Milton Blake sifted through ahead of Alfred, who paused to check for other survivors. There were none. He closed the door.

"This way," he stammered, passing Blake in the small corridor and jogging toward the kitchen.

A hand landed on his shoulder, slowing him to a walk. Milton Blake's grip was almost painful, and he could feel the man's body heat against his back.

"How did you know that James was a demon?"

"I didn't. I saw the smoke and thought there was a fire. I was trying to put it out."

"Funny, Alfred, the smoke was clearly coming from the other men, but your water landed on James."

Alfred narrowed his eyes. How did Milton Blake know his real name? His name tag read Francis. "I'm a bad shot I guess. I was aiming for Bakewell. James was very close."

"Hmm."

The clanking sounds of a bustling kitchen soothed Alfred. Almost there. There was a phone in the kitchen to call security. Milton Blake gripped his shoulder tighter, causing pain to shoot up his neck. He stopped short. The hand spun him around.

"The thing you should know about lying, Alfred, is that you can't lie to a liar. And, if you are going to try, you should make damn sure you aren't lying to the Prince of Lies. Look into my eyes."

Alfred had no choice but to do as the man asked. Blake had gripped him by the neck and pulled him flush against his chest. Nose to nose, he stared into the man's baby blue irises, but beyond their innocent exterior, Alfred's mind was bombarded with unimaginable horrors. Burning flesh, wretched screams, twisted and beaten men in a hopeless sea of darkness. He gagged and tried to close his eyes.

"Why did you throw the water on James?"

"I was following orders. He was supposed to drink the water, but he didn't."

"Why?"

Alfred didn't answer, but his eyes flicked to his boutonniere. Milton Blake used his free hand to crush the white rose and the tiny camera inside. The fist he formed was aimed at Alfred's heart.

"Idiot do-gooders. When will you ever learn?"

Blake's fist smashed through Alfred's ribcage, leaving him with no time to consider who the man was, what his words meant, or what would happen to the camera's live transmission, beamed wirelessly and automatically to a handful of the nation's top journalists.

* * * * *

Malini could not believe what she was seeing. "Jacob, Grace, come quick."

The two Soulkeepers entered Sanctuary from the kitchen. Grace dropped the towel she was holding when she saw the television.

The local news station was replaying a video clip again and again, clearly showing Asher James transform into a demon and Milton Blake murder a man. The Council for the Eradication of the Unholy had been dismantled. In fact, the members were all dead. A sharply dressed news reporter kept repeating the same thing: *Harrington Security found to be a scam. People are flocking in record numbers to churches around the globe to use holy water to remove their brands. Brands no longer required for the purchase of goods. Chaos in the streets as demons attack.*

"It's a miracle," Grace said. "We've won! The challenge is ours."

Jacob was still gaping silently at the image of black wings spread over Bakewell's dead body.

"I wish I could say you were right, Grace, but my gut tells me this is the beginning, not the end," Malini said.

"What? Why?" Jacob asked, finding his voice.

"This is the fifth gift. It exposes Lucifer for what he is. But the Devil isn't going to run. After the second gift, when the Watchers were exposed, what did he do?"

"He had the Watchers attack, then used the terror to his benefit," Jacob said.

"Lucifer is backed into a corner. When have we ever seen him back down in that situation?"

"Do you know what it will be?" Grace asked.

A scream pierced the night from the direction of the street. Malini prayed for Cheveyo, Dane, and Ethan, who were on patrol. This war was far from over.

"I don't. Not yet. Grace, go get Samantha, Ghost, and Lillian from the laundry room."

Grace took off toward the rectory.

"Where's Katrina?" Malini asked Jacob.

"She left a few hours ago with Father Raymond for Paris."

"Good. She'll be safer there. Where's Hope?"

"She was fussy and coughing. Bonnie took her into the shower to see if the steam would help," Jacob said.

"I'll get her," Malini said. "When Grace gets back, tell everyone they are needed in the field as soon as possible."

"What about Dane?" Jacob asked.

"He needs to stay here with Hope and me. He won't have a power to borrow."

Jacob paused. "You're not coming?"

"No. I need to consult the immortals. We have to use every advantage at our disposal."

"It's not that I'm disappointed. I want you to be safe. Just be careful. There will be no one here to protect you."

Glancing over her shoulder, she locked eyes with the boy she loved. "I can take care of myself, Jacob. I'm the Healer."

Jacob nodded and then turned away as Grace arrived with the others.

Malini continued through the door to the large sitting area connected to the bathroom and shower. This used to be a bride's room, where brides would dress, do their makeup, and wait to walk down the aisle on their wedding day. It used to be a hopeful place, not the overused facility for a set of war-torn, black-blood-covered warriors. Inside, the sound of sobs and a labored cough broke through the heavy steam.

"Malini, thank God," Bonnie said. Her face was moist with droplets of steam, but the trails down her cheeks made it clear she'd been the one crying. "Hope stopped breathing. She started again, but look, her lips are blue."

Bonnie handed her the baby. "You've got to heal her."

"I will," Malini said softly.

"Why isn't it working? You've healed her before. She keeps getting sick again, every time worse than the last. What's wrong with her?"

Malini glanced at the floor and made a decision. "What is wrong with Hope is something I cannot heal. When you brought Abigail to the In Between through the red stone, a piece of Hope's soul stayed there. Hope is outgrowing the piece that is left in her body. She's disconnected. If I can't figure out a way to bring her soul back, she'll die."

Bonnie shook her head. "But she's a Soulkeeper. She's Abigail's daughter. She can't die. We need her."

"I know. I'm going to figure out a way."

"I couldn't stand it if she died," Bonnie sobbed. "When she came, it was like a message from God."

"She was. She is. She was the bringer of the third gift. Something about her and you together changed Cord."

Bonnie's eyebrows drew together. "Are you sure? Maybe he was going to change anyway."

Jacob busted through the door. "Bonnie, we gotta go."

"There's no time," Malini said. "The fifth gift has come to pass. It's complete chaos out there. I need you to help protect the humans until dawn."

"I'll fill her in," Jacob said.

With a look of confusion, Bonnie followed Jacob from the room. Malini cradled Hope in her arms. The baby broke into a fit of coughing again, and a guilty weight settled over the Healer's chest. She had to find a way to save the girl so that the girl could save them all.

Chapter 18
A Demon's Plaything

Cord woke in a dark room with a single candle, wrists bound, chained to one of four black walls. There wasn't much more in the room: a table, the candle, and a set of sharp metal instruments that glinted in the flickering light. A door in the wall across from him was closed. A tile floor chilled his bare feet, the type of floor that was easy to clean. A floor not easily stained by blood.

Focusing on the light, he tried to fold into it in order to free himself, but his power fizzled. His body remained bound.

"It's cursed," Auriel said. She'd materialized in the room without opening the door. "This light is enough to help you heal but insufficient for you to escape. Ten feet of pitch black surrounds you on all sides."

"Why heal me? Why not kill me?"

She stepped forward until their cheeks almost touched. Almost. Actually touching would be painful for both of them. "Death would be too easy for you," she whispered. "No, I'm going to rip everything you know about the Soulkeepers out of your body one silvery chunk at a time. Then, when you are in so much pain that you can't bear to take your next breath, I'll turn on the lights and watch you stitch back together so I can do it all over again."

Cord gagged a little. His horror was made more acute by the familiarity of her face. He had memories of a long relationship with Auriel, although he couldn't characterize it based on the scenes that played out in his head.

"We were friends once," he said.

"Friends?" She laughed. "We were competitors for Lucifer's attention. I was his right, and you were his left."

Cord allowed his thoughts to journey into the past, to dredge up the personal history he would have rather not remembered. "No," he said slowly, deliberately. "I was the right, and you were the left. And we *were* friends. You sent me f...fingers for my collection when you didn't have to."

She turned her face away. "You never did understand your place."

"Explain it to me." If he could keep her talking, he might … he might, what? Delay the inevitable? He knew the Soulkeepers couldn't risk coming to his aid. He'd been incredibly stupid doing what he did alone and against the rules. Only, the chance to do something truly good and selfless was enough of a motivation to drive him forward. So, if he were meant to die, he would distract this Watcher for as long as possible. One less for the Soulkeepers to deal with.

"You, Cord, were being used. You thought you were Lucifer's right, and you sucked up to him and me like a calf to a heifer's teat, but you were always the rube. We used you and nothing more."

"*We* used you. Don't you mean that Lucifer used us both, just like he uses everyone?"

She shook her head. "When all of this is done, I will be queen of everything, Watcher and human alike. Lucifer and I will rule, side by side."

"That's not what it looked like to me. When I was hovering in that conference room, it looked like the Wicked Brethren were being groomed for the job."

She growled. He was getting to her.

"Free me, Auriel. If I can become an angel, you can too. You can leave your Watcher ways behind and go where you are truly needed."

She paced over to the table of implements, selecting a silver tool with a curled end like a pig's tail. Twirling it between her fingers, he could see her jaw working beside her platinum hair, the anger tightening the muscles under her illusion.

"How *did* you become an angel, Cord?" Auriel asked.

He couldn't tell her about Bonnie or Hope. Truth was he didn't fully understand how the miracle had occurred. So he said nothing.

"Just as I thought." She took a step toward him. "Thank you for not answering. This way I get to ask again, and then I get to do the torture thing."

Cord shook his head. "But I don't know the answer to your question. I'm not sure how it happened."

Auriel smiled and stepped closer. She plunged the razor-sharp tip into his gut.

The scream stuck in Cord's throat, the pain so intense as to render him silent. Something hot and wet dripped onto his toes. Silver blood. His blood. Finally the scream came, and he tipped his head back to let it out. He knew little about his anatomy as an angel, but the thought crossed his mind that he couldn't live through much more than this. Surely this was as bad as it could get.

But he was wrong.

With a grin worthy of evil incarnate, she twisted the sharp tool in his side, and a new wave of agony overcame him.

* * * * *

Bonnie couldn't stop thinking about Cord, but acting on those thoughts was far from possible at the moment. Merged with her sister, she swung a heavy metal club at a Watcher, knocking the beast's head off its winged shoulders. Its human prey staggered away, bloody and injured but strong enough to get up and run for the nearest building.

From a bag tied around her waist, she tossed the man a Ziploc of holy water. "On the door," she ordered. The man nodded and dragged himself inside, splashing the contents wildly as he entered. Good enough.

Bonnie scanned the now empty street. "I think we lost Lillian on Second Street. Let's double back. She always knows where the action is."

"Fine, but only if you get your head in the game," Sam said through the set of lips they presently shared.

"What is *that* supposed to mean?"

"You keep thinking about Cord. We're sharing a brain. Kind of hard to keep it a secret."

Bonnie sighed. "Can we separate for a second? I want to talk to you face to face."

The familiar tug started at her belly button, a spinning top whose force expanded like a supernova, then collapsed in on itself, leaving both of them on the outside of its gravitational pull.

Samantha used both hands to heave the club onto her shoulder, much heavier now that she was half the size. Smoothing her long red hair into a high ponytail, she pulled a dagger from a sheath on her forearm. "Talk," she said. She lumbered in the direction of Second Street, and Bonnie fell into step beside her.

"About Cord, I think we should make an attempt to rescue him."

"Malini says no. He broke the rules. We can't risk anyone else."

"I know what she said."

"Then why do you insist on fighting it? You're always questioning the Healer. She's the Healer for a reason, you know?"

"I know, but—"

"But what, Bonnie?" Samantha asked incredulously.

Bonnie watched their shoes fall in perfect rhythm on the sidewalk. "Do you remember much about Dad?"

"A little. Images mostly." Sam shook her head.

"I have this memory of him reading the story of Jonah and the whale. Do you remember it?"

"I think so."

"Well, God tells Jonah to preach to this city called Nineveh because the people there are corrupt. Jonah doesn't want to do it. So, instead, he jumps a ship and sails in the complete opposite direction. God isn't happy about this and sends a storm to rough up the ship. The crew, suspecting Jonah is to blame, throws him overboard where he is swallowed by a giant fish, and after three days is vomited on the shores of Nineveh." Bonnie hoped it was an accurate summary. She hadn't memorized the story word for word.

"And this has to do with what?" Samantha looked frustrated.

"I remember Dad telling me something about Jonah, about why he didn't want to preach to Nineveh. Jonah was Jewish, and the people who lived in Nineveh weren't. Plus they did awful, sinful things there."

"So?"

"So, Jonah didn't want to go there to preach because he was afraid *it might work*. He did not want the Ninevites to be saved. Dad said Jonah allowed his own prejudices to get in the way of God's work."

Samantha groaned, clearly not following what this had to do with Cord.

"Don't you see? I am Jonah. I didn't want to forgive Cord even when his transformation was clearly a gift from God. It took him saving my life twice, my own personal fish swallowing, for me to accept His will."

Rolling her eyes, Samantha stopped and turned toward her sister. "Don't you think you are overanalyzing the situation? Bonnie, you are a Soulkeeper. He was a Watcher. No one expected you to welcome him with open arms. You are not Jonah. Lillian still doesn't believe he's an angel, but you do. You eventually accepted him."

"Still, there must have been a reason God changed him. Why him? God could have changed any Watcher. Cord has a purpose, a purpose we should have been figuring out all that time I was starving him in the pantry. I think we need him back."

"Malini says—"

"I know what she says, but the fact is, if I hadn't been so hard on Cord, maybe he wouldn't have felt the need to prove himself to us. Maybe it's my fault, my pushing him away, that has left us without our God-given angel. If I had been more open and forgiving, if I had trusted in his redemption, would he have left without permission?"

Sam shrugged. "Who knows? It might not have had anything to do with you."

"I need to get him back."

"You don't know where he is."

"I think I do."

"Huh?"

"I have this really strong feeling he's in Lucifer's penthouse. Shit is hitting the fan for Harrington, Samantha. Lucifer is going to be distracted while this Asher thing blows up. Now's my chance to find out if my intuition is correct."

"Oh, Bonnie, you can't go alone. It's too dangerous."

"Then come with me."

Samantha balked, glancing down at her Mizunos and repositioning the dagger in her hand. "I can't come with you. I get what you're saying, I do. You feel guilty about something you've done, and you want to set it right. But I'm not guilty, and I think the idea is reckless. What if you die? What if they capture you? I can't be part of this."

Righteous indignation burned within Bonnie's chest until she paused long enough to digest what her sister was saying. "You won't go, but you aren't going to stop me, are you?"

"Stop you? Who could stop Bonnie Guillian? You're practically swallowed by a fish."

"Thank you. You won't be sorry."

"I'm already sorry. Sorry I didn't kick your ass about this a month ago when it would have made a difference. Are you equipped?"

Bonnie checked the blades on her arms and down her back. "I think so."

"Your appearance?"

"I don't think the wanted posters have the same kind of power anymore. Still, can you give me a few pounds?"

Sam nodded and gripped her hand, shifting mass in her direction. Bonnie incorporated her sister's gift, but maintained her identical appearance. Still, the potential was there, right below the surface, to disguise herself if needed.

"You're twenty minutes from the penthouse," Sam said. "You have an hour. After that, if you're not back, I'm telling Malini."

"Deal."

Her sister wrapped her arms around her neck and squeezed. Bonnie could feel the stiff form of the weapon holster she was wearing under her shirt. "Don't do anything else stupid. Love you."

"Love you too, sister."

Bonnie scanned the street then took off running toward Lucifer's penthouse.

Chapter 19
The Devil's Due

Lucifer arrived at his penthouse with a singular purpose, wrath. Anger consumed him. What happened today was inexcusable. Disastrous. Closing his eyes, he called the Wicked Brethren from shadow. Auriel, on the other hand, arrived first, without request or invitation, apron and rubber gloves covered in silver. Careful not to get Cord's blood on her skin, she stripped the soiled garments off and dumped them in the kitchen sink.

"Is there anything left of him?" Lucifer asked.

"A few gurgling parts."

As upset as he was, he gave her a weak grin. Auriel was truly without conscience. He could respect that. Perhaps he hadn't given her enough credit. Before he could soothe himself with the tale of Cord's torture, three columns of smoke formed in the center of the room: Damien, Levi, and Asher.

"What has happened?" Auriel asked at the sight of their distraught expressions.

Lucifer paced to the brethren, eyes narrowing as they fell on Asher. Striking his chest, Lucifer fisted Asher's shirt, the skin of his hand peeling back from his talons. He lifted the sizable demon from the ground as if he weighed nothing.

"You revealed yourself. The world knows what you are," the Devil hissed, quiet as a whisper but with more venom.

"What?" Auriel eyed Asher scornfully. "You idiot!"

Asher's aqua blue eyes flashed. "I did no such thing. I did not *reveal* myself. I was revealed. Bastard human doused me in holy water, and not your usual run-of-the-mill corner church variety. The damage hurt like a bitch. It was the real deal." Grasping Lucifer's wrist, he struggled and kicked his feet.

Lucifer let go, sending Asher crashing to the carpet. "Oh, I have no doubt it was, as you say, the real deal. I smelled the Great Oppressor's signature all over that conference room. Your incompetence proved a useful vessel for delivering the fifth gift."

Asher rolled onto his hands and knees. "What of it, then? The damage is done."

Without warning, Lucifer delivered a swift kick to Asher's ribs, sending him flying into the sofa. While he paced, deciding how to punish Asher further, Damien and Levi positioned themselves in a protective, albeit cautious, stance near his unconscious body.

Awkwardly, Auriel interjected her opinion. "Surely you, the master of lies, can spin a tale to cover the damage. Perhaps a demon broke in and was confused for Asher?"

"Unfortunately, while you were here playing in the dark with our captive, a video of Asher *ingesting* the Council for the Eradication of the Unholy was transmitted around the globe. The association between Milton Blake and Asher James is well known. The humans are turning away in record numbers, soaking off my seal in holy water. Harrington stock is tanking."

"A quarter of our human employees have already resigned," Damien said.

"Some will undoubtedly stay. Winners want to be on the winning side, after all," Auriel said hopefully.

Levi swept his hair back from his eyes, his Mediterranean complexion reddening with anger. "You took me from a well-fed existence on a Romanian hillside for *this*? What is your plan, Lucifer? Or has the Great Oppressor gotten the best of you?"

In a heartbeat, Lucifer crossed the room, gripped Levi's neck, and bent him backward until his spine threatened to snap. He brought his face within a half-inch of Levi's.

"You will do as I tell you to do, when I tell you to do it." Lucifer's teeth ground together. He let go abruptly, and Levi's body slapped the floor.

"Call in the Watchers," Lucifer said.

"Which ones?" Levi asked, scrambling to his feet.

"All of them."

Damien turned a confused visage toward his lord and master. "There are thousands. Where should we have them come?"

"For my sixth curse, it is imperative that my Watchers are in my physical presence. There must be a place in this city large enough for us to entertain them."

"The humans have large gatherings at the United Center," Auriel offered.

"Very well. Levi, order the Watchers to meet in the United Center. I want them there tomorrow night. We will enchant the building for our purposes."

"Yes, my lord."

"The rest of you, prepare for our guests."

"What preparations should we make?" Damien asked.

"I will need equipment so that every attending Watcher can see my face. And we will need a suitable security system to keep out the undesirables."

"The Soulkeepers," Auriel clarified.

Lucifer grinned. "Do you know what the benefit is of having that angel almost dead in the next room?"

Damien smirked. "His protection is no more."

Lucifer nodded and closed his eyes. A column of black smoke funneled into the middle of the room, and soon the persistent pain in his side, Malini, formed behind the magical glass that separated him from her soul.

Her eyes grew wide when she saw where she was.

"Lucifer," she spat.

"Yes," he said. "It appears your protective mechanism has been eliminated, which means I again have the ability to call your soul to me."

"Eliminated," Malini murmured inside her glass cell.

"Don't tell me you didn't know," Lucifer said, laughing. "The presence of an angel hinders my ability to find your soul."

"Cord," Malini muttered.

"You sent your shield to spy on me." He shook his head and clucked his tongue. "And now your spy is a puddle of silver on the floor of my dungeon, and your soul is mine to call again."

Malini's face hardened. "What do you want, Lucifer?"

"I want you to know that it is just a matter of time before I find you. I can sense your soul and track your location." He laughed wickedly. "When it pleases me, I will come for you, and I promise my vengeance will not be quick."

The Healer attempted to hide her terror, but Lucifer could see the fear ripple across her skin. He could smell the musk of it in the air.

He waggled his fingers in a patronizing wave. "See you soon, Healer." With a snap, she dissolved again, sucked out of the room as quickly as she'd come.

"When do we attack?" Damien mused. "Before or after the sixth curse?"

"Neither. My message to the Healer was meant to intimidate and keep her out of our way. She'll be too busy trying to protect her fellow Soulkeepers to interfere with our gathering."

"What if you're wrong? Soulkeepers are notorious for acting on the greater good," Damien said.

"Do not question me. Without their angel, the Soulkeepers are vulnerable. If they are stupid enough to come for us, we will be ready. I will crush them, and then nothing will stand between me and the world."

Auriel cheered. "Yes! What will the sixth temptation be? How will you win human hearts back to our side?"

"To ensure our success in the future, we must look to the past, to the strategy of our enemy. In the time of Moses, the Great Oppressor sent the angel of death into Egypt to kill the firstborn son of any who did not have His mark. The Angel of Death passed over the Israelites who painted their doors with lamb's blood. The Great Oppressor won the freedom of his people through selective death.

"We will win this challenge in the same way. The winner is judged based on the number of living human hearts aligned with me at the time the last gift is given. To win, all we have to do is make less human hearts. Either they align with us, or they die."

"We kill the humans aligned with good," Levi repeated.

"And then, all who are left will be ours," Auriel said.

"Exactly." Lucifer folded his hands behind his back and stared out the window to the chaos below. "My final curse will be death, and my vessel, every Watcher on Earth. They will spread my deadly curse across the world, and only those who still bear my seal will survive. Now, go. Prepare. We can leave nothing to chance."

* * * * *

There was one good thing about the chaos going on outside the doors of the skyscraper on North Wabash Avenue: the lobby was empty. No one opened the door for her, and there was no one behind the front desk. With a powerful kick that would have been impossible for a mere human, she busted the door to the security office open, finding a large bald man cowering in a corner.

"What are you doing in here?" Bonnie asked.

"Hiding from the demons," the man said breathily as if the answer was all too obvious.

Bonnie noticed the scar on the back of his right hand. He'd had the seal but burned it off. Good for him; she'd let him live. She moved to the wall cabinet and selected the same key to the penthouse Ghost had obtained for them when they'd rescued Abigail. Palming it, she turned on her heel.

"Wait. Where are you going?" the man asked.

"To kill the demons," Bonnie said by way of explanation.

"You're one of them, aren't you? From the poster. Harrington's most wanted."

Bonnie gave a little half smile. "I'm a Soulkeeper. If you value anything good in this life, you won't tell anyone you saw me."

He shook his head vigorously. "I won't, but that key will only get you upstairs, it won't get you inside."

"What?"

"That key is for the elevator to the penthouse, but this—" He snagged an unlabeled gold key from a hook. "This will get you in the front door. We always keep one for every unit, in case of emergency."

"Excellent." Bonnie looked at the man's name tag. "Thank you, Ian."

He nodded. "You're welcome."

"I apologize in advance, but I need to borrow something else from you, Ian."

"Anything."

Folding in on herself, Bonnie transformed into the man, security uniform and all. "Anything," she repeated, then said it again an octave lower. "Anything."

The man crossed himself.

"Later." Bonnie rushed for the open elevator, slipping the key into the slot. The doors closed. The elevator ascended. Music piped into the mirrored compartment, a wordless version of Sting's *Desert Rose*. The song was almost over when the doors slid open to the penthouse foyer she remembered from before. The same plastic potted plant greeted her. There was a door to her right and her left.

On light feet, she padded toward the one on her left, the one she'd gone through the first time she was here. If she remembered correctly, it led to the kitchen and the family room. She pressed her ear against the wood.

"Now go. Prepare. We can leave nothing to chance," she heard Lucifer say. She jogged backward at the sound of approaching footsteps. She needed to hide. The elevator was already gone. Only one other place to go. She slid the key from Ian into the opposite door, slipping inside and pulling it closed behind her. Four sets of footsteps filtered under the door, along with the murmur of excited voices. She held her breath until the sound of the elevator ushered the voices away. Silence.

Heart pounding, Bonnie turned into the empty corridor. She remembered searching for Abigail in these rooms. The penthouse was shaped like a doughnut with the elevator and foyer the hole in the middle. The hallway was dark now, without the benefit of sunlight from the wall of glass that made up the building's exterior. Still, a trickle of illumination from what city lights survived across the Chicago skyline was enough for her to make her way.

She tried the first door, listening for any signs that the four sets of footsteps she'd heard leaving weren't the only ones in the penthouse. A bedroom. She swept through and found it empty along with the adjoining bathroom. She begged Fate and then God that Cord's prison was one she could see and not one like Abigail's. Back in the hall, she checked the next room and the next. Her hands began to sweat. She had to find him. She had to make this right.

Her fingers gripped the next knob, willing Cord to be inside. The iron tarried willfully against her palm. Locked.

"Cord," she whispered. She pressed her ear against the door. There was no answer but a soft hiss. Whether it was her angel or a pit of vipers she did not know, but she backed across the hall and jumped a few times to build her momentum. With a deep breath, she bound against the opposite wall, finding purchase and propelling her body across the corridor as her foot shot out toward the door. As before, she couldn't break the lock, but she could break the wood. The frame cracked, the lock and mechanism still engaged, and the door swung open on its hinges.

Bonnie landed at the threshold. The room was not filled with pit vipers, but her brain could not digest what she saw there. The window in this room had been painted over. The walls were dark, the space a black hole. The only thing she could see was a shiny film on the floor, a silvery slick that glowed dimly against the black. A piece of the slick rippled and the hiss came again. She inhaled sharply, and the scent of citrus and ocean filled her nostrils.

An icy chill scampered like an army of ants from Bonnie's toes to the base of her skull. Foolishly, she slipped inside the room. She patted the wall for the light switch. When she flipped it, a dome light flickered and then gave off an intense, brassy glow.

Bonnie pressed a hand over her lips to stifle a scream.

Cord. He had to be dead. Wings limp, his torso lay facedown on the floor in a pool of silver blood. One arm dangled from a cuff chained to the wall. The other was free but shredded, as though it had been torn forcibly, flesh and all, from its cuff. The bend and twist of his legs and spine was contrary to the proper alignment of bones.

Thick with grief, Bonnie ran to Cord's side, flipped him over, and wiped the hair back from his lifeless eyes. "Cord. I'm sorry. I'm so sorry." Her tears fell like rain on his neck and chest, carving trails through the silver blood. The light from above wavered iridescent against the silver, creating a sickly river of death.

What was this place? There was a table of torturous implements next to his head—gougers, knives, and scrapers—all covered in silver death. She closed her eyes against images of the unspeakable acts he must have suffered.

She couldn't stand seeing him like this. No way would she leave Cord's body to these monsters. Gently resting his head in her lap, she reached for the chain on the wall and used her dagger to pry open the restraint. What would she do with his body? She could not, would not, leave him, but even in her current form, carrying Cord would not be easy.

"What are you doing in here?" Auriel asked. She'd formed in the shadowed corner of the room, her sapphire blue eyes piercing the darkness like a predatory animal.

For a moment, Bonnie forgot she was wearing the image of the security guard, but as she gently repositioned Cord so she could stand, she noticed Ian's thick, callused fingers on the angel's skin. She cleared her throat.

"Question is, what are you doing? This man is injured. He needs help," she said in Ian's voice, two octaves lower than her own. She was covered in silver blood, a fact that was surely masking her Soulkeeper smell.

"Stay where you are," Auriel demanded, positioning herself in front of the door. "I can't let you tell anyone about this." She snatched Bonnie's right hand, no doubt checking for a seal. Auriel bared her teeth when she saw the unblemished skin.

With the snap of overstretched elastic, Bonnie retracted her hand and drew one of her daggers. She readied herself for a fight.

"Stupid human. Don't you see that alignment with us is the future? We are your only chance of survival." She laughed, glancing at Bonnie's smooth right hand. "But, since you made your choice, and I have made myself hungry with my efforts tonight..." Her fangs flashed in the fluorescent light.

Bonnie shook Ian's image from her body like a dog shakes water from its coat. "Bring it on, Auriel."

"Soulkeeper," Auriel hissed. Her skin morphed black as she shed her illusion.

With a banshee scream, Bonnie hurled herself at Auriel, wanting nothing more than to do to the Watcher exactly what she'd done to Cord.

Chapter 20
A Light in the Darkness

Malini held baby Hope against her chest, stroking her hair and rubbing circles over her tiny spine. Against her russet skin, Hope's complexion looked almost gray, and her lips had taken on a blue tint. The infant's breath sounded pinched and ragged. Concentrating her Healing power, Malini placed her left hand on the back of Hope's neck and flooded her with her gift, feeling the burn until the baby's cheeks pinked.

She'd done this over and over again. The problem was, as soon as she pulled her hand away, Hope's condition would gradually worsen again. In a few hours, she'd be back to the brink of death. The healing was temporary and draining, a condition that couldn't come at a worse time for the Healer.

Unfortunately, Malini needed to be fresh and energized, now more than ever.

Lucifer had called her soul and made it clear that he could find her and the other Soulkeepers at any time. To think, Cord was their protection all along. His presence had kept them safe, and in return, they'd made him feel guilty enough to risk his life for information on the sixth curse.

She was alone tonight. The Soulkeepers were all out trying their best to protect the humans in the chaos that ensued after Lucifer's exposure. Even now Malini could hear screams from the street as the Watchers fed indiscriminately. There was no illusion of safety anymore. Lucifer's seal offered no protection now that it didn't serve his purposes.

For Hope's protection, Malini had taken cover near the holy water font. If the Watchers came for her, she planned to climb into the water and wait for the sun to rise or the other Soulkeepers to return. But Hope's worsening condition meant she could not delay council. With Hope in her arms, she leaned against the side of the font and cleared her head, her soul falling backward into the In Between.

"Finally," Fatima said, her immortal eyes wet with tears. "We've been waiting for you." Fate grabbed Malini's elbow and pulled her toward the front of her villa. "She's sick."

Noting her empty arms, Malini didn't need to ask who Fatima was talking about. As expected, Hope's guide, the missing piece of her soul, lay on a hospital bed. Mara and Henry stood vigil on either side of her. The girl's form had faded to a dark transparency, ghostlike and unconscious.

"She's fading," Mara said. "I cannot see her future."

Henry frowned. "Her physical body is dying. I've tried to hold this piece of her soul here, but I cannot. It's as if she is being washed from existence."

Fatima held up the tapestry she was weaving. "Her thread dulls in my creation. It was purple to begin with. Now it is barely blue."

Malini shook her head, weeping openly. "I came here for answers. Are you telling me you have none?"

The three immortals stared back at her, despondent and pleading.

"Only God has the answer," Mara said. Her black eyes fixated on Malini. "You've come to the wrong place. Don't you understand that her existence was a gift from the creator, the third gift? Only He knows her purpose."

"Then why isn't he telling us what to do?" Malini asked. "How do we save her?"

Hope's eyes flipped open. She blinked up at the ceiling and swallowed in a way that seemed painful. "The question is valid," she said.

Malini reached for her hand while the immortals pressed in around her, waiting for her to speak.

With a wave of Hope's hand, blossoms fell from thin air and piled on the girl's stomach. She ran her fingers through the flower petals and then answered with trembling lips. "You will save me by releasing your power into the world."

Malini shook her head. "I don't understand."

Hope smiled. "All humans are made from God. They come from God. Each is a gift, just like me. But like me, some are disconnected from the piece of themselves that is eternal. A human soul is an ancient, powerful thing. Cut a person off from their soul, and you make them a shell whose only purpose is their current unremarkable existence. My tiny body is dying. Did I have a purpose, Malini?"

Malini wiped tears from her eyes. "Of course you did. We all love you, Hope."

Hope nodded. "Every person has a purpose. *Everyone.* Not just the people who understand it. A person connected to their soul will choose God, because they are made of God."

"Made of God? I don't understand. How will I reconnect you with your body?"

"You must destroy what you are."

Malini froze. Jaw clenched, she hugged her stomach, the truth plowing through her like a runaway freight train.

Hope closed her eyes. "There can only be one Healer." The girl drifted off again, her breathing falling into an even rhythm.

"Did she just say what I think she said?" Malini's voice cracked and tears spilled over her lower lids. Her eyes darted to Mara, Henry, and Fatima. Each shook their heads.

"Do I have to die for Hope to live? Do I have to die for her to save the world?"

Henry's brow knit. "If that *is* the only way, we have a problem. You can't die, Malini. Only Hope, the new Healer, can release the soul of the old Healer. Remember how you released Panctu?"

Wiping under her eyes, Malini hunched her shoulders, defeated by the truth in Henry's words.

"If you *do* need to die for Hope to save the world, only she can make that happen. And that would require her to have full access to her power on Earth. I'm sure you can appreciate the paradox."

* * * * *

Bonnie's dagger narrowly missed Auriel's heart. The Watcher broke apart and re-formed a foot to the left, talons swiping at her throat in retaliation. Bonnie avoided the strike by somersaulting backward into a handstand and using her boot to kick Auriel's hand aside. She halted at the apex of the movement, then jackknifed, planting both feet on Auriel's chest. The Watcher flew backward, breaking apart before she hit the far wall.

Hastily righting herself, Bonnie pivoted in fighting stance, waiting for her enemy to form again. *Rip.* Claws tore across her back and caught in her ponytail. She screamed as her neck snapped back and the poison leached into her skin. Twisting and turning, she attempted to yank her hair away while avoiding Auriel's flapping leather wings and razor-sharp assault. In the end, there was only one thing she could do. Her blade sliced through her hair, leaving Auriel with a handful of ponytail. At the same time, she tossed the blade at the Watcher's chest.

Auriel dodged right, not fast enough. The blade sliced through the black flesh above her collarbone and lodged in her wing. With a howl of pain, she broke apart. The knife clanked to the floor. Bonnie didn't bother to pick it up. She withdrew another from the sheath on her opposite arm and readied herself for another attack. Retaliation came quickly. Auriel formed within the circle of Bonnie's arms, fangs sinking into her jaw.

Bonnie shrieked, stabbing Auriel again and again in the side. She fell to the floor, but Auriel came with her. Teeth, claws, and daggers dug in. The two rolled until their bodies hit the wall. Bonnie was trapped, pressed into the floor by Auriel's weight and wings, held in place by searing fangs. Blood flooded her mouth. Her body stiffened, seizing from the effects of the poison.

All at once, Auriel's teeth retracted, an unholy scream piercing the room. She reared up, her hands reaching, grabbing behind her back. Through dusky vision, Bonnie saw her salvation. Cord stood in the corner of the room where she'd lost her first blade. That dagger now protruded from the center of Auriel's back. The Watcher tipped forward, face slapping the floor as she writhed in torment.

"Come," Cord said in a raspy voice. He crossed to Bonnie, placing a hand on her cheek. A faint glow later and the bleeding had stopped, although she was far from healed. "I'm too weak to do much more."

Painfully, Bonnie got to her feet, bracing herself against Cord until they were both upright. They used each other to limp past Auriel's thrashing limbs and escape into the hall.

"Let's hope we don't run into any more of them on the way out," Bonnie said, spitting blood. "I can barely stand. I won't be able to fight. My back." She pointed her thumb at the crippling sore spreading behind her shoulders.

Cord nodded, glancing pleadingly at the dim hallway light. A few painful steps and a shiver passed over his body. Inhaling sharply, he turned to look her in the eye. Then he began limping more quickly, dragging her along, down the hallway toward the great room.

"No, Cord, the elevator is the other way. We have to get out of here," she rasped.

It was no use. As if possessed, he hurried her aching body along the corridor until they stood at the wall of windows that overlooked the Chicago skyline. He stopped in front of the glass.

"What are you—?" Bonnie paused. Low, behind the buildings, an orangey pink ball of fire rose to the east. As she watched, rays of light broke over and between silver and glass skyscrapers, fanning out to chase away the darkness. Cord's body glowed. He drank in the light. A golden health washed over him, straightening his wing and healing the oozing wounds in his arms and legs. His sapphire eyes met hers as the glow intensified, and the sunrise cleared the rooftops. She staggered sideways in the glare. He caught her shoulders, his healing energy flowing into her, warming her torso, then her back, and finally from her face all the way to her toes. She blinked at him, speechless with gratitude as the pain left her body.

"Thank you for coming for me, Bonnie."

"It was what I was supposed to do," she whispered.

He laughed, a sound like baritone church bells. "And now I will do what *I* am supposed to do." He rolled her into his chest, folding his wings around her body. Lifting his face to the sun, they blended into the light, and he carried her home.

Chapter 21
Preparing for War

Around the table at Sanctuary, the Soulkeepers gathered to listen to Cord and Bonnie's unbelievable story of escape. The two had arrived at dawn, Bonnie with a new dagger-made haircut that she corrected as soon as she had contact with her sister, and Cord, who had fully healed aside from the bright white scars that now decorated his exposed skin. As he told of his capture and torture, Malini was sure his scars ran deeper than their superficial appearance. Moreover, she thanked God for the return of his protective presence.

"I just want to apologize for doubting you," Grace said. "It's clear you were trying to do the right thing."

Lillian added, "Right. I'm not happy you broke the rules, but I know you did it for the right reasons. I'm sorry it took something like this for me to see you for what you are. Please forgive us."

Cord bowed his head. "I understand why you didn't trust me. I wouldn't have trusted me. I forgive you for it. But now, we all must learn to trust each other because I have news of the sixth curse."

"Did Auriel tell you what it would be?" Malini asked.

"No." He scoffed. "I heard Lucifer and the Wicked Brethren talking about it in the penthouse. Auriel's torture did not affect my angel hearing."

"Please, we need to know," Malini said.

"Lucifer is calling in the Watchers. All of them. From every corner of the globe. His last curse will be death."

"Death?" Jacob asked. "How does he plan to win hearts with death?"

"He will give his Watchers the ability to see inside human hearts and order them to kill any who have not sworn allegiance to him," Cord said. "I heard him compare it to the Passover. He plans to win the challenge by killing off the competition."

Malini inhaled sharply. "Did you hear when? How long do we have to prepare?"

"The Wicked Brethren will call the Watchers in tonight. They will enchant the United Center to hold them all. Lucifer has to have close contact with the Watchers to transfer his power."

"Tonight. How do we stop him?" Lillian asked, voice pinched. "There are eleven of us. We're good, but we're not that good. We can't take them all out."

Malini cupped her chin, running her fingers along her jawline.

"Maybe you don't have to." Cord cleared his throat. "In the past, there has always been a physical element to Lucifer's curses."

"Like?"

"When I was the vessel, he cut his finger off and placed it in my ear. That is how he infected me with his power."

A collective groan rose from the table of Soulkeepers.

"He doesn't have that many fingers," Malini said, frowning. "But if flesh or blood is required, likely it will be something on a grand scale. He'll need to pack them in. There will be sorcery involved."

"So," Cord continued, "if we can stop Lucifer from making physical contact with the Watchers, we can delay the curse."

"Good," Malini said. "That will be plan A. One team will be responsible for intercepting whatever method Lucifer uses to infect the Watchers and eliminating it." She walked to the whiteboard and wrote the idea down.

"What's plan B?" Grace asked.

"We fight. We kill as many as we can before they kill us," Lillian said.

"Ghost," Malini said.

"Yeah," Ghost said.

"Go to city hall, to the building inspector's office. See if you can find blueprints for the United Center. We'll need them to plan our attack."

Ghost nodded slowly and disappeared.

"I can flood the place," Jacob said.

"It won't be like it was in Nod," Malini said. "God sent holy water then. This will be the regular variety. It won't kill them."

"Unless we turn the water in the pipes to holy water," Jacob said. "If I bring blessed water and force it up the pipes, I might be able to get it into the sprinkler system."

She nodded. "Great idea. We have a plan B, counterattack." She jotted the plan on the whiteboard under plan A. "Other ideas."

"Malini, you can raise the dead again like you did in Nod," Dane said.

The Healer glanced at the floor. "I don't think so. The United Center is surrounded by concrete, not cemeteries. Even if I could find bodies to call, it might take them too long to get there to be of any use to us."

"Not to be a dick or anything, but do we have a plan C?" Ethan asked. "These things are tough, and there will be thousands. Cutting off Lucifer's method of infection only delays the inevitable, and even with all of us doing our part, Lucifer is not going to back down this time. Eleven people can't bring down tens of thousands."

Malini glanced toward the makeshift cradle Hope was sleeping in. She walked over to the infant and kissed her head. It was time to share the truth about Abigail and Gideon's daughter. She glanced at Dane and at Cord. "Hope is a Soulkeeper."

"You mean she has the Soulkeeper gene," Grace clarified.

"No. I mean she's an actual Soulkeeper."

Grace shook her head. "I would have sensed her."

"Her soul isn't in her body. It's locked inside the stone." Malini pulled the red disc from her pocket and dangled it between her fingers. "And she's not just a Soulkeeper. She's a Healer."

The table erupted in whispers and darting glances.

"I believe that Hope transformed Cord, and I think she can transform the others."

Cheveyo shook his head. "Wait. You think Hope was what turned Cord from a Watcher into an angel? She'd just been born. How could her Soulkeeper gene have been triggered?"

"I believe God did it. Hope was the third gift."

"And now you want to try to use Hope to turn the Watchers into angels?" Cheveyo asked.

"In short."

"Are you sure it was her?" Samantha glanced at her sister. "If her soul is trapped within the stone, how was she able to exercise her power? She's a baby. How would she know what to do?"

"Cord changed when he saw Bonnie holding Hope. We know it wasn't Bonnie, because the entire time we've been fighting Watchers she hasn't changed another. It had to be Hope."

"Maybe we should test the theory. I could capture a Watcher, and we could try to reproduce the phenomenon."

Hot tears pricked at the corners of Malini's eyes, and her lips trembled. She couldn't explain everything to them. She didn't understand Hope's prediction and didn't want to burden them with the paradox. "The immortals and I do not fully understand Hope's situation. Her soul is split. A portion remains in her body, but another part, an ancient part, survives in the In Between."

"Like you and your guide," Cheveyo said.

"Right. Only, unlike me, the two pieces of Hope's soul are disconnected and the part left in her body isn't enough to sustain her."

"I remember," Bonnie said. "When we rescued Abigail and passed between the Cherubim to reach Eden, I thought it was strange that we couldn't see the baby's soul."

"She wasn't even born yet, Bon," Samantha said.

"I know. But when Cheveyo's soul was inside of Dane, we all saw him. The Cherubim sifted him, outside of Dane's body. Abigail was pregnant. Hope was inside of her. If she'd had a complete soul, it would have been logical for us to see her being sifted."

"What are you saying? What does it mean that her body is disconnected from her soul?" Samantha asked.

Malini took a deep breath. "She's not just sick. She's dying. She changed Cord when she was just born. When she was healthy. Today, she is not. Hope's ability to transform Watchers is a manifestation of her healing energy. There is always a price to pay for healing, even with an intact soul."

Cord frowned. "So we can't test your theory because it could kill her."

"Which means using her to battle Lucifer could also kill her," Lillian said sadly.

"Yes," Malini admitted.

Jacob shook his head. "There's got to be another way."

"If we could reunite Hope with her soul on the other side, she'd be stronger, but we've been trying for weeks. Nothing works," Malini said.

"We?" Lillian asked. "Someone else knew about this?" She glanced around the table.

Dane scowled. "Yes. I knew she was sick, and Malini asked me to try to help her, but I had no idea she'd be delivered to her death by the people who love her." He stood from the table, arms crossed over his chest.

"We have no choice," Malini snapped. "Don't you dare make me feel like I'm sacrificing her. God sent us Hope for a reason. She's dying. Whether we attempt to use her for her purpose or not, she's dying. I don't make the rules. All I know is, tonight, when the sun goes down, thousands upon thousands of Watchers are going to converge a few miles from here, and if we don't do something, they are going to wipe out what currently amounts to half of the people on Earth." She swallowed. "I have to have faith that God is going to present a way for Hope to be whole again at the proper moment. Can I have a little compassion? A bit of empathy? Do you think I don't love her as much as any of you?"

The room fell silent. None of them could look Malini in the eye, least of all Dane, who focused on a patch of table in front of her.

"I'm sorry," Dane said.

At that moment, Ghost popped into the room, breaking the uncomfortable silence, a large roll of paper in his hands. "What did I miss?" he said upon seeing the solemn faces around the table. Samantha grabbed his hand and pressed a finger over her lips.

"Everyone get some rest. I'll draw up teams. We leave at sundown." Malini snatched the blueprints out of Ghost's hand and unrolled them on the table.

The Soulkeepers scattered as a confused Ghost looked on.

"Go ask Samantha," Malini said.

He dissolved, and she returned to her work.

* * * * *

With Hope sleeping on her chest, Malini maneuvered through the rubble to the front of the church, near where the altar used to be. She could've used a long talk with Father Raymond, but he hadn't returned yet from dropping off Katrina in Paris. Instead, she used her foot to right a toppled pew and took a seat under the massive crucifix still mounted on the wall. It wasn't what she was used to. This was a Catholic church. Her Protestant church displayed a plain cross and a statue of the resurrection. It also wasn't how she pictured God anymore. There was no statue for that, no image that could possibly incorporate the enormous and versatile source for good she'd come to know. Still, it was all she had now and would have to do.

"I suppose I should pray more," she began, staring at the crucifix. "I'm not very good at it, and there never seems to be enough time. To be honest, there is nothing I can say to you that you don't already know. I suppose then, you are aware that I have failed you. I do not know how to save Hope. I do not understand how to reconnect her spirit. I know she said I must give my power to the world. There can only be one Healer. But I can't die, and without her full power, she can't kill me. If there is a way to save her, some further purpose I should play in all of this, then you must be more direct. You must tell me what to do."

Malini closed her lips tightly, realizing she'd crossed a line snapping at God as she did. Her heart sank.

"I don't mean to be ungrateful. You gave us a safe place to stay here. I know that was you who whispered in my ear how to gain Father Raymond's trust. All of your gifts have been appreciated. Cord's redemption especially, as I realize now it was his presence that kept us safe for so long. Plus, you gave us each other. Not a small thing.

"But what good is all of it if we go to our deaths now? We don't stand a chance without your help. We can't possibly survive this without your guidance. I've been to the In Between, and not even the immortals know what to do. The tapestries are no help either. The future shifts and changes color. It is impossible to predict. I am a Healer. I am supposed to be their leader. Don't make me lead them to their deaths. Especially Hope. Why bring her into this world just to have her die? It doesn't make any sense."

Malini rubbed Hope's tiny back and pressed her tear-stained cheek against the side of her soft head.

"Well? Answer me? How do I save her? What should we do next? Am I going in the right direction?"

Her voice echoed in the empty church, only the rubble witness to her plea. The crucifix didn't respond. There was no burning bush or choir of angels. The silence was almost deafening, and her heart broke to know they'd been abandoned.

Minutes passed. Malini was about to give up and return to Sanctuary when a strong wind picked up outside, knocking against the wall of the church and causing a painting to fall from its hook and crack against the floor. After the deafening silence, Malini started at the sound.

She stood slowly, a shiver raising the hair on her neck. Step by step, she made her way over to the painting and lifted it by the frame to get a better look. The art contained the image of a dove descending from a glowing red sun. Beams of light ignited every corner of the canvas. She read the inscription aloud. *"For I know the plans I have for you, declares the Lord, plans to prosper you and not to harm you, plans to give you hope and a future. Then you will call on me and come and pray to me, and I will listen to you. You will seek me and find me when you seek me with all your heart. Jeremiah 29:11-13."*

Swallowing hard, she read it again and again. "Plans to give me hope and a future, huh? Okay. So pretty much you are saying to trust you and stay the course."

No answers came from the silent rubble. They didn't need to. Malini could feel the answer in her bones.

"Come on, Hope. If you are going to help us save the world, you shouldn't do it on an empty stomach." With new energy, she jogged toward the kitchen to make the baby a bottle of formula and finish preparing for the battle to come.

She would step out in faith, go to battle against Lucifer without all of the answers, and trust that when the time came, she would know the path to take.

Even if that meant her ultimate demise.

Chapter 22
Labyrinth

"Cord, I'll need you to take Hope."

Cord turned to face Malini in surprise. She supposed after everything that had happened, he didn't expect to be a key member of the plan. Even though Lillian and Grace had apologized for doubting his loyalty, his face said it all; Cord felt like an outsider.

"She requires constant healing, but for my plan to work, I can't take her. She must remain with Bonnie and so must you," Malini said.

Eyebrows knit, Cord reached for the baby obediently, a soft healing glow engulfing Hope as he folded her into his arms. "Of course, I'll help in any way I can."

"Why does Bonnie need to stay with Hope?" Grace asked.

Malini's heart sank to have to put Grace in this position again. How hard it must be as the mother of a Soulkeeper. "We need to recreate the conditions that changed Cord. I think Bonnie acted as an amplifier of Hope's power from inside the stone. Bonnie will wear the stone and hold the baby exactly as before."

"You're sure it has to be her?" Grace murmured. "I would be happy to do it."

Bonnie shook her head vigorously. "No, Mom, I can't let you do that."

"Yes. It has to be her," Malini said. "Amplification isn't something every Soulkeeper possesses. If I am right and Bonnie amplified Hope's latent power, she is likely the only one of us who can do it."

With a sigh, Bonnie nodded. "So, I'll have to stand at the center of them all, where all of the Watchers can see Hope, in order for it to work."

"Cord will hand you the baby at the last possible second. I'm not sure Hope will last any longer. And yes, get yourself to the place most visible."

"We know where that will be. Wherever Lucifer is," Bonnie said, voice shaking.

Malini nodded, feeling like she might be sick.

"Your team will enter here." She pressed a finger to the blueprint. "It's the closest to the most likely staging area. Lucifer will have to be on some sort of platform, probably broadcasting across the arena to his followers. Use that to your advantage. Cord and Ghost will protect you and Hope and, of course, your sister, Samantha. Cord and Ghost, your job is to get Bonnie where she needs to be at the proper moment. Are you guys up to the task?"

Cord glanced toward Bonnie, who was holding hands with Sam, an anxious-looking Ghost behind her. "I'll protect her. As long as I'm still moving, she will make it to that platform."

Ghost agreed. "I'm in."

Samantha tossed up her hands. "You know I am."

"Where will we be?" Jacob asked Malini.

"You, Grace, and I will enter here." She pointed to a service entrance to the back of the building. "We'll find a water source, a sink or a fountain. You will force holy water up the pipe and contaminate the rest of the building. Then, you'll make it rain."

Jacob nodded. "Looking forward to it."

"Lillian, Ethan, Dane, and Cheveyo will enter here." She pointed at the most likely hub for food preparation in the stadium. "You will attempt to find the way Lucifer intends to dole out the physical element for the spell. Perhaps he will place his blood in something they will eat or drink. Stop whatever it is from reaching the Watchers."

"Piece of cake," Cheveyo said, laughing. Everyone stopped and looked at him. "Get it? Cake, because his blood might be in the cake." He grinned.

Lillian groaned. "We get it, Chevy. It's just not funny."

Cheveyo made a face as if he were injured.

Solemnly, Lillian continued to arm herself from the stack of newly soaked weapons on the table. She handed a deadly looking dagger to Dane, who glanced at Ethan. No words were needed to know they were the first offensive and likely the first to see combat. The job was dangerous enough, but Dane added a level of complexity. He was inhumanly fast but didn't have any powers of his own. That meant the other three would have the added responsibility of protecting him.

Malini was surprised when Lillian didn't question it. But then, maybe she realized that this mission was equally deadly for all of them, and no one's role could be underestimated. Besides, there was no way Dane would be convinced to stay behind.

"Cord, has the sun gone down?" Malini asked, arming herself with as many weapons as she could carry.

The angel's eyes flicked toward the ceiling. "Almost. The sun is low in the sky. It is twilight."

"Lillian's team will go first. Then mine. Then Cord's." Malini looked around the room, meeting the eyes of each of the Soulkeepers one by one. Lillian moved toward the door. "Wait." Malini held out her hand.

One by one the Soulkeepers joined hands in a giant circle and bowed their heads. "Lord, we come to you just as we are, imperfect, vulnerable, and scared. We ask for your protection and guidance tonight as we go into the darkness to do your work. If it is your will, safeguard us from harm, and if not, take us home."

Cheveyo cleared his throat. "Oh great spirit, we pray for your help to return our Mother Earth to a purified, healthy, and peaceful planet. We sing for strength and wisdom for the good of all people. Our hope is not yet lost. Help us to restore the health of our Mother Earth for lasting peace and happiness."

"Amen," Malini said.

"We say *Techqua Ikachi*—for Land and Life," Cheveyo said.

Jacob raised a fist in the air. "Amen and *Techqua Ikachi*."

The others joined in, repeating the phrase until it was obvious they could delay their quest no longer. Malini raised one hand, suddenly feeling ancient, seventy rather than seventeen. "Be careful out there."

The group broke out in a chain reaction of cautious hugging, each aware that the other was concealing a small arsenal. Then Lillian made a whistling sound and led Dane, Ethan, and Cheveyo to the door.

"Godspeed," Malini whispered behind them.

* * * * *

Full black, the sky showed no moon, no stars. Nature was not responsible for the total darkness. A flock of Watchers, thousands of them, blotted out the sky wing to wing like an oil slick might coat the ocean. From his hiding place in the cold underbelly of a patch of evergreens, Dane stared, openmouthed, at their arrival. Even in Nod he hadn't seen this many, or been so intimidated by their militarism.

"Damn, there's a lot of them," Ethan whispered in his ear. "Yeah."

"I think I wet my pants," Cheveyo said into his other. "No ... no ... I didn't. But only because my bladder is officially frozen."

Crouched in the branches behind them, Lillian laughed under her breath. "The good news is, I don't see any in the streets. They are all flying in and fast. Lucifer must have rattled their chains."

"What's the plan?" Dane asked. "Do we wait for the sky to clear or chance it?"

A stretch of silence indicated Lillian was weighing the options. "I think we chance it, with caution. No more than five hundred feet at a time. We stick together, and we stay hidden."

Dane contorted his body on the cold ground to see her better, although in the darkness, he could barely make out her silhouette. "Following you," he said. One of his weapons poked into his side, and he repositioned himself.

"One, two ... three." Lillian bolted from the underbrush. Dane followed, Ethan and Cheveyo behind him. On quick, light feet, they crossed a street and ducked into an alley. As they were trained to do, all four quieted, listening.

"Clear," Dane whispered.

"Clear," said Cheveyo.

Lillian held up one hand. "One, two ... three."

* * * * *

After what seemed like forever, Dane arrived at the door to the United Center, the one Malini had suggested they use. The sky was conspicuously empty. While they were traveling, the flock had arrived, and although Dane could hear them inside, he could see none in the area.

Lillian placed her hand on the door pull, digging in her pocket for the skeleton key she used to navigate locked doors. "Everyone ready?" she whispered.

Dane nodded. Ethan's pinky finger bumped his and Dane gave him a small smile.

"It's already unlocked," Lillian whispered. Cheveyo shuffled to the door, cutting in front of Dane, a measure meant to protect but which came with a side order of humiliation.

"Brace yourself." Lillian pulled open the door. Inside was a concrete corridor typical of a stadium, dark except for the square of moonlight that filtered in around their bodies. Cheveyo entered first. When he gave an okay sign, the all clear, Dane and Ethan followed. The door swung closed behind Lillian.

The click of the door closing corresponded with a light clicking on overhead, a streetlight. The four shuffled like roaches, flattening their bodies against the nearest wall, which turned from concrete to wood under their touch.

"What's going on?" Cheveyo whispered.

Dane's eyes darted around the scene that had formed. It looked as though they were on a cobblestone street in front of a shop with three windows. Each window was empty, aside from a wooden chair. The façade was of a European village.

"Retreat," Lillian whispered. But when they turned back toward the door, it was gone. A smooth concrete wall had replaced it.

Dane trailed his hand over the place the door had been. "It's a trap." He turned around, toward the group. "I think." He glanced up and down the street.

"It's a labyrinth," Ethan said.

"What?" Lillian turned a circle, dagger in hand.

"This is why the door wasn't locked. Watchers would know how to navigate this sorcery. We're in a maze. If we make it through, we find ourselves at the party, if not…"

"We'll be dead," Dane finished.

Cheveyo turned his head left and right. "Hate to break it to you guys, but the street ends in either direction. We are currently locked in a room with no doors and no windows."

Lillian inhaled sharply and began patting and stroking the wall. "Check for a hidden exit. Any seam or ripple could be a clue."

The four split up. Dane followed the cobblestone to the fake storefront. His fingers tested every crevice. His toes overturned each and every stone. It was as if they were trapped inside a movie set, characters in some impromptu play. Eventually, each of them ran out of wall and ended up standing in front of the three windows.

"Are we supposed to break one?" Dane asked.

Lillian shrugged.

"Which one?" Cheveyo took a step forward and reached out to touch the glass. On contact, a red light came on over the chair, and a door at the back of the shop window opened.

A dark-haired woman stepped into the doorframe, her shapely leg breaking the slit of the long pencil skirt she was wearing. She stared at Cheveyo and licked her ruby red lips. Toying with the tie of her white wraparound blouse with one hand, she ran her other along the edge of her plunging neckline.

"Come to me," her husky voice said from behind the glass. She extended one gloved hand, beckoning.

Cheveyo's eyebrows shot up, and his mouth dropped open. He moved to break the glass. Dane's hand clamped down on his wrist. "Not a good idea."

The woman started to dance, using her teeth to tug off one glove and then the other. One high-heeled boot landed on the seat of the chair. She leaned forward, tugging at the neck of her blouse and making direct eye contact with Cheveyo.

"She looks a little like Raine," he said absently. He stepped closer until his breath fogged the glass. "What if she's trapped in there?" He pressed both hands against the glass as the woman sashayed her hips and let her skirt fall to the floor. Underneath was an indecent pair of shorts.

"Cheveyo, that girl is nothing like Raine. Whatever this is, it's deadly. Look at yourself. It's pulling you in," Dane said.

Lillian placed a hand on Cheveyo's shoulder. "You know it's probably an illusion, right? This is sorcery."

Ethan furrowed his brow as Cheveyo pressed in even closer to the glass. "Yeah, buddy. Maybe take a step back until we know what we are dealing with."

Cheveyo pulled back a fraction of an inch, but did not look away from the woman, who had removed the pins from her hair and was rolling her neck, flinging her raven locks.

"Leave me alone." Cheveyo shrugged off the hands on his shoulders. "What do you guys know? This is a person. She's trapped behind glass. She's probably being forced to strip her clothes off. We're Soulkeepers. It's our job to help her!"

Fists clenched at his side, Cheveyo's pupils dilated and his face flushed.

"Come on, Cheveyo. Look at me. You're not acting like yourself, man," Dane said, pressing one hand into his chest.

"I said, leave me alone." Cheveyo stepped back, and then his brown fist shot out, aimed at Dane's temple. Dane dodged out of the way. Big mistake.

Cheveyo's knuckles collided with the window. *CRASH.*

Chapter 23
Plan B

"This is the door," Malini said, approaching their planned entrance to the United Center. Her stomach flip-flopped with unease. Thousands of Watchers had filled the night sky a moment ago, flying in formation, wing to wing, but in the blink of an eye, they'd disappeared, evaporating like so much smoke. Jacob pressed into her side, a shiver running the length of his body. He'd seen it too. They all had.

"Where do you think they went?" Grace asked.

"They're here. Inside," Malini said. "I think I can hear them."

"I've never seen them so organized," Grace whispered.

"Lucifer has them by the short hairs," Jacob said.

"We're wasting time. Pop the lock," Malini said.

Channeling water from his flask, he did as she asked, but halted when the freezing water met no resistance. "It's unlocked."

Malini's eyes widened, and Grace's head whipped around.

"A trap?" Grace eyeballed the door skeptically.

Pausing, Malini tapped into the ancient part of her wisdom for guidance. "This is the only road."

Grace tipped her head to the side. "Then we must travel it."

With a curt nod, Malini gave her blessing. Jacob braced himself and pulled the door open. Inside, a concrete corridor was lit only by a dim safety light on the far wall. Jacob entered first. When there was no immediate danger, Malini and Grace followed. The door clicked closed behind them, plunging the area into total darkness.

"What happened to the light?" Grace whispered.

As if in answer to her question, a torch blazed to life in the corner.

"What is this?" Jacob asked.

The walls were made of gold bricks and covered in hieroglyphs. Gems of every type, jewelry, gold coins, goblets, and diamond tiaras were heaped in every corner of the room. Three painted sarcophagi overlooked the treasure.

"I've got a bad feeling about this," Malini said. She turned back toward the door. "It's gone." She'd only taken a single step inside, but the place where they'd entered was now a solid wall. She ran her hand along it.

"No exit," Jacob said. "In what direction did your power say the road would take us?"

"There must be a way out. It's a test. We have to battle our way through to get inside."

Jacob scanned the hieroglyphs on the walls. "Woe to those who enter here. Greed is your demise and death the only doorway."

"It kills me that you can read that and I can't," Malini said. "Maybe it's not a warning but a riddle. There has to be a way inside."

Grace toyed with the cross around her neck. "I wonder if all of the Watchers had to pass through a similar test?"

"If that's the case, then the riddle won't test our worth but our evil intent. We'll have to think like a Watcher to get through." Malini walked the periphery of the room, eyes passing over the treasures inside. Her gaze locked on the three sarcophagi propped against the walls. She pivoted, noting their position.

"The sarcophagi form a triangle." She pointed at the floor at the center of the room. "There's a triangle on the floor."

"It's in the opposite direction," Grace said.

Jacob shrugged. "Maybe if we moved them to match the pattern?"

"Like a key. Death is the only doorway. The sarcophagi represent death," Malini said.

"It's worth a try," Grace said.

Malini chose one at random, the Egyptian face on the front reminding her of Tutankhamen's. "Help me move this one over there." She motioned toward the point of the triangle.

Jacob and Grace waded into the mound of jewels. Silently, they positioned themselves, Jacob and Malini on either side, Grace near the feet. There were no handles. They would have to carry it from the bottom.

"Tip it toward me," Jacob said. "Then you guys can get under it." He reached out and grabbed the ornate gold coffin.

Malini stopped short before making contact. The box rattled violently. A quick check with Grace found her hands in the air. "What's going on?"

"Uh-oh," Jacob said. He stepped back, tripping in the pile of gold coins and goblets behind him. He landed hands and knees in the treasure. "There's something happening. It's grabbing me." He struggled to his feet. Shiny silver chains snaked around his wrists and legs, the treasure bulging and swarming around his body. "Mal?"

"Hold still, Jacob," Malini ordered. "Maybe your movement provokes it."

He froze, but the treasure continued to rise around him.

Grace leapt to the cleared area of the floor, drawing a chain from Eden from her hip. With a flick of her wrist, she cast it over Jacob's shoulder, hard enough for the end to wrap around his torso. With a firm tug, she yanked him toward her.

"Ow! Ah, this stuff is biting into me," Jacob yelled.

Waist deep now, Jacob's arms turned purple as Grace continued her tug of war against the treasure. "Malini, I need your help. I can't budge him."

Beside her, the sarcophagus rocked ominously, a cantankerous banging against the lid. Malini bent her knees and leapt. She landed on the edge of the treasure and jogged to Grace's side. "It didn't grab me," she said. "I think it's because he touched the sarcophagus. Hold on, Jake. We'll get you out of this." She grabbed the chain and pulled with Grace. It was no use.

The treasure climbed to Jacob's neck. "Help! Ahh. Ahhh!"

"No. No, Jake, no. God, no, Jake." Malini tugged with everything she had until her fingers ached. Grace's hands bled from the effort, but it was like pulling stone. The living treasure mounded around Jacob until a final surge swallowed his screaming head.

"Jacob!" Malini dropped the chain. Throwing caution to the wind, she scrambled through the treasure toward him, digging in the stuff for her beloved.

A sharp, screeching sound turned her face toward the sarcophagus. The lid swung partially open, and the sharp tang of resin permeated the room. A bandage wrapped hand gripped the corner of the lid.

"Is that?" Grace paled and drew a blade from the sheath on her leg.

Malini reached for the sword on her back and glanced toward Grace. "Mummy!"

* * * * *

Bonnie toyed with the stone around her neck and glanced at her sister. They'd found their assigned entrance unlocked without even one Watcher anywhere in the vicinity.

"I don't like this," Cord said from the open door, Hope buried in his shoulder.

Ghost broke apart and re-formed under the emergency light at the end of the corridor. "It looks the same in both directions," he said. "Do you want me to go farther inside?"

"No, Jesse," Samantha said. "We should stay together."

"Well, come on, then," Ghost said, fidgeting as he stared down the corridor. I have a weird feeling we need to hurry."

"I feel it too," Bonnie said. She turned on her heel. "Cord, close the door. Maybe someone is coming."

Cord frowned but took a single step forward, allowing the door to close behind him. The lights went out. Bonnie couldn't even see Cord despite his natural glow. When they came on again, she screamed.

She was in a room of mirrors. Circling right then left, she found herself alone in a maze of warped and polished silver. "Sam? Cord? Ghost?"

"I'm here," Sam said. "Only I can't see you. There are mirrors. Oh." She made a gagging sound that seemed to bounce around the maze, impossible for Bonnie to narrow in on.

"What's wrong?" Bonnie called.

"I think the mirrors are enchanted. Don't look, Bonnie."

Ghost's voice rang tinny through the labyrinth. "Keep talking, Sam. I'll find you."

"Oh damn, Jesse, I can't open my eyes. It's horrible, horrible what I saw. Please hurry."

"I'm trying. Hold on. Oh crap. Hell. Don't look in the mirrors."

Bonnie turned in the direction of Ghost's voice and came face to face with her full-length reflection. At first the image was normal, stretchy black pants and dark winter jacket, but then her likeness changed. She knew she should look away. She'd heard the warnings. But, as hard as she tried, she could not pry her eyes from the mirror.

Her winter clothes morphed into a gray, short-sleeved dress, and her skin wrinkled. The fiery red of her hair faded to gray. Before her eyes, her spine deformed. She'd become an old woman, thin and crippled.

Inside the reflection, a church topped the hill behind her aged body. The bell in the belfry began to ring, and she joined a crowd of gatherers moving for the door. Her sister stepped in beside her.

"Sam? Is that you?" It looked like Samantha, only she was older. Her hair was red, although likely colored, and Jesse was on her arm. Three young men stood at their side, strapping red-haired sons. Samantha's children.

Bonnie's heart sank as she followed after her sister's family. She had no one with her, no one to help her. She was pushed and shoved within the crowd, away from her sister. Finally inside, the churchgoers forced her toward the altar.

The crowd retracted, leaving her standing alone in front of a casket. Was this a funeral? She smoothed her dress and staggered back toward the pews. All of the seats were taken. Exhausted, she rested in the aisle, leaning against one of the ornate wooden benches.

Samantha walked to the front of the church and positioned herself behind the pulpit. *No*, Bonnie thought. *Was this her mother's funeral? Why else would Sam be speaking?*

Her sister looked at Jesse and straightened a paper on the podium. Then, she began to speak. "We all knew this would happen one day. After all the years she spent, plodding through life on her own, it was inevitable. But part of me always hoped Bonnie would find love."

Bonnie startled. Had Samantha just said her name?

"All of us wanted her to get help when she went mad. Jesse and I tried to do what was right. But there wasn't any reason for her to want to get better." Samantha looked directly at her. "Bonnie had nothing. She lived for no one and died with no one."

Another person named Bonnie? A terrible mistake? Bonnie's mind threw out explanations as her legs hobbled toward the coffin at the front of the church. Every step hurt. Her twisted spine made walking difficult, and her head pounded with the effort. She fell forward, catching herself on the satin-lined edge, and peered inside.

The coffin was empty.

Hands shoved her. Up and over, she dropped into the coffin. Her head landed on the satin pillow. Her arms crossed over her chest of their own accord. She tried to scream, but her mouth wouldn't work. Her lips felt as if they'd been glued together. All that came was a kind of hum from deep in her throat that seemed to float away from her.

Half the coffin lid was up, and Jesse and Samantha's faces appeared above her.

"Finally, Jesse. Finally, I am free of her. All my life, I've been forced to be her twin. Now I can be my own person and have my own life."

His hand rubbed her back. "It must be such a relief."

"It is," she said. "You can't imagine what a burden it was to always be the good one, the better one … the favorite. And then to constantly try to deny it to her so that I wouldn't hurt her feelings." Samantha shook her head.

Jesse's hand gripped the edge of the lid. "It's over now, Sam. We finally have our own life."

"What will happen to her body?"

"She'll be cremated. Say goodbye. It's time."

"Goodbye, Bonnie," Samantha said. Jesse began to close the lid.

Bonnie tried her best to scream. She thrashed inside her skin to no avail. She couldn't even twitch her finger.

The lid *thunked* closed. Total darkness. By fear or panic, her blessed hands finally moved. Fingers found her lips, dug into the corner of her mouth, catching on something that felt like dental floss. The crushing realization that her lips were sewn together gripped her like a vice. Prying and tearing, she worked the string out of her flesh. The process was painful, but fear strengthened her resolve. Frantically, she continued until her bloody lips parted on a gasp.

She banged on the lid of the coffin with her fists. "I'm not dead. I'm not dead!"

Chapter 24
Consequences

Blood and glass exploded around Cheveyo's fist. Instinctively, Dane closed his eyes and turned his back on the spray. Razor-sharp debris blasted toward him, and he tightened his lips against the onslaught. But Cheveyo was not as careful. His piercing howl cut through the sound of shattering glass.

"I got it," Ethan said.

Dane unraveled to see the glass hovering in front of the shop window, broken but safely contained. Ethan had it in his telekinetic grip, the dancing woman concealed by a thick fog that had formed within the small room.

"Good job, Ethan," Lillian said. "Let it go."

Harmlessly, the shards tumbled to the floor. Thick fog rolled from the small room, coating the floor and the tops of their feet. The shuffle of footsteps, the hiss of an animal, and the wood on floor clunk of the chair toppling over reached Dane's ears.

"Hey, are you okay in there?" Cheveyo reached into the room.

Ethan grabbed his shirt and pulled him back. "Hold it, Kemo Sabe."

The intervention came just in time. Out of the broken glass and fog, the head of a giant red insect with two slate-black eyes surfaced. Dane took a step back, drawing his sword. Lillian sank into attack mode.

A set of red legs as long as he was tall carried the head out the window. Creeping legs on a long, scaly body. Enormous pincers. Antennae. "It's a giant centipede," Dane cried, retreating as the bug snapped at his head.

Ethan dragged Cheveyo backward despite the boy's continued wide-eyed struggle toward the creature. "I love you," Cheveyo called, arms open to the writhing thing. It scuttled into the room on a thousand legs.

Dane stabbed, landing a blow between the centipede's eyes. The bug reared, a drop of green blood forming at the point of contact.

"Don't hurt her!" Cheveyo screamed. "What's wrong with you?"

"Look out," Lillian called. The beast charged. Dane dodged left, the centipede narrowly missing him and scurrying up the far wall.

"That thing must be ten feet long," Ethan said.

"And it's not alone," Lillian said. Another centipede emerged from the broken window and another.

"Careful, they're poisonous," Lillian said, dodging the snap of razor-sharp pincers.

Dane shook his head. The sight of the two bugs made his skin crawl. "What? A centipede bite won't kill you."

"Yeah, when it's one-one thousandth of the size of this one, but they do have venom. Don't get too close."

"Great plan," Dane said, back to back with her. "How are we supposed to kill these things without getting too close?"

Ethan joined them in the center of the cobblestone street, Cheveyo struggling in his grip. Without warning, Dane's blade slipped from his fingers and stabbed through the center of the first beast, effectively pinning its body to the wall. The centipede squirmed and curled around the sword, a high-pitched squeal piercing his ears.

"By using me," Ethan said. "Lillian, can I have your assistance with two and three?"

"Why? Why did you do that to her?" Cheveyo shouted, almost frantic with his struggle to get to the giant bug.

Lillian tossed two daggers into the air. With ease, Ethan shot them toward the second and third bugs, this time aiming for the heads. Both died on impact, spraying green blood across the room. "Bull's-eye."

Hysterical now, Cheveyo thrashed wildly, freeing himself from Ethan's arms. Dane took over, bear-hugging the guy.

"We've got to get him out of here," Ethan said.

"Look. This way." Lillian pointed through the broken window. The fog had dissipated. On the other side of the small room was an open door. She drew a fresh blade from her back. "I'll go first."

Jumping up on the platform, she kicked the chair aside and passed through. "All clear," she called. "But don't get your hopes up. Looks like this is far from over."

Dane was more than happy to leave the green dripping blood and writhing forms of the centipedes behind. He wrestled Cheveyo through the chamber, following Ethan's lead. The Hopi boy relaxed as soon as they cleared the threshold. The door slammed shut behind them.

Gradually, Cheveyo's pupils shrank to their normal size. He shook his head as if clearing it of cobwebs. "What the hell?" He tapped his temple with the heel of his palm.

"Yeah, you were really out of it," Dane said. "You tried to make out with a centipede, dude."

Pitching forward, Cheveyo caught himself on his knees and hurled. "Just give me a minute. I'm sorry. I don't know what came over me."

"This place is enchanted," Lillian said. "We need to be more careful from now on."

"You don't have to tell me twice," Cheveyo said.

Dane looked around their new surroundings. They were standing amid a ghost town of midway games. Wide-eyed

Kewpie dolls on either side of the trodden path watched them from their dangling homes above each booth. "What's this all about?"

"Sign says Freak Show." Lillian pointed to a large red arrow painted on a wooden fence.

"Can't wait," Ethan said sarcastically.

The team followed the path to a black-and-white striped tent. Conveniently, the entrance flap had been pinned open, revealing only darkness inside. Ethan held up a hand, motioning that he'd go in first. Silently, he stepped into the darkness. A second passed, and then another. His hand shot out, beckoning them inside.

Dane walked into the tent on Cheveyo's heels, side by side with Lillian. Beyond the entryway was a typical circus scene, a lighted ring surrounded by stadium seating. At the center of the ring was an ornately sculpted crystal bowl that reminded Dane of the one his mother often filled with fresh tulips in the spring. As large as a swimming pool, the bowl belonged in an art exhibit, artistically designed and lit from within. It glowed like a Christmas luminaria at the center of the ring.

Dane squinted against the light to get a better look. Ethan and Lillian moved forward with him, similarly spellbound. A stream of bubbles passed, followed by something with long, lean muscles. He pressed his palms against the glass. *Flash.* Taut, alabaster flesh contorted in a way that wasn't quite human. *Flash.* A man's broad chest skimmed and twisted against the glass, then retracting into the bowl. *Flash.* A cloud of bubbles parted to reveal a woman's shoulder, her naked back, her silhouette writhing against the light.

Swirls of aqua and purple danced within the crystal. Dane pressed his nose against the glass, taking in the two serpentine figures deep inside the bowl. The two seemed to wrap around each other, combine, and separate in a graceful dance. Was that a tail? Yes, shimmering, gossamer scales from hips to fluke. Merfolk.

Dane swallowed, entranced by their beauty. Spotting him, the merfolk swam to the edge. Their two heads broke the surface, spilling water over the side of the bowl. Dane stepped back to get a better look. The female's long blond hair dried and lifted immediately when it hit the air, and she scanned the room with iridescent purple eyes that locked on Cheveyo just outside the ring. The male emerged next to her, closer to Dane. He looked a bit like Ethan—dark hair, sharp features, but with vibrant turquoise eyes. Light cascaded from the bowl behind his head.

Just when Dane thought he'd never experienced anything so beautiful, he was proved wrong when the merfolk started to sing. Voices like bells rang out across the tent, the melody sending an electric heat over Dane's skin. Sweat broke out on his upper lip, and his entire body tingled, yearning to be touched. More than anything, he wanted to swim in that bowl, to be closer to the magic pulsating through the tent.

Fervently, Dane tugged his shirt off and then worked at the sheath of weapons around his waist. As he unbuttoned his pants, he was vaguely aware of someone yelling his name.

There was something else he was supposed to be doing, only Dane didn't want to do it. Kicking shoes and socks off as he went, he stumbled toward the tank, mind buzzing with the promise of pleasure the fishbowl offered. The merman reached for his hand to help him in, and he obliged, longing for the touch.

Whoosh. The bowl shattered, glass and water sweeping him back across the sandy circus ring. Bereft of water, the merfolk twisted and writhed, bodies stretching and straining. Mouths gaping. Until both transformed into carnivorous eels, twisting and gasping on the sand.

Dane shook his head, stumbling to his feet and looking back toward the bowl in horror. Cheveyo stood in the center of the ring, one hand over his eyes and a silver hatchet from Eden in his hand.

"Are they dead?" he asked.

"Not yet," Dane shot back. Across the ring, Lillian, in nothing but her underwear, brought around her sword, slicing through the eel's heads like butter.

"It's done," she said.

Cheveyo dropped his hand. "I'm making a new rule. Stay away from the glass. Also, I think it's important to note that we are damn lucky we have different tastes in, uh, partners."

Ethan glanced at Dane, who suddenly realized he was also only in his underwear. Eyebrows shooting through the roof, he scrambled for his clothes, trying his best to cover himself with his arms.

"I did enjoy the show," Cheveyo said, brushing his eyebrow piercing and giggling. "If we ever get out of here, I am so telling everyone about this."

Dane shot him a nasty look before pulling his shirt over his head. "Paybacks are hell, centipede boy."

"Enough," Lillian said. She strapped on the remainder of her weapons and pulled on her boots. "We've got to find a way out of here. Shit. *Into* here. We are trying to get in. Damn, I don't know what's up or down anymore." She wiped a hand over her face.

Fully dressed again, although still dripping a little, Ethan slicked back his dark hair from his face and pointed at the other side of the tent. "Only one way out."

Dane stepped to his side, bumping his fist with his own. "Who goes first?"

Ethan glanced in his direction. "I will."

Chapter 25
The Living Dead

Malini gripped her blade, back to back with Grace in the center of the ring of treasure that had swallowed Jacob. Resin-stained bandages, reeking of death, hobbled toward her. A mummy. The other two sarcophagi had joined in the shake-and-bang routine, and two more walking dead burst forth on stiff legs.

"Revenge of the mummy," Grace murmured.

"What?" Malini gasped.

"I saw a movie like this once. If they are mummies, they are all hollowed out inside. Nothing but bandages holding them together. Aim for their limbs."

Malini rotated the hilt of her sword in her hand. As the Healer, she rarely had to fight in this way. The weapon felt heavy and unfamiliar in her palm. While she was working up her confidence, Grace attacked mummy number one, slicing off one bandaged arm. The limb dropped to the gold brick floor with an ominous thud.

"The fingers are still moving," Malini yelled.

"Oh hell, that's not the worst of it." Grace pointed with her blade toward the shoulder of their attacker. A scarab beetle scurried from the wound and dropped to the floor. Another creature, a scorpion, wiggled a claw out of the hole and tumbled from the shoulder.

"No," Malini whispered, staring at a long, hairy leg that protruded from the hole. A spider scampered down the stiff body. "I fricking hate spiders." She jumped as her backside hit the stretch of wall behind her and stared in horror as the three bugs doubled and then tripled in size.

"Don't, I repeat, don't cut off the limbs of the mummies," Grace said, poking at the giant pincers of the scarab beetle. "How do you kill something that's already dead?"

"Mummies are dead *people*." Malini stiffened.

Grace stabbed. The beetle reared. "Blatant statement of the obvious, young lady."

Malini sheathed her sword and tore the flesh glove from her right hand. The skeletal arm Death had given her so long ago gleamed pearlescent in the gold room. She rotated the wrist, finding the metaphysical string that connected the hand to the living dead.

"Ugh," she moaned. "They're old and hardly human. But they still have ... human hearts. I think I remember something from school about the Egyptians leaving them in during the mummification process." She bent the bone fingers, the *crick-crack* of bone on bone almost as unsettling as the snapping pincers that Grace held at bay with her blade.

"While I find Egyptian history fascinating, Malini, I will remind you that I'm over sixty. Get on with it."

She focused, upper arm beginning to smoke as her power took hold. The mummies stopped, turning bandaged, faceless heads in her direction. "Kill the beetle," she commanded. A groan like a hollow wind passed through the cavern. They obeyed, tackling the bug to the floor and ripping its legs and pincers from its body.

"Watch out," Grace dodged in front of Malini, blade slicing through the scorpion's stinger as it moved toward her head. The creature scampered back in pain, snapping its claws. Unfortunately, the spider wasn't taking turns or playing fair. It dropped from the ceiling, fangs sinking into Grace's shoulder.

"The spider. Kill the spider," Malini ordered, drawing her sword with her left hand and stabbing the creature in the head.

It released Grace and tried to climb its web but was soon overwhelmed by the walking dead. As Grace toppled to the floor, shoulder swelling and mouth foaming, the scorpion attacked.

"Grace!" Malini yelled, thrusting at the snapping beast. The burn, a consequence of her healing power, had worked its way up the side of her neck and across half her chest. She forced herself to move through the pain. Recalling all she'd learned from Lillian, she thrust and parried until, with a painful surge of adrenaline, her blade sliced through one of the claws. The injury gave her enough time to realign her troops.

"Kill the scorpion," she commanded, pointing a bony finger at the beast.

The mummies stopped immediately, changing direction to do as she asked. They pounded on the shell and tore off its legs. The scorpion's last working pincer snapped around the one-armed mummy, crushing its abdomen. Malini doubled over in pain but didn't release the strings to her puppets. With relief, she watched the scorpion shiver and then quit under the assault of the other two. Dead.

The crispy ache of the burn traveled down the back of her legs, but she could not release the mummies, not yet. "Dig. Jacob. Out," she commanded, pointing to the mound of treasure that had swallowed her one and only true love.

The three did, casting aside gold goblets and coins, silver chains, and gemstones of all shapes and sizes. When they reached Jacob, Malini heard a sharp intake of breath and then her puppets freed him from the gripping, shredding riches. They released him at her feet, bloody and bruised but alive.

"Which way is out?" she rasped to the one-armed mummy, who pointed at his sarcophagus. Malini swallowed. Her eyesight was failing, but she thought she saw a flash of light behind the lid. "Good. Now lock yourselves inside those two." She pointed to the other two sarcophagi, and watched the dead retreat. They closed themselves inside, magically sealing the opening.

Malini collapsed between Grace and Jacob, moaning in pain. On her back, she pulled her flesh glove over her right hand, knowing one touch might mean the death of one of her friends. Once she was done, she turned her burnt face toward Jacob and focused on her breath.

Beside her, he curled into the fetal position. One of his legs didn't obey, hanging crooked and slightly behind the rest of his body. But his hands found his flask and soon Malini was doused with water, her skin easing at its touch. She placed her left hand on his cheek, healing his wounds at the same time he gave her what she needed to heal herself. This was their relationship. Symbiotic. Selfless. For a moment, she lost herself in it, closing her eyes and giving herself over to Jacob's comfort.

"Grace," she said, pulling her hand away. Jacob wasn't completely healed, but seemed to understand her urgency. He nodded.

Malini reached for Grace. The Helper's body was swollen to the point of being unrecognizable. White foam oozed from the side of her puffy lips, and her eyes were buried under an excess of edematous flesh. Malini might believe she were dead if she couldn't hear the faintest heartbeat under it all. Parting Grace's shirt collar, she placed her left hand directly over her heart, willing healing energy into her. She met resistance.

"There's something wrong," Malini said, trying harder. The heartbeat slowed beneath her fingers. "No, no, no." She could feel the woman slipping away beneath her touch.

Jacob pulled the water back into his flask and crawled to Grace's side, across from Malini. He turned Grace's head and swept her mouth with his fingers. "Her tongue and throat are swollen shut. She's not breathing."

Malini shifted her hand to Grace's swollen neck. She focused her power on opening the throat. "It's not working," she rasped.

A high-pitched wheeze echoed through the gold room. Grace coughed weakly and a plume of black ooze spewed from her mouth, narrowly missing Jacob.

"Watcher blood," Jacob said.

"The bite must have been enchanted. This is sorcery. That's why it's so difficult to heal." Malini redoubled her efforts, stretching out on the floor next to Grace as her tender skin began to burn again. Minutes passed.

"Malini?" Jacob rasped, breaking the silence.

"Yeah?"

"I just want this to be over." His voice was barely audible.

"It's just beginning," she said sadly.

Thankfully, Grace sputtered, drawing deep, rumbling breaths. "Grace?" Malini shook her slightly. "She's breathing but still unconscious."

"Do you think we'll survive this one?" Jacob asked, pain evident in his voice.

"I'm not sure."

"If we do, will you marry me?"

Malini grinned, barely lifting her pounding head from the gold floor to see his face better. "Where's my ring?"

Jacob pointed toward the stack of treasure where several jeweled rings poked from the pile.

"Cursed treasure, Jacob? Hardly appropriate."

Lying back until his head hit the floor, Jacob smirked. "Let's just shake on it, then."

Malini laughed and offered him her gloved hand. He hooked his fingers into hers and squeezed. She moaned. The burn was traveling again, up the side of her face.

"More water?"

"Yes, Jacob. Please."

He obliged.

* * * * *

Trapped inside the coffin, Bonnie screamed until her voice cracked with inescapable hoarseness. Nearly hysterical, she pounded on the lid until her fists bled. Her torturous fate seemed sealed until a blue light formed around the edges of her consciousness, quieting her screams. The lid lifted. As her eyes adjusted to the intense light, she saw him, her angel. Cord held out a hand to her, pulling her up into his arms. As the warmth of his touch permeated her skin, the illusion of age fell away. Her wrinkles smoothed. Her back straightened. The church and everyone in it was swept away by his light.

She focused on his sapphire eyes and gripped his shoulders ever tighter.

"You are okay, Bonnie Guillian. I've broken the illusion. You are healthy and alive."

Bonnie heard the words he was saying, but it took her a full minute to understand. She glanced around, finding herself back in the mirrored maze, inside her own skin.

"What is this place?"

"Enchanted labyrinth. The mirrors show you your greatest fears."

Bonnie closed her eyes and wept. "What did it show *you*?" she asked in lieu of reliving her own harrowing experience.

"I became a Watcher again and ate Hope. Thankfully, my angel energy showed the illusion for what it was."

Only then did Bonnie notice the baby on his shoulder, looking blue and barely breathing.

"She's worse."

"Yes. We must hurry."

Bonnie's eyes darted right then left, but all she could see was her reflection, no way out. "How do we get out of here? How did you get to me?"

Cord's eyes drifted to Hope. "Did you know there are different types of angels?"

"Uh, sure, I guess. Fallen ones and regular ones."

Cord cocked his head to the side and smirked. "I mean different types of regular ones."

"Not really."

"There are nine different types. Gideon and Gabriel were messenger angels, but there are others. Seraphim never leave

Heaven; they guard the throne of our Lord. Cherubim are also guards, but here on Earth."

Bonnie nodded. "Two cherubim guarded Eden. I didn't think of them as angels, but I guess they were."

"And then there are archangels," Cord said quickly. "Archangels guard people, and they have a certain set of skills to do just that." He lowered his chin and looked at her through his lashes.

"And you are?"

"I didn't know what I was until I heard you scream." Carefully, he handed Hope to Bonnie. "If you would hold her for a moment, I'll show you what happened."

She took the baby, tucking her sleeping form into the side of her neck.

Glowing brighter, Cord clapped his hands and became a supernova. She shielded her eyes and took a step back. A flaming sword erupted between his palms, burning purple and infusing the space with warmth. At the same time, he spread his wings, now blue with holy fire.

"I am an archangel, Bonnie. I was sent to protect you and Hope, and I will do so, even if it means my death."

"Wow," was all she could manage.

He gave a tight smile and turned toward the mirrors. "This labyrinth is constructed of sorcery, and if there is anything an archangel is good for, it is battling sorcery." His sword sliced through the mirror that had trapped her, the mirror where she had seen her death. The walls of the maze came apart stitch by stitch as if someone had found a loose thread and was slowly unraveling the scene before her.

"Sam," she called when her sister came into view. Ghost was standing next to her, looking dazed as the mirrors melted around him. Bonnie pulled her sister into a tight, one-armed hug and kissed her cheek. They were in the concourse of the United Center, in front of an abandoned burger booth.

Ghost raised an eyebrow at Cord's flaming sword. "That's a cool trick." He turned a circle. "But you may want to be discreet."

A gathering cheer rang out from within the stadium, ten thousand raving Watchers lapping up whatever milk Lucifer was throwing their way. Bonnie glanced up and down the concrete walkway lined with empty vendor booths. A small screen in the corner silently televised the show. Lucifer lifted a wine glass full of dark liquid. The Watchers cheered again.

"We're in. Really in. We made it through the labyrinth," Samantha whispered. "Do you think the others are still in there? Without Cord, how would they break through the sorcery?"

Bonnie opened her mouth to answer but was distracted when Hope coughed once, then twice, then gasped for air as her tiny body shook with the effort of clearing her lungs. "Cord, she needs you." She turned to hand the baby over, but the angel wasn't alone.

Levi, the member of the Wicked Brethren who had tried to kill her at the Quik N Smart, faced Cord with fists clenched and eyes blazing. "You shouldn't be here. How did you escape my labyrinth?"

"You and your brothers aren't as clever as you presume to be," Cord said. He clapped his hands together, and the sword blazed to life.

Levi raised an eyebrow. "An archangel? You, Cord?" The demon laughed low and haughtily. "It won't help you. Baby angels are all the same. Big swords and not a clue how to use them." With a circle of his arms, Levi produced a weapon of his own, blazing orange with a black center that reminded Bonnie of an eye.

Angel rounded demon, and Levi's blade flashed. Cord blocked the blow, but the power brought him to his knees. Bonnie gasped, reaching for her dagger. A hand clamped down on her shoulder. Ghost.

"No way." With one hand on her elbow and the other on Samantha's, Jesse tugged her behind the counter of the burger booth. "Hide here. This is going to get ugly."

"We need to help him," Bonnie whispered.

"No." Ghost shook his head. "Our mission is to get you and Hope to that platform."

Placing a hand on her forearm, Samantha nodded in agreement.

With Hope still struggling to breathe on her shoulder, Bonnie raised up on her knees to peek through the multicolored beer taps and nacho cheese dispenser. Cord was back on his feet. Levi's red blade pummeled Cord's purple one, pounding down again and again on the angel's locked arms and bent knees. Sparks flew with each connection, raining gold and silver fire on the concrete.

"Jesse," Bonnie whispered. "What if the other Soulkeepers are stuck somewhere in the labyrinth?"

Ghost broke apart and came back together. "What if they are, Bon? I'm not Cord. I can't cut through the sorcery like he can."

"But what if the other two teams are trapped?"

Grabbing Bonnie's shoulder, Samantha gave her a little shake. "Stop worrying about everyone else. Malini is the Healer. She was probably the first one out of that damned thing. Trust in the plan. We've got enough trouble staying alive and doing our part."

Chapter 26
Healer

"You can't move it at all?" Malini said, the high pitch of her voice a hint of the stress within. She tried her best to conceal her mounting panic. Grace had enough to worry about without bringing Malini's insecurities into it.

"No," Grace said. "There's no feeling from the shoulder down." The older woman adjusted herself on her sit bones, wiping the last bits of black ooze from her face with her left hand. Her right was gray tinged and limp in her lap.

Malini lifted the dead hand again and tried to bombard Grace with healing energy, to no effect. "My power is telling me you're healed. I'm sorry, Grace. Whatever this is, my power can't touch it."

"You can't heal the dead," Jacob said gravely. "What if Grace's arm was dead before you started the healing?"

"Can that happen? Her arm is dead but not the rest of her?"

"I'm not a doctor, but maybe the spider's venom killed the cells it was able to spread to. Dead."

"But—"

Grace cut her off. "It doesn't matter why. It just is. You two have to leave me here. I'm right-handed. I can't fight like this. I'll be more of a liability than a help."

"No," Jacob and Malini said together. "We came in together, and we leave together."

Grace pursed her lips, jaw tight and brow showing her age. She gave each of them a long, hard look, and then allowed her eyes to rest on her dead hand.

"None of us know where we are going to end up in this world." She shook her curly red head. "Who would have thought a cattle rancher's kid and timid Catholic school girl would end up here, battling giant scorpions and mummies." Her green eyes flashed to the body of the dead spider. "I knew when I walked in the door I might never walk out."

"Grace—"

She held up her good hand. "Stop. This is my decision. Leave me here. If you succeed in thwarting Lucifer, I might still be here when you return. And if you don't? Well, none of us will have long to live anyway, will we?"

The full force of Grace's stare drilled into Malini. Once again, the Healer was put in the position to choose: the life of one versus the lives of many. The labyrinth was deadly; Malini knew this for certain. The chance Grace would still be alive if they left her here was slim. Still, this was what the Soulkeepers were called to do. If they took her with them, she'd be vulnerable, easily captured and used as a bargaining chip, or worse, killed. Grace would never forgive herself if she became the reason for their mission's failure.

"Okay," Malini said.

"You can't mean that," Jacob said.

Malini placed a dagger in Grace's left hand. "Use the short blade. It will be easier with your non-dominant hand."

Grace nodded.

"You can't be serious. We can't just leave her here," Jacob said again.

Malini grabbed Jacob's shoulders and gave him a look that said just how serious she was. "Come on. We're behind schedule."

She gathered her fallen weapons, checked that her glove was on properly, and walked toward the sarcophagus the mummy showed her was the exit to the tomb. She paused when Jacob didn't immediately follow. Knee-deep in treasure, her spine tingled with the instinct to move on. They were on borrowed time. "Jake."

Jacob stared at Grace with his hands on his hips. She turned away, frowning. "Fine," he said, dusting some invisible substance from his hands. "This is not on me." He pushed past Malini and led the way through the passageway.

Sure that his words had cut her to the quick, Malini followed.

The corridor was dark and became darker as the walkway descended. With fingers hitched to Jacob's back, Malini's other hand trailed along a rough-hewn wall that crumbled beneath her touch. She patted down her pockets and utility belt until she found the small flashlight she'd packed, her long tapered fingers pausing on the switch. Light was a powerful thing, and so she hesitated, worried turning it on would cause some sort of calamity.

Click. Jacob's flashlight glowed to life.

"That was incredibly stupid," Malini hissed.

"No more stupid than continuing to walk in the dark. What the hell is this place?"

"That's the question of the day, isn't it?" Malini snapped on her flashlight and pointed it at the wall. A million gems sparkled like diamonds. She moved her face closer to one, then pivoted to shine her light past Jacob, who was staring at something on the ceiling. A mine cart on a track marked the center of the cavern. The alternate wall glittered with the same gems. She walked to the cart and looked inside. Dozens of yellow, white, and amber gems glinted back at her.

"I think this is a diamond mine," Malini said.

"Yeah?" Jacob swallowed hard, his pale face still staring at the ceiling.

"What are you looking at?" Malini returned to his side and followed the beam of light from his flashlight to the black ceiling of the cave. There were no sparkling gems in his beam. Instead, the top of the cavern seemed leathery and dead black.

"It's moving," Jacob said.

"What's moving?"

"The ceiling."

Malini squinted her eyes and pointed her light to join with Jacob's. In the brightened beam, a piece of the ceiling shifted, and a set of reflective eyes blinked at her. "What is that thing?"

"Correction, what are those things?" Jacob asked. Dozens of yellow eyes and white flashing teeth were now focused on them.

"Giant bats?" Malini asked.

Jacob shook his head. With his flashlight, he followed an oily blob as it dripped down the wall to the floor in front of them and formed into something that might look like a mangy dog if it wasn't ten thousand times worse. "Hellhounds!"

Malini yanked Jacob away, cursing as the hounds rained from the ceiling. She'd been right. The light woke them up, and now they would pay the price.

"Come on." She climbed into the mine cart, tugging him in after her, and lifted the handbrake. He pushed off with one leg, the hellhound's claws narrowly missing his receding heel. As the cart began to roll, Malini stabbed and swung her blade, back to back with Jacob, trying desperately to keep the oily bodies outside the cart. Slowly but surely, they picked up speed, leaving the hounds panting behind them.

"We're headed downhill," Malini said, gripping the sides of the cart until her knuckles turned white. The entire thing shook violently, enough for her to fear the track might come apart.

"The speed isn't half as bad as where we're headed," Jacob said, pointing into the distance where the track bent and then disappeared to be replaced by a wide-mouthed gorge. "Track's out."

"Jump!"

One foot on the edge, Malini leapt over, dropping into a roll on the painfully rough ground. Jacob landed next to her and barrel-rolled to a stop. "Ow."

"Shhh. Don't turn your light back on. Those things are probably right behind us," she whispered.

"Then how do we get out of here?"

"I don't know."

Jacob sighed. She could hear his rhythmic breathing in the darkness. "This is unreal," he said.

"Don't give me a hard time, Jake. I'm thinking, all right?"

"No. I mean it. This isn't real. We are physically in the United Center in Chicago, Illinois. That means everything around us is an illusion. The mummy's tomb, the treasure, this cavern—it wouldn't all fit in the space. It's not real."

Malini's mouth dropped open. Why hadn't she considered that before? This was sorcery and illusion. She grabbed Jacob's head in the dark and plowed a kiss into the side of his temple. "You are so smart."

"Huh?"

She hooked two fingers in the crook of her elbow and peeled the flesh from her right hand. Then, concentrating on the magic of her skeletal limb, she thrust it into the wall of the cavern. As predicted, her bones sliced through the stone like butter. When she pulled her hand back, the hole she punched glowed radioactive green, the energy eating away at the stone like a cancer.

"Whoa," Jacob said.

The cavern melted away, and they found themselves standing on the main floor concourse of the United Center, next to the darkened window of a sports apparel shop. On instinct, Jacob flattened himself against the wall, pulling Malini along with him.

Lucifer's voice echoed against the concrete, making him jump. "Drink, my children. Drink of me, and I will give you power beyond your wildest dreams."

Malini's eyes swept the concourse for the source of the voice, finding a television screen at the entrance to the stadium. Lucifer's face smiled at her, holding up a wine glass of dark liquid to toast the crowd. He drained the glass, and Malini's heart sank.

"Lillian's team didn't make it. His blood was in the wine. The Watchers have had his flesh; he can cast the spell."

"We're too late," Jacob said.

"A day late and a dollar short," came a conceited voice from behind them.

Malini whirled to see Damien in a suit that hung like it was made for him and leather shoes that looked soft as butter. Jacob's sword was already frozen in his grip.

The Watcher folded his hands behind his back and raised his chin. He glared at Jacob's weapon as if it were a toy. "Do you know how much my businesses are worth?" Damien asked.

Taken aback, Malini shook her head.

"Over one billion. I live where I want. I eat whom I want. I do what I want."

Malini snorted. "As long as it serves Lucifer."

Damien's face fell. "It wasn't always so. The Wicked Brethren have, in the past, served their own masters."

"Greed," Jacob said. "You serve greed."

Damien bowed at the waist. "The thing about money is it can buy you anything else in this world. I had a good thing going before the evil bastard started yanking my chain."

"Get to the point, Damien."

"The point is that it was never in our contract that I should have to fight the Healer directly. I feel that this situation is a breach of what I agreed to and a threat to my viability." He stroked the lapel of his suit with his palm.

"Are you going to let us go without a fight?" Jacob scoffed at the thought.

Damien pinched the bridge of his nose with his thumb and forefinger. "I am a businessman. I do not fight with fists but with words, with deals. I wish to offer you an agreement."

"Which is?" Malini asked.

"I let you go now with the understanding that, should the tide turn in your favor, you will do the same for me."

"Never," Jacob said self-righteously.

Damien ignored Jacob and turned the full force of his stare on Malini. "Think about it, girl. I am not your typical Watcher, growing fat and lazy on prisoners in Nod. I have lived above ground since Lucifer's fall. There are some who compare my power to his. We could fight, and it is true that you would likely win, considering I'd have to pull you apart to kill you and your blood would burn me like acid. But in the time it takes you to fight me, Lucifer will have cast his spell. Thousands of Watchers will have accepted his curse. You will never make it out alive."

"So if I take your agreement?"

"I turn my back as you go about your business, and should God win the challenge, you do the same, for me. Deal?"

Malini stared into Damien's gray eyes and scanned his meticulously kept clothes. "Deal."

"Malini?" Jacob looked at her as if he'd never seen her before.

Damien gave her a short salute. "Nice doing business with you." He folded into the nearest shadow and was gone.

"How could you do that?" Jacob asked incredulously.

She grabbed his hand and pulled him down the hall to the nearest restroom. "Because, Jacob, he was right. We don't have time for a fight. And besides, if the rest of this mission goes as planned, I won't be the one to kill him."

Chapter 27
Asher

Dane shifted from foot to foot, wishing he could be the one to step through the flap of the circus tent to whatever lay beyond. But he was the liability here, powerful yet powerless. It made sense for Ethan to lead the way. He could use his telekinesis from a safe distance against anything that attacked.

Only, now that Dane thought about it, the real danger of the labyrinth wasn't what attacked them from afar but the lure of the illusions that drew them in.

"Have you guys noticed that everything in this labyrinth is sexual?"

Ethan paused at the threshold and glanced over his shoulder at Dane. Lillian and Cheveyo had to pull up short to stop from plowing into him.

Dane continued. "On the city street, the stripper in the window appeared when Cheveyo touched the glass. Her appearance was engineered to be exactly the type of woman he was attracted to. If we hadn't been there, he would have been centipede chow."

Cheveyo's head bobbed. "Yep. Totally sucked into her spell. I can't explain it."

"And the fishbowl. There was nothing but a stream of bubbles in there until Lillian and I touched the glass. Then, before we know it, we are all stripping down to our skivvies to feed ourselves to the eels."

The bright blush on Lillian's face voiced her agreement. She scratched behind her ear. "The male looked like Charlie to me, Jacob's dad."

"And looked like Ethan to me," Dane said.

Ethan laughed. "It looked like you."

"So the only reason I was able to save your asses was because I didn't touch the glass. All I saw was a male and female merfolk. They didn't look like anyone to me."

"Exactly."

Lillian's eyes darted around the tent. "This place isn't real. It's all sorcery, illusion."

"Not just sorcery. Sorcery based on lust," Dane said, raising an eyebrow.

"Asher." Ethan placed his hands on his hips.

"Exactly what I was thinking," Dane said.

"So, how do we get out of here?" Cheveyo asked Lillian. As the matriarch of the group, it was natural they looked to her for answers.

She shrugged. "Evil sorcery can only be negated with something equally good. Malini's hand, an angel's touch. Good and evil cannot exist in the same place at the same time."

"Like how my power works," Cheveyo said.

"Exactly, although I'm not sure you could possess the labyrinth itself," Lillian said.

"Maybe we can make it through and find our way out, now that we know the secret. Don't touch any glass," Ethan said.

In a sea of darting glances, no one seemed to want to move, until, finally, Lillian motioned Ethan on with a small wave of her hand.

"Cool. Let's do this, then." He pushed through the flap and led the way into the dim corridor made of canvas.

Dane followed at the rear of the group, dagger in hand. For some reason, knowing Asher was behind these tests didn't put him at ease. In fact, his heart raced and his palms sweat. When he stopped to think about it, he would have chosen any of the Wicked Brethren over Asher. He'd spent much of his life denying his sexuality, and even now, with Ethan, he'd chosen to remain celibate to give their relationship time to mature.

What if all of the waiting had left him a throbbing, raw hormone that would cave at the slightest provocation? Sure, he'd like to believe his virginity made him stronger. When he shared that piece of himself with someone, it would be precious and permanent. That's why Asher scared him so much. Losing himself to lust, when he'd waited so long for the person who would be his permanent partner, would be the ultimate self-betrayal. He swallowed hard, resolved to make it out of here in the same state he entered.

"What the?" Ethan said. "So much for sticking to the plan. There's no glass in this room."

At the back of the line, Dane couldn't see what Ethan saw, but he could hear the whooshing of falling canvas behind him. "The corridor is collapsing," he yelled, pushing into Cheveyo, who forced Lillian and Ethan forward. The entire tent collapsed behind him, brushing down his back as he entered the next challenge just in time.

The floor gave slightly under his feet as if he were walking on a thick gymnastics pad. He glanced down to find red silk sheets layered under his shoes. The red silk didn't stop at the floor. It cascaded up the walls and lined the ceiling of the circular room. Swaths of it draped from ceiling to floor in random intervals. Large square silk pillows were scattered around the room.

"There's no way out," Lillian said.

"Maybe behind one of the curtains?" Cheveyo said, reaching for the edge of one.

"Don't touch that, man," Ethan said.

"We can't stand here forever," Cheveyo argued.

Dane held up his dagger and moved toward the wall. With the tip, he pushed aside the drapes one by one. No exit presented itself, but as he removed his dagger, the drapes began to sway.

"Whoa," Cheveyo said, gaze darting toward his feet.

The entire floor roiled, and Dane bent his knees to surf the wave. "Looks like we stirred up the snakes."

Ethan pointed to the corner of the room. A human body danced beneath the silk, a woman with long limbs and large breasts. The silk skimmed over her skin. A dark head of hair broke the surface of the sheets, followed by pale skin and large brown eyes. She smiled, clutching the silk to her collarbone as she arched her back beneath the fabric.

Cheveyo cleared his throat. "I'm going to close my eyes," he squeaked.

Dane chose to look away, but in the opposite direction, the muscles of a man's back broke the surface, flexing and stretching, the silk catching just below the dimples of his hips.

"Cover your eyes," Lillian said. "It's started."

Dane did, pressing his palm into his face. It didn't help. Two silky hands worked their way over his feet and up his shins. A hand caressed the inside of his thigh, sending a shiver to the base of his scalp. His knees buckled. He caught himself on his thigh, fighting the urge to lie down in the soft massaging coils of silk. "It's touching me," he said.

"Me too," Cheveyo said. "This is freaking me out. It's snakes. You know they're probably snakes."

The thought of snakes brought Dane to his senses. His spine straightened, and he remembered the dagger in his hand. It was a blessed weapon from Eden. Perhaps if he stabbed it into the floor, he could shred this illusion. Then again, touching the dagger to the silk had been a disaster. What he needed was something good and pure. Something that would send the evil of this place running.

Something like Soulkeeper blood.

Silk hands rubbed up his back, over his shoulders, pulling him down toward the floor. "I'm going to try something," Dane said. Eyes tightly closed, he pressed his dagger into his opposite palm and squeezed. There was a sharp pain and then warm, wet blood oozed and dripped from his fist.

Screeching pierced his ears. He opened his eyes. Where his blood fell, the illusion came apart stitch by stitch. He looked to the others. Cheveyo was doing all right, but Ethan and Lillian were on their hands and knees in the silk.

"Cheveyo, help Lillian," Dane said. "Use your blood. Soulkeeper blood damages the illusion."

Dane raced to Ethan's side to help him up.

"No," Ethan howled, slapping his hand away.

"Ethan, it's me," Dane said. "Oh hell." He held his still bleeding hand just over the patch of silk around Ethan. "Open your eyes."

Ethan did, gasping in relief as the silk came apart strand by strand, replaced by cold, hard concrete. "Thank God. I thought you were one of them."

"Our blood breaks the spell," he said again. Turning, he saw that Cheveyo had jumped in to help, cutting his forearm and destroying his section of the tent. He'd also helped Lillian to her feet. Standing together, he watched the last bits of the illusion come apart, replaced by the concrete walkway of an upper level of the United Center, just outside a ramp to the seating within. The hideous cheers of thousands of Watchers tumbled out at their feet.

"We made it," Lillian whispered. "We're in the stadium."

Clap. Clap. Clap. Asher stepped from the shadows, dark wings stretched behind his rock-star good looks. He plunged his hands into the pockets of his skinny jeans. "I'm almost impressed the four of you survived my challenge. Then again, I hadn't expected that two of you would be so annoyingly innocent. Lust begins in the mind, you know. Hardly entertaining to be prudish."

With her daggers in hand, Lillian stepped in front of Dane, prepared for an attack. Asher's face fell. "As a rule, I'm a lover not a fighter." He eyed Lillian from toes to breasts but stopped before he reached her face. "Unfortunately, Lucifer would digest me if I let you go. He's at an important stage in his work and cannot be disturbed."

"Then bring it on, oil slick," Ethan said.

Asher spread his wings, fangs dropping as he hissed. Fire flew from his hand, orange and red and hot enough to send

Dane diving over the nearest counter to avoid the blast. Ethan blocked the flow of fire with his mind while Lillian hurled her blades into Asher's chest and side. He didn't let up. Instead, the flamethrower technique blasted from his other hand, straight at Lillian. She flipped behind a hot dog cart.

Sheltered by a row of beer taps, Dane watched the flames melt the canopy and the plastic smiling hot dog off the front of Lillian's hiding place. Crap, she wouldn't last long in that. And Asher seemed to have an endless amount of firepower. Ethan was sweating from the effort of holding back the heat. Cheveyo ... Where was Cheveyo?

The Hopi boy emerged from a women's bathroom behind Asher. He must have ducked into the entrance next to the beer vendor and walked through. He tiptoed toward Asher's back, a finger over his lips. As if Dane was going to announce his attack or something.

"Ahh!" Ethan screamed as his nose began to bleed and Asher's flames licked one side of his face. He fell to his knees and then collapsed to the ground.

"Now!" Dane yelled at Cheveyo. Asher narrowed his eyes in Dane's direction, giving Ethan a half-second of relief. Cheveyo's body hit the floor.

The flames stopped. Asher grabbed his throat, bending at the waist and heaving.

"Not going to throw that one up," Dane said, rushing to Ethan's side. He tucked his partner's burnt face into his shoulder. "Hold your breath."

The oily explosion that filled the corridor was the biggest he'd ever seen.

Chapter 28
Hope's End

Bonnie bit her bottom lip as she watched Cord tangle with Levi. Angel against Watcher, the two forces of nature collided, showering the corridor with red and purple fireworks. She'd been here before. Behind the Quik N Smart, she'd watched Levi almost destroy Cord before he was able to escape through the sunlight.

Cord couldn't run now. He had to protect her and Hope, to see the Soulkeepers' mission through.

In a blur of darkness, Levi dropped to the floor and kicked under Cord's sword, into his gut. The angel soared into the concrete wall of the concourse, weapon dissipating on impact. Cord slumped to the floor, silver-white blood oozing from a gash on the side of his head.

Levi shook his dark waves and swaggered in Cord's direction. "Pity you weren't more of a challenge. I'd heard the Watcher Cord was truly terrible. Looks like the Great Oppressor clipped your wings."

Cord floundered, attempted to stand, but couldn't. A tear welled over Bonnie's lower lid, her heart pounding at the sight. That monster, Levi, was going to kill him. He raised his burning blade over Cord's heart. Weeping, Bonnie squeezed Hope to her.

Hope.

Bonnie burst from behind the counter, throwing off Ghost and Samantha's pleading hands, and shrieked, "Wait!" At the same time, she turned Hope to face Levi, tugging aside the collar of her shirt to expose the stone.

Levi sneered in her direction, then stopped. The flaming sword in his hand disappeared, and his body shivered as if he were having a seizure. The Watcher collapsed to his knees, twitching, a glow beginning in his fingertips and working up his arms.

Hope gasped and coughed.

"She's dying." Samantha wept, reaching for the baby. Bonnie shrugged her off.

Hope's little body was gray instead of pink, and she'd curled up in pain although she seemed too weak to cry. Just a little longer. She had to save Cord. Levi growled and shook his head, straining to escape Hope's spell.

"She's not breathing, Bonnie. Stop this." Samantha tugged at her elbow.

Thank the Lord, she didn't have to choose whom to save. Cord leapt to his feet, clapped his hands together, and with a renewed vigor produced the burning purple sword of an archangel. He stepped forward and swung.

Levi's head departed his neck, skipping down the hall from the force of the blow. The demon's muscled body swayed for a beat, then flopped to the concrete like a dead fish. Black blood bubbled from the neck. Like acid, it ate away the body from the inside out, leaving a puddle of oily black behind.

As soon as he was sure the deed was done, Cord pulled his sword inside and ran for Hope. He lifted her lifeless form from Bonnie's hands and tucked her next to his heart. In awe, Bonnie watched as Cord's radiance gathered and blazed, engulfing her tiny body in healing energy.

Hope gasped and then coughed. Blue eyes fluttering, her skin pinked.

"Thank the Lord," Samantha said, crossing herself. But Ghost's face looked grave. He popped between them, holding his hand up in alarm.

"Flipping one Watcher almost killed her, how are we going to change all of them?" he said.

A cheer rose up in the background, a reminder of how close they were to a legion of Watchers. Bonnie's eyes shifted to Hope, so sweet and innocent in Cord's arms. She desperately wanted to flee with her, with both of them. What kind of God would do this to a baby? Maybe none of this was worth the fight.

"Pose as Levi," Samantha said suddenly. "If you transform into him, you can walk right up to Lucifer with Hope on your shoulder."

"Yeah, until he smells me."

"By then it will be too late. You transform the Watchers, and it's over. The new angels will defend you and the baby."

"Hope will be dead."

"Not if Cord blends into the light and heals her at the same time as you magnify her power. No one even needs to know he's there. Lucifer is standing under a huge spotlight."

"That might work," Ghost said.

"And I'll be close enough to defend you if something goes wrong," Cord said.

"Sam and I will be nearby. We'll engage if things go sour."

Bonnie's eyes hardened as she stared at baby Hope, snuggled into Cord's chest and sucking on her fingers. "Seems like the wrong thing to do, bringing a baby into a pit of vipers."

Samantha met her sister's eyes and toyed with the cross around her neck. "Dad would have wanted you to do what was right for the greater good. That's what he did every day as a police officer. That's what Mom would say if she were here, too. And I'll tell you something else, Bonnie, I know that look in your eye. I know you want to take Hope and run and go hide under the covers, but you can't get away from this. These Watchers will eventually find you. And because your heart is pure, they will kill you, and Hope too if she's

still alive. You said it yourself. You are Jonah. You've been
called to this. You won't get away from it."

The words slapped Bonnie's face as sure as if it had been
Samantha's open palm. She gaped at first, and then the truth
of it seeped into her heart. A wave of preeminent grief
washed from the pit of her stomach to the bridge of her nose,
aching there like the root of a raw nerve. They both would go
then, she and Hope, sacrificial lambs to the Devil's table, and
if God were with them, He would give them the strength to
be enough when the time came.

"Okay," she said, wiping under her eyes. "I'll take her."
She looked each of them in the eye. Ghost and Samantha
wept for her. But not Cord. His face was a model of faith.

"I've lived a life without God, Bonnie. You don't want to
live that life. Whatever the outcome for us, have no regrets
that you walked this road. You're making the right choice."
He handed her Hope.

"Wait," she said, holding up her hand. She reached for
Samantha, flesh merging with her sister's, and transformed
into an exact replica of Levi. Her sister was smaller now, like
a child, but her size wasn't indicative of her power. If need
be, she'd become a Watcher-killing hurricane. Bonnie
adjusted the stone around her neck so that it was clearly
visible, then reached for Hope.

Cord handed her over. "You look eerily evil, although
your scent gives you away."

"Nothing I can do about that."

"Maybe." Cord stared at her for a moment and then gathered a handful of brown napkins from the counter. With an expression of pain, he mopped up some of the oily black puddle that used to be Levi and painted it over Bonnie's clothing, careful not to touch her skin. "Better."

She nodded. Another round of cheers rose up from the stadium. "Sounds like Lucifer is giving the speech of his existence." She cocked her head to the side. "Here goes nothing."

* * * * *

Tucking Hope under the lapel of the leather coat Levi had been wearing, Bonnie entered the stadium from the first-floor concourse, trying her best not to think about the tens of thousands of Watchers in the seats around her. She had to look badass. Her simple presence, from the way she held her shoulders to the set of her mouth, must elicit fear or Lucifer would see her coming.

From the shadow of the concrete walls of the entrance ramp, she emerged into a cesspool of evil. Lucifer stood on an elevated platform at the center of a sea of perfect faces, each illusion more flawless than the next. Fluffy pink, purple, and orange wings stretched from the backs of tall, thin runway model types. Even the men appeared graceful and gorgeous. It was an illusion, but the force of their collective presence had an immediate effect on her. Was her portrayal of Levi perfect enough?

Why did these creatures insist on their illusions, even when only in each other's presence? As she walked the aisle toward Lucifer, who was babbling on about taking over the world and forcing humans to pay them the respect they deserved, she supposed that illusion was a necessity as a Watcher. A Watcher would never accept another in his or her natural state. They exercised no forgiveness, no compassion, and definitely no love. She was standing in the middle of a room of beings that thought each of their individual desires was more important than anything. Lucifer was tolerated out of necessity; he pulled their metaphysical strings. These creatures were not free, but slaves to evil. Slaves to their selfishness.

But Bonnie with Hope would set them free from that bondage.

Lucifer held up the empty glass he was holding and turned in a circle. "Now, my Watchers, that you have tasted of my blood, I give you my sixth and final curse. Death."

A rumble rose up around her and then settled into a restless silence.

"I give you the Devil's Passover. You shall go forth from this place with the ability to see into the hearts of men. Humans with hearts for evil shall be passed over, while those with a heart for God shall die."

The crowd roared, Watchers pumping their fists in the air. Not one of them questioned her as Bonnie, disguised as Levi, placed her foot on the first step to ascend the platform. She took another step and caught the deadly gaze of Auriel from the front row. Another step and Auriel stood from her chair.

Bonnie sneered at her in a way she thought Levi might, and she sat back down.

Distracted with his sorcery, Lucifer did not notice when Bonnie joined him on the platform. He raised his hands above his head and a black wind blew through the complex, tongues of inky sorcery licking down on the Watchers' heads, all those who had drunk of Lucifer's blood. Of course, the magic avoided Bonnie, drawing more visual ire from Auriel. Did she know? Did the way the sorcery moved around her give her away?

Luckily, at that moment, Auriel and the rest of the Watchers twitched and froze, internal wiring scrambled by the unholy fire filtering into their bodies. On shaking legs, Bonnie forced herself to continue forward, walking the platform to an area behind Lucifer. She looked up and saw Levi's face on the giant screen above her. This was it. All the Watchers seeing Lucifer would also see her.

With Lucifer distracted by the delivery of his final curse, Bonnie peeled back the leather jacket to expose the stone and turned Hope's beautiful face toward the camera. Unfortunately, the Watchers, writhing under the force of the spell, were not looking at the mega screen above their heads. In the throes of pain, most squeezed their yellow eyes shut.

Lucifer dropped his hands. Bonnie froze only steps behind his back.

One by one the Watchers stopped their violent conversion and raised their faces to Lucifer, which meant they also saw Hope. Bonnie watched in horror as her tiny body was bled of life, her skin graying again and her breath coming in small, tight gasps. In return, a few Watchers at the front of the crowd fell into a sort of stupor, fingers sparkling slightly. All the rest of them just looked angry.

"It's not working," Cord whispered from the light next to her ear. He was touching Hope, but she wasn't healing.

Lucifer whirled at Cord's voice and balked at the sight of the baby. His lips peeled back from his teeth. "What is this? What are you doing?"

Chapter 29
The Still, Small Voice

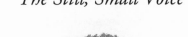

"Hurry, Jacob," Malini said. "I have a bad feeling."

Jacob held one of his flasks over the sink in the bathroom and willed the holy water up the spout, into the pipes. Sweat broke out on his forehead. He worked against the pressure, water into water. Not the easiest of tasks but, like a virus, the blessing spread. He could feel it branch and bloom in the pipes above his head. When the holy water took on a life of its own, traveling beyond his reach, he let it go.

"It's done," he said. "The blessing will continue to spread on its own."

"Good. Come on. We've got to find Bonnie and Hope." Malini threaded her fingers with his and tugged him into the concourse. They both pulled up short when they saw the video feed.

"Oh no," Jacob said. Hope slouched in Levi's hands. No, wait, those were Bonnie's disguised hands; the stone around her neck gave her away.

"Lucifer knows," Malini said. "We're doomed."

"Oh, I wouldn't say that."

Malini whirled around to see the source of the still, small voice behind her. She came face to face with ... herself. Realizing who it was, she dropped to her knees. God often appeared in the image of the viewer.

"Please, we don't have time. The sixth temptation has been given, now you must help me deliver the sixth gift."

"What can we do?" Malini asked. Jacob was speechless, unable to fathom that the Lord God Almighty was standing less than a foot in front of him.

"We must release your healing power and reconnect Hope with her soul," God said.

Malini nodded. "There can only be one Healer," she whispered. "Will it hurt when I die?"

"Die?" Jacob shook his head. "What?"

The Lord smiled Malini's smile. "Peace, Soulkeeper. Malini need not die."

"Then how?" Malini asked.

"Only Jacob can do it." God smiled. "Water is alive, Jacob. It is the beginning and ending of all things, agile enough to enter the tiniest crevices and powerful enough to carve mountains."

He nodded. "Do you want me to flood the stadium?"

"No."

Jacob started. "Then what?"

"Destroy the red stone."

Malini and Jacob glanced at each other. "My red stone?" Malini asked. "The one around Bonnie's neck?"

"Yes. Destroy it." The Lord placed Her hands on Jacob's shoulders and looked him deep in the eyes. "Hope is my vessel for the sixth gift, but she cannot do my work disconnected from her soul. Her soul is trapped inside the stone. Free her and I will do the rest."

Jacob glanced at the screen above his head. Cord formed between Lucifer and the baby and was protecting Hope.

"How?" he asked quickly. "How can I destroy the stone?"

"It can only be done by you. Use the water. Direct it into the stone." The Lord pointed one small brown hand toward the stadium. "Go now. Hope's life is in danger."

Malini stepped back as a huge wash of water arced from Jacob's flask into his hand. He stormed past her and charged up the ramp to the seating area at a full run. Malini took one last look toward God before joining the fray, but She was already gone.

The two made it halfway to the platform before the Watchers descended.

* * * * *

Covered in Watcher blood, Dane helped Ethan to the relative safety of the dark booth. "Your face is burnt."

"I'm okay. It isn't that bad." He tried to stand on his own, but failed. Blood gushed from his nose, and the skin over his neck and cheek had already started to blister. Dane handed him a wad of brown napkins from the dispenser.

"Are you seeing this?" Cheveyo asked from the concourse. He was pointing at the video monitor. Dane lowered Ethan to the floor behind the counter, holding up one finger to let him know he'd be back, and jogged out from behind the concessions stand to join Lillian and Cheveyo.

The first thing he noticed was that Levi had Hope in his clutches, but when he saw the stone around his neck, he figured it was actually Bonnie. Cord was battling Lucifer in front of her and, *wow*, he had some new skills. He was wielding a fiery sword like something the Lord made, which of course he was. The Watchers quivered in their seats in various states of confusion.

"Are they having a collective fit or something?" Dane asked.

"I think it's a side effect of Lucifer's sixth curse," Lillian said.

"What's happening on the floor?" A few Watchers battled at the base of the platform. Heads flew from the crowd at regular intervals.

"Jacob," Dane said. "We've got to help them."

"Why isn't Hope working?" Lillian asked. "They can all see her."

"She's dying. She's disconnected from her soul," Cheveyo said.

Lillian drew the sword she kept sheathed on her back. "Then we'll have to kill them the old-fashioned way."

"Dane," Ethan rasped.

Dane leapt over the counter, landing next to his partner. "What's going on, Ethan? You going to be okay?"

"You've got to take my power. I'm done. My body has completely given out."

"Huh?"

"Borrow my telekinesis. It's wasted on me."

Dane wanted to protest, but the plan made too much sense. Ethan would be safer here anyway. He nodded and held out his hand. Ethan placed his shaking fingers in his, and Dane drew out his power as gently as possible. Still, Ethan's body jolted from the loss, then passed out on the cold floor.

"We've got to go," Cheveyo said.

Dane placed a dagger in Ethan's right hand and kissed him gently. Then he retrieved the arsenal of throwing stars and boomerang weapons his partner always wore and strapped them on his arms, ankles, and waist. He bounded over the counter and headed for the entrance to the stadium proper.

"I'm ready. Let's go."

* * * * *

The worst thing about the war going on around Bonnie was the sound. While she held Hope in one hand and a blessed hammer in the other, a horrific din rose up around her like a fog. The gurgle of black blood gushing from Watcher bodies, the sizzle of burning flesh, and the rhythmic explosion of power that sparked all around her. The first was caused by Jacob, doing his best to clear a path to the platform. The second was thanks to Malini, using her healing hand to do the same, and the last was due to Cord, defending her from Lucifer with a growing power worthy of an archangel.

She would have liked to help, but in her position behind the Cord-Lucifer conflict, she was painfully aware that she was the only thing standing between a wave of Watchers recovering from Lucifer's spell and Hope, who was barely breathing. At this moment, Auriel was gathering herself, stepping toward her on uncertain legs with death in her eyes.

"Archangels are such a pain in the ass," Lucifer said, wielding a stormy mass of power in Cord's direction.

Cord slashed it aside with his fiery blade. "Must have hurt when Michael tossed you off the edge of Heaven onto your ass." He swung, clipping Lucifer's wrist. The Devil staggered backward. "I hope you learned from your mistake. If not I'll show you a replay."

Lucifer laughed wickedly, circling him on the platform, fangs and talons protruding from his illusion. "Michael was over ten thousand years old. You've been an angel for as long as it takes me to sneeze. I will crush you."

Wings spread from one side of the platform to the other, Cord smirked and curled his upturned fingers. "I'm waiting to see you try."

The clash that ensued was so bright Bonnie turned away, which brought her gaze to Auriel's. The Watcher staggered up the stairs toward her with increasing conviction. Bonnie readied herself for an attack.

Inconceivably, a barrage of throwing stars landed in Auriel's spine, causing her to arch and howl. She pivoted, casting the weapons out of her skin by shedding her illusion and unfurling her large, leathery wings.

Above them, balanced on the railing of the second-floor seating area, Dane pointed and yelled, "Auriel!" He goaded her from above with a barrage of weapons.

Thankfully, Dane's taunt was enough to distract Auriel. Spreading her leathery wings, she flew to the second level, and the battle began anew. Bonnie could tell Dane had borrowed Ethan's abilities. Circular blades flew at Auriel from all directions in a tornado of blessed steel. Behind him, Cheveyo made use of his explosive skills, giving the nearby Watchers pause. That hesitation was enough for Lillian to take advantage of. By her sword, Watcher heads tumbled, flying over the second level railing on either side of Dane as he battled Auriel.

Vengefully, Auriel's sorcery blazed. She swatted the weapons and heads aside like so many gnats. The stress on Dane was obvious. None of the Soulkeepers could wield their power without consequences, and since Dane was borrowing his, the toll was double. She watched as he jumped down from the railing and backed down the aisle in retreat. The look of defeat on his face said it all. He was done for.

With a flap of her mighty wings, Auriel pursued him, teeth bared.

"Dane, run!" Bonnie cried. Her voice was lost in the noise around her. Worse, more Watchers were coming, staring at Hope as if she were their next meal. Bonnie gripped the baby tighter against her chest. That was how she noticed.

Hope wasn't breathing.

"Hope!"

* * * * *

Dane staggered back into the concourse, drawing the katana he'd worn on his back, the long curved blade giving welcome weight to his hand. Auriel glided in and landed in front of him, transforming behind a swirl of smoke into the girl he'd met years ago.

"So we meet again," she said, tucking a strand of her platinum hair back into her French twist. It was a wholly unnecessary motion. Every inch of her illusion was under her control. Messing with the hair was a way to distract him, as was the way she was dressed.

"Was the St. Mary's uniform necessary?"

"You seemed to like it the day we met."

"You'd drugged me with elixir. I would have liked you in a pair of discount sweats."

She rested her hands on her hips, twisting back and forth. "Not nearly as ironic."

He circled her in a wide arc, maintaining the space between them. "Come on, Auriel. Let's end this," Dane said. He sank deeper into his stance, sword slashing across his field of vision.

"We both know how this fight will end. Twice now, I could have killed you. If it wasn't for Jacob, I would have finished you off in the Paris High School parking lot."

"Seems like I remember impaling you with something a lot less dangerous than this in Nod."

She laughed. Her heels clicked on the concrete as she circled him, and he pivoted slowly to keep up. "We both know if Malini's zombies weren't there to distract me, you'd be history."

"No better time than now to test the theory."

"I could free you, you know." She met his eyes.

"Free me from what?"

"Your … abnormality. A little sorcery and *poof,* cured of your homosexuality. Swear your allegiance to me, and I will take care of everything."

It was Dane's turn to laugh. "Auriel, there is nothing in this world or the next that would make me want to change who I am or, God forbid, be like *you.* I'm willing to bet even the Devil has no use for you."

Dane's last words sent her over the edge. Auriel attacked in a flurry of shredding claws and slashing teeth. He dodged and scurried, swiped and sliced. The tip of his blade connected with her hand, and a piece of her talon flew off and hit the wall. She never touched him. When she got too close, he pushed her away with his mind. And although his nose had started to bleed, the adrenaline took care of any fatigue.

Heart hammering in his chest, he attacked, blade singing through the air. *Ping.* Metal met bone. Her right wing dropped to the floor and sizzled.

She moaned and grabbed the stump. "Dane, how could you? Is this what you've become? A man who attacks women?" Stumbling back, she pouted and began to cry.

"No. I'm a man who vanquishes evil." He thrust toward her heart.

She broke apart, funneling into black mist just out of reach. He drove forward, hoping to catch her essence on his blessed blade. Another blade did the job first.

Ethan's dagger knocked Auriel from shadow. She tumbled from the darkness, shrieking. Her injuries made it impossible for her to hold her illusion, and she formed in front of him all black scaly skin and yellow eyes. Her mouth opened, no doubt to tempt him with some other promise, but Dane was done with hesitations or empty promises. He swung his blade, slicing through her neck.

Auriel ended in a black oil slick in front of a Burger Barn.

"Damn good job," Ethan said from behind the counter.

"All I can say is I was glad she looked like a Watcher when I killed her."

"Yeah?"

"Funny what illusions can do to you, you know? When she looked human, some part of me always wanted to save her ... even while she tried to kill me."

Ethan lowered his chin. "Hey, you okay?"

Dane smiled slowly, meeting his eyes. "Yeah, I am."

"Sounds like war in there," Ethan said, gesturing toward the stadium.

"We'd better help." Dane swayed. The next time he opened his eyes, he was sitting on the floor, and Ethan was in front of him.

"My turn." Ethan gripped Dane's hand, allowing his power to flow back to the source. Then he kissed Dane on the forehead and ran full speed into the war.

Chapter 30
Winner

Of all the reasons Bonnie had called out Hope's name, she'd never thought of the consequences. Amid the fighting and the bloodshed, the one person who heard her, the one face that turned, was Cord's. He stopped and made a slight motion toward Hope, a simple shift of his weight. It was enough. In that fraction of a second, when Cord's thoughts shifted to her, Lucifer pounced.

One of the Devil's hands slapped Cord's wrist, dissipating his weapon with the force of impact. Cord staggered backward, but Lucifer was too quick. He caught the angel behind the neck and thrust his hand into his chest. Bonnie screamed in horror as Lucifer brought his lips to Cord's. As he laid that deadly kiss upon the angel's lips, he tore his silver heart from his chest.

Bonnie gasped as Cord's body dropped lifelessly to the platform. For her, the fall was timeless. In a moment, it repeated itself in her brain. She rushed forward, reaching her hand out to break his fall. When his head hit her palm, he broke apart into a billow of glittery dust that sifted through her fingers. The pieces lifted and blew away in a swirl that tornadoed toward the ceiling and beyond. The death of an angel was an ironically beautiful affair while equally devastating, a visual representation of everything good, all of the kindness in the world, taking to the wind, sucked out of the room with all of the oxygen.

Her lungs collapsed, her chest aching with the loss. He'd protected her. He'd given his life for her. Time sagged with the scattering of light. Blurred faces passed her by. The baby in her arms, Hope, was dead. Gone. Replaced by infinite sadness. The clamor of war and death raged on around her, yet produced a deafening silence only broken by the sound of her own breath.

Strong hands gripped her shoulders and shook. Jacob. What was he saying? His sword pressed against her neck. Was the whole world going mad? Or did he believe she was really Levi? Perhaps he would kill her before he realized the truth.

Wait. The red stone fell into his hand. It was not her neck he was cutting but the leather strap holding the stone. He tossed the gem on the platform.

Bonnie was strangely aware of the Devil racing toward them, but the slow-motion effect from Cord's scattering ashes applied to him as well. The only one who seemed to be moving at normal speed was Jacob. His sword of ice collided with the stone, melting into the cracks and drilling into the red. The pressure mounted, the stone shivering with the force, and then it exploded.

A supernova of red light formed in the space between her and Lucifer, and then a silhouette walked from the burning center. A ghost with golden-brown hair and ice-blue eyes glided straight for Bonnie. When she reached Hope's body, she smiled.

"It is not too late," she said. Then the soul dropped a hand into the baby's chest and disappeared.

The red boom rolled out to the walls and washed back in, both Watchers and Soulkeepers staring in stunned silence at the fireworks display. A sound Bonnie never thought she would hear again—a baby's cry, Hope's cry—filled the stadium. As pink as she was angry, Hope screamed, a swift, strong scream. Bonnie held her up for all the Watchers to see.

It started in the front row. The Watchers fell to their knees, the blue glow sweeping over them, turning their serpent skin to radiant flesh. Those newly turned angels began to fight the Watchers behind them. Even the upper rows on the second and third floors began to change. The mega screen projected Hope's face for every Watcher in the entire stadium to see, and all fell like dominoes to her power.

The newly formed angels stared at their hands and eventually fought to control the Watchers who were still changing. In the end, the only evil left in the stadium was Lucifer.

"Nooo!" Lucifer wailed. "My Watchers." He strode for baby Hope, his face a mask of rage. Bonnie braced herself for his attack. It didn't come. He walked, then jogged toward her, but the platform stretched, and lengthened, so that as fast as he walked, he never reached the baby.

A man formed between them, distinctly Jewish looking with olive skin and long wavy dark hair. He wore a Journey T-Shirt and cargo pants.

"The carpenter," Malini whispered to Jacob.

"God has come in the image of the maintenance man?" Jacob's face twisted in question.

"Shhh."

"My final gift is redemptive love," God said with an unblinking stare. "The challenge is complete."

Lucifer seethed. "You cheated. You already gave that gift when you changed Cord."

God folded His hands behind his back. "The transformation of the Watcher named Cord was Hope's doing. My gift was her existence. I triggered her Soulkeeper gene before her time. She did the rest."

"Bah! Your gift is invalid. The contest was for human hearts. All you changed was my Watchers."

"There was no stipulation against such a gift," God said. "No rules, remember, except that the humans must have free will. The challenge is over. Let us see where we stand." He snapped His fingers, and the roof opened up. The scorekeeper descended, marble wings now living and supple, still blindfolded and holding her scales. She landed on the platform and solidified, wings outstretched.

The swaying scales came to rest, and God's side was clearly lower. The crystal globe in the angels other hand glowed with pinpoints of light.

"It appears seeing you for what you are has driven the humans back to me, Lucifer. You have lost the challenge." God stuck his hands in his pockets and shrugged, with a calm, matter-of-fact countenance that seemed human, but better.

"You," Lucifer hissed, punching the air with his fists. "You knew you would win. You cheated. You deceived me."

"You know I am incapable of both, and you are incapable of winning this challenge."

"I'll show you what I am capable of." Lucifer charged, a cloud of sorcery building between his hands.

The earth began to shake. A giant chasm opened in the platform behind Lucifer, sending angels and Soulkeepers scattering for safe ground. The hole widened until it pressed against Lucifer's heels. He circled his arms to keep his balance, and the sorcery he'd been brewing dissolved.

"The challenge is complete," the hollow voice of the scorekeeper boomed. "Lucifer is sentenced to one thousand years in Hell."

From a safe distance, Bonnie could see the hole behind Lucifer burn red, smell the sulfur wafting from it through the stadium, and hear the howls of hellhounds echoing from below. Perched on the edge, Lucifer contorted his body to keep from falling, but seemed incapable of regaining his balance. Gravity overcame will, and he fell backward into the pit.

Only to be caught by God. The carpenter had grabbed Lucifer's flailing arm at the last second, holding the Devil fast at a forty-five degree angle over his gaping fate. Lucifer's fingers closed around God's wrist, and he met the carpenter's eyes with a questioning and skeptical gaze.

"My grace is infinite and free," God said. "Repent and follow me. I will pull you up."

"What is he doing?" Jacob whispered to Malini. "He can't possibly forgive Lucifer, not after everything. He's the Devil."

God turned his head to look at Jacob and smiled. "You are one to talk, Jacob Laudner, with your anger and your shifting moral compass. Are you saying my compassion is too freely given?"

Jacob closed his gaping mouth and forced a swallow. "Uh, no. I'm good."

"Thought so." God turned His attention back to Lucifer. "Your choice?"

For a moment, Bonnie thought it was over. What being wouldn't jump at the chance for redemption? Of escaping an eternity of torment? But then a wave of arrogance passed over

Lucifer's features. His eyes hardened and tightened at the corners.

"I don't need you or your grace," he spat, and then, Bonnie gasped as he peeled his fingers away and jerked his hand from God's grip. He did not scream as he fell into the abyss. Lucifer dropped to his fate with his arms crossed over his chest.

The earth swallowed him into its depths.

Chapter 31
The Last Soulkeeper

God straightened and dusted his callused hands off on his pants. He turned a half smile on Malini. "Well that was something, wasn't it?"

She nodded dumbly.

"As of today, Lucifer is detained in Hell for one thousand years."

A cheer rose up, a chorus of newly made angels. Malini couldn't help but clap too, although it seemed a silly and trite thing to do given the magnitude of what she'd just experienced.

Hope, still nestled in Bonnie's arms, giggled and kicked, pink cheeks dimpling with her smile.

The Lord approached her with arms outstretched, lifting her from Bonnie's hands and tossing her above His head before catching her again. "You look just like your mom and dad, Hope," He said. "Now, my Soulkeepers, I have some instructions for you. Gather 'round."

Lillian, Dane, Ethan, Samantha, Cheveyo, and Ghost came down from where they'd ended their fight, covered in black blood and grosser things, to bathe in the light of goodness in their presence. They stood at the base of the platform, staring with wide eyes at the carpenter holding the baby and waiting for the mysterious instructions he promised.

"Aren't you forgetting someone?" he asked.

At that moment, Grace walked through the door, one arm dangling limply at her side.

"Grace." Malini and Jacob met her halfway, pulling her into their arms.

"Some of you are injured. Please, allow me to help," God said. Malini and Jacob stepped aside. With a wave of God's hand, Grace's arm returned to normal, Ethan's face healed, and a number of scratches, gashes, and festering abrasions disappeared from the rest of them.

"Thank you," Lillian blubbered, tears of gratitude rushing from her eyes. The others followed with a chorus of appreciation.

"Enough. I cannot stay long, and there are things you need to know. Lucifer is gone—" Cheering again from the angels. God raised his hand, and they silenced. "But his echo remains." He pointed to the scales, tilted only slightly in the favor of good. "There are a lot of people out there who thought someone else should be in charge. They will carry on his legacy. They learned a lot while he was here."

"We can handle humans," Malini said.

God placed his workman hand on one hip. "I am sure you will, Malini, but not the way you are used to."

She raised her eyebrows, knowing something more was coming.

"In everything, there must be balance. Soulkeepers were created as a balance against Watchers."

"And now there are no Watchers," Jacob mumbled to Malini.

God laughed. "I can still hear you, Jacob."

Jacob blushed.

"Ah, never mind it all. You are correct … mostly. There is one Watcher left on this Earth."

Malini's eyes darted around the stadium.

"He's not here. He left when he had the chance."

"Damien," Malini said.

"Always more interested in doing things the human way, that one."

"So do we kill him?" Malini asked.

God sighed and a warm breeze coursed through the room, making Hope laugh. "As I was saying, there has to be balance. One Watcher, one Soulkeeper. That Soulkeeper is Hope." He tickled her belly. "Hope is the last Soulkeeper, a

Healer with the power of redemptive love. The most powerful Soulkeeper I have ever created."

"What about us?" Jacob asked, not bothering with the whisper this time.

"As of this moment, your powers are no more."

Malini knew. She'd felt it like a change in the barometric pressure. Still, she dug her fingers in the crook of her right arm and succeeded only in creating a bright red mark there. Her arm was her own. Across from her, Ghost stood as solid and vibrant as anyone, and Bonnie had returned to her own shape and size. Next to her, Jacob was staring at his hand and then at his flask as if one of his limbs had simply stopped working. Quiet tears slipped over Lillian's cheeks.

"You are normal humans again, but that doesn't mean I am done with you. Now, more than ever, I need you to lead. Be a force for good in this world, not because you are different from those around you but because you are the same. You have seen evil. You've walked among it. Teach the world to see it too and to reject it."

"But haven't they already seen it?" Grace asked, looking around her.

God smiled. "When I leave here, I will set things right. My final gift to each of you is that you will be the only ones to carry the memories of the challenge. Life will go forward without the burden of these last days."

Bounding down the stairs to the main floor, God approached Malini and Jacob. "Now, one more thing," he said. "It is my will that you two should raise Hope as your own."

Malini gasped. "What? I don't know how to raise a baby." The panic in her voice surprised even Jacob.

God laughed. "Malini Gupta, you raised the dead. You slayed hundreds of Watchers in my name. Is a baby such a burden?"

Her jaw snapped shut.

Jacob reached out for Hope and gathered her into his arms. "We'll figure it out."

"She's yours, Malini. Your parents were disappointed but supportive."

Wide-eyed, Malini bobbed her head.

"You must teach her about me and about her power, and when she is old enough, she will become a great leader and defender of humanity."

While Malini backed into a chair and sat down, Jacob poked Hope's giggling belly and said, "Great leader? Let's start with great eater. I bet you're a hungry girl." He kissed her forehead.

God returned to the platform and stood next to the scorekeeper. "Home," he said. With a gesture of his hand, all of the angels and the scorekeeper ascended through the hole in the roof.

"Wait," Bonnie pleaded. She threw herself at the platform. "Please, what about … Abigail and Gideon? What about Master Lee? When you set things right, will you bring them back?"

"I will not disturb their peace. I know it is difficult for you to understand, but it would be evil for me to do so."

"What about Cord?" Her voice broke.

God squatted down and took her hand in His. "Do you know, Bonnie, that you played a part in his redemption? Malini was correct that you amplified Hope's power that day, but it was what you did after he became an angel that made him powerful."

"I treated him like dirt."

"In the beginning, but then he loved you and love, the ability to love another, even if that love is not returned, is a gift, a transformative miracle."

"It was returned," she whispered.

"I know."

"But, he wasn't human." Her voice faltered. "So, is he just gone?"

"Energy, Bonnie, has no beginning or end, it simply changes form. Angels are made of positive energy. Cord's energy has returned to me."

Bonnie wiped under her eyes, thankful for her mother, who wrapped an arm around her and guided her away.

"Now, all of you, I recommend you leave this place as soon as possible and find your way home. Grace, Samantha, and Bonnie you have a restaurant to run."

The three Guillians looked at each other in surprise.

"Malini, Jacob, and Dane, you have finals. Lillian, you are already late for work. Yes, Laudner's Flowers and Gifts is back in business, and John, Carolyn, and Katrina have no memory of its ruin. Cheveyo, your tribe needs you."

"What about me?" Jesse asked. "I have no one left."

"Perhaps Grace would make a place for you?"

The redheaded woman smiled and nodded. Samantha pulled him into a tight hug.

Everyone turned to look at Ethan.

"Oh, I think Ethan knows exactly where home is for him," God said, laughing.

Without another word, not even a goodbye, the carpenter broke apart into a column of light, and they never saw him again for as long as they lived.

Epilogue
The Service

Eight years later.

"Hope, why aren't you in your dress?" Jacob coughed to clear the tickle in his throat and straightened his tie. Perched on the side of her bed, he appealed to her across her pink bedspread.

"I don't want to wear a dress. Why can't I wear pants?" Hope held up a pair of stretchy pink yoga pants. Hope loved pink. Her walls were pink. The carpet was pink. Even her toothpaste matched the theme. Ironically, the first time Jacob had seen eyes just like hers, he was living in a pink room—the day Abigail came to his window.

"Because it's a special occasion. Grandma is going to be there."

"I thought Grandma was at her other house."

"She flew in last night." Jacob was looking forward to seeing his mom after so long. Lillian spent her winters in Hawaii now that he was managing Laudner's Flowers and Gifts full time. He missed her.

"What about Mom?"

"Her flight from Tel Aviv came in late. She's going to meet us at the church." Jacob coughed again. Okay, now it was more than a tickle. He was definitely getting sick. Probably the flu that was going around.

"I want to see her show." Hope crossed her arms across her chest.

"Now? We're going to be late." He coughed again, shaking his head.

"I'll put on my dress," Hope singsonged, raising her eyebrows in promise.

"This is blackmail, you know." Jacob stood to pluck a tissue from the box on her desk and blew his nose. Definitely, getting the flu.

Hope stood on her bed and placed her arms around his neck, planting a kiss on his cheek. A familiar warm flow of energy seeped through him, clearing his head and chest. Jacob tossed the tissue into the garbage, not needing it any longer. "Thanks, but you had me at the dress."

She grinned.

He turned on her television and found Malini's latest broadcast on the DVR. They called her the Peace Warrior. Her show on CNBC focused on highlighting leaders and causes across the world working for peace. As the youngest journalist ever to anchor a news show, Malini traveled nonstop and was rarely home these days. Hope missed her, but Malini loved it. This was what she'd wanted to do for as long as she could remember.

Jacob could have felt bitter or lonely to be left behind to care for Hope while she followed her dream, but he didn't. He felt proud. He felt like this was how it was supposed to be. He didn't realize it until it happened, but his family was his greatest love. Caring for Hope was his joy and accomplishment. If he wasn't coaching her softball team, he was volunteering at her school or teaching her about Abigail. Everyone loved her. She couldn't go anywhere in Paris without a familiar pair of eyes looking out for her. As much as he had once hated it there, the small town had become his one true home and the perfect place to raise Hope.

Malini's latest show featured her interview with the Dalai Lama at Tel Aviv University. Dressed in a red suit and seated in a teal-blue chair against a gray backdrop, she looked the ruby and saffron-robed man in the eye and asked her first question.

Your Holiness, thank you for allowing me to interview you, Malini said.

The Dalai Lama nodded graciously.

*On the eve of the third annual Peace Gathering in Tel Aviv,
what do you think is the most important ingredient for a
peaceful world?*

The Dalai Lama answered in his distinctive accent. *One
word, compassion. Each of us, everyone, wants to be happy, but
too often we focus only on ourselves and our problems. We think
more money, more things, will bring happiness. True peace, true
happiness, comes when we expand our minds to value and respect
others as our brothers and sisters. If we do this, then we know we
must treat them with compassion.*

*When you say our brothers and sisters, are you talking about
those who are similar to us in religion and heritage?*

The Dalai Lama smiled. *Compassion toward those who are
like us is much easier, but true peace comes when we exercise
compassion for all. Some believe in God, others do not, but we
are all human, all striving for the same happiness, the same end
of suffering. We breathe the same air, and we drink the same
water. Acceptance of each other, different cultures, and different
environments is vital. A single reality, a single truth like God,
can naturally be interpreted differently among diverse peoples.
Compassion and universal responsibility, therefore, are key to
peace.*

Jacob raised an eyebrow at Hope. With one eye on the
screen, she picked the dress off her bed and removed it from
the hanger. He backed out of her room to let her get dressed.
The ringtone Jacob reserved for Malini sounded from the
kitchen, and he jogged down the hall of their sprawling
modern home to retrieve his cell phone. He toyed with the

wedding band on his finger as he answered it. She'd arrived and was safe. She'd meet him at the church.

He smiled. He couldn't wait to see his wife today.

* * * * *

Across town, Dane Michaels leaned over his sink to get a better view in the mirror as he shaved a path through the foamy cream on his face. He was looking forward to seeing everyone at the service today. Jesse and Samantha had missed the reunion this year with the birth of their twins. Boys he'd heard, with red hair just like their mom.

"We're going to be late," Ethan said from behind him, slipping a tie through the collar of his dress shirt.

"How's Mom?"

"Resting comfortably. I gave her a pain pill. The nurse will be here soon. She'll be fine while we're gone."

"Maybe we should ask for Hope?"

Reflected in the mirror, a smile slashed across Ethan's face. "She had her gallbladder removed, not open heart surgery. She's going to be fine. Besides, you know that Jacob and Malini are trying to limit how often Hope uses her power. It's already suspicious that no one in her third grade class ever gets sick."

"I guess."

Ethan wrapped his arms around Dane's shoulders and kissed the patch of just shaved skin on his face. "Stop worrying." He pulled back and wiped away a blob of misguided shaving cream.

"I'll tell you what I'm really worried about," Dane said.

"What?"

"The nine pounds I've gained since we got married. It's like the words 'I do' completely stopped my metabolism."

"You look great." Ethan tied his tie and buttoned his cuffs.

"My dress pants are tight."

Ethan caught Dane's gaze in the mirror. "You look great. Buy bigger pants."

Dane finished shaving and rinsed his face in the sink. "Jesse and Sam are bringing the twins."

"I heard. I can't wait," Ethan said, moving into the bedroom.

"Do you think they're too young for kids?"

"They're in their mid-twenties. Couldn't be a better time."

"We're in our mid-twenties." Dane punched one arm up the sleeve of his jacket and allowed his thoughts to drift as he finished putting it on. The words hung like a rain-bloated cloud over the bathroom. Maybe it was too soon to have this conversation. Maybe Ethan hadn't even heard him in the connecting bedroom.

A full minute later, Ethan appeared in the doorframe, mouth pressed into a straight line and face pale. "Do you think you're ready for a baby?"

"Who is ever ready?"

"People are going to talk. We will get hate mail from half the town about how a gay couple should not be allowed to adopt children."

"Half the town? You said the same thing about our wedding, and more than half showed up to support us. Do you think Carolyn Laudner is going to refuse the chance to hold a new baby? I bet her feet never touch the ground."

"Her?"

Dane shrugged. "I pictured us with a girl." Heart thudding in his chest, he stared at Ethan, waiting for some reaction. Relief flooded him when the corners of his partner's eyes lifted, the start of tiny smile lines folding above his cheeks.

"I think there's an adoption agency in Terre Haute. I can call this week," Ethan said.

Dane beamed.

"Now come on. We're going to be late."

* * * * *

At the appropriate time in the service, Bonnie positioned herself at the center of the altar at the front of the church. Out of the corner of her eye, she saw Jacob and Malini in the third row. The two sat so close together their shoulders touched, Malini's fingers tangled with Jacob's and resting on his thigh. Hope, in a fluffy pink dress, looked content tucked protectively under Malini's free arm and next to her grandma, Lillian, who smiled encouragingly at Bonnie.

On the other side of the church, her sister, Samantha, with her husband, Jesse, each bounced a ginger-haired baby boy on their laps—Gideon and Gabriel. Her mother, Grace, reached for the one in Samantha's arms—Bonnie couldn't tell them apart yet—and cuddled the baby against her shoulder. Near the back of the church, Bonnie grinned when she saw Dane and Ethan, but it was the couple next to them that sent her mood through the roof. Cheveyo and Raine had come all the way from Arizona. She guessed Dane or Malini had paid for their tickets. The two didn't make much money living on the Hopi reservation.

It was time for her to begin. All at once, she was tempted to hide behind the pulpit. Something about the rectangle of wood always made her feel more confident and secure. But in seminary, she'd learned that this more vulnerable position, out in the open, connected better with the congregation. Her hands began to sweat and her mouth went dry and cottony. She adjusted her microphone. Could she do this?

Wings. Amid the sound of rustling bulletins and the occasional throat clearing, the shadow of two outstretched wings spread across the carpet in front of her toes. She raised her face to the skylight window in the roof above and saw a dove there, stretched and flapping against the glass. *Cord*, she thought as she looked into the light. The scene reminded her of waking up in his arms the day he healed her.

All that tragedy was over now, but somehow this bird in the sun gave her comfort. Cord's presence seemed to surround her, to remind her of why she was there.

"If you haven't met me yet, my name is Bonnie Guillian," she began. "I have accepted the call to be your new pastor." Absentmindedly, she ran a finger under the clerical collar at her throat. "This is my first sermon here. I hope I won't disappoint you. I'm not nearly as longwinded as my predecessor."

As the church erupted in laughter and she continued with her sermon, Bonnie made a point to meet the eyes of each of the Soulkeepers. Awash in gratitude, she couldn't help but think of their journey together. Her time as a Soulkeeper, her successes and her failures, her moments of pride and of regret, had brought her to this. Cord's life and death had moved her to pursue seminary school, to pursue her greatest love, connecting people with their creator. Oddly, losing Cord had taught her to value every day as if it were her last, and value every person as if he or she might fall through her fingers at any moment. The loss had changed her.

Then again, none of the Soulkeepers had been the same since the day they vanquished Lucifer. And, in her modest opinion, that was a good and purposeful thing.

About the Author

G.P. Ching is the bestselling author of The Soulkeepers Series and Grounded. She specializes in cross-genre YA novels with paranormal elements and surprising twists. The Soulkeepers was named a 2013 iBookstore Breakout Book.

G.P. lives in central Illinois with her husband, two children, and a Brittany spaniel named Riptide Jack. Learn more about G.P. and her books at www.gpching.com.

Follow G.P. on:
    Twitter: @gpching
    Facebook: G.P. Ching
    Facebook: The Soulkeepers Series

Sign up for her exclusive newsletter at www.gpching.com to be the first to know about new releases!

The greatest compliment you can give an author is a positive review. If you've enjoyed this title, please consider reviewing it at your place of purchase.

Acknowledgements

As I bring this series to a close, my deepest appreciation goes out to Karly Kirkpatrick and Angela Carlie, whose support, encouragement, and careful eye helped make the series what it is today. These two have been a part of the development of this series from start to finish. On that note, another big literary hug to H. "Dani" Crabtree who edited all six books.

I also want to thank Leta Gail Doerr and Nida Kazim for reading an early version of the Soulkeepers and encouraging me to pursue the idea. The series wouldn't have grown to what it is today without their reassurance that the manuscript did not belong in the rubbish bin. Also, thank you to Brenda Rothert who offered to beta read The Last Soulkeeper. I can't begin to convey how much her fresh eyes helped with this novel.

Additionally, I need to thank my family for standing by me during the ups and downs, and there have been quite a few of both. Days spent hunched at the computer, even during vacations and special events. Nights spent pacing the halls when writing and publishing complications kept me from sleeping.

Finally, thank you to the fans who have made this series what it is today. In the end, you are what really matters, and I am so thankful you've come along this journey with me. The next book I write will be for YOU—not for the money, not to add another book to the list, but to entertain you. I appreciate each and every one of you.

Book Club Discussion Questions

1. Who do you think changed the most over the course of the series and why?

2. Do you think the Soulkeepers were too hard on Cord?

3. If the story was real and you needed the brand to buy, sell, or earn anything, would you allow the mark on your hand?

4. Why do you think God chose Tom Sawyer as the symbol of the society that would undermine Lucifer's curse?

5. The Hedonic Party offered a government that would allow total freedom and no consequences. Would you like to live that way? Do we need our government?

6. In the end, Damien chooses to walk away from a fight with Malini and save himself. Do you think Malini did the right thing to let him go?

7. Do you believe someone who has done evil in the past can truly be redeemed?

8. Which of the challenges in the labyrinth did you find
    most disturbing and why?

9. Were you surprised Lucifer did not accept God's offer of
    redemption in the end?

10. Did Bonnie's choice of careers surprise you? What do you
    think will become of Hope?

11951352R00191

Printed in Great Britain
by Amazon.co.uk, Ltd.,
Marston Gate.